A Song for Menafee

FUNERAL SINGER

Book Two

Lillian I. Wolfe

Pynhavyn Press

This book edition is published in 2016 by:
Pynhavyn Press

TM

http://www.pynhavyn.com

First Edition: August 2016

Copyright © 2016 Lillian I. Wolfe

All rights reserved.

ISBN-13: 978-1-942622-09-3

ISBN-10: 1-942622-09-0

Cover Design: SelfPubbookCovers/FantasyArt

Books by Lillian I. Wolfe

Funeral Singer Series

Funeral Singer: A Song for Marielle
A Song for Menafee

Science Fiction Fantasy

O'Ceagan's Saga Series
O'Ceagan's Legacy

Young Adult Urban Fantasy

Isles of Magic Series

Dew Dropping Hour – coming soon

Dedication

For my great grandfather, Menafee Womack Tatum, whose name alone inspired me. I never knew you, but I know you would have told great stories. Thank you.

Acknowledgements

Many thanks to everyone who contributed to this book, especially to my family and the pets, who tolerated being ignored while I worked on it. To my beta readers, Pati Bagley, Nancy and Steve Sorbets, Peggy Hancock, and Patricia Kelly, my deepest gratitude for your honest observations.

To my High Sierra Writers critique group, my thanks and appreciation. You folks are all awesome and I offer my gratitude to Nicole Frens, Brian Cave, Lucas Ledbetter, Mark Bacon, and Don Huggins for your help, suggestions, and support. My work is much better for it.

A huge thank you to my editor, Julie A. Richards, who did her absolute best to keep me on the straight and narrow path. Any mistakes left in this work are completely mine.

Big thanks to the artist known as Fantasy Art at SelfPubBookCovers.com. I was fortunate to find the moody, wonderful book cover that fits this story so well.

Finally, thanks to Pynhavyn Press for the book design, layout, and everything else I haven't mentioned.

Contents

ONE

A spurt of adrenalin shot through my body as the sharp snicking-sound of a blade snapping into place came from behind me and registered in my brain. In an instant, I spun around, crouching lower as I completed the turn.

Across from me a bearded mountain of a man, who looked like he could lift a truck, came at me with his arms held out to each side and ready to attack. In his right hand, he brandished the switchblade knife that had made the noise. Only the lights from the four ceiling-high windows spilled into the dojo, simulating the lighting of an encounter at dusk.

Dropping into defensive mode, I bent my knees more and took an easy stance to shift direction as I would need to do when he came at me. I kept my arms loose, swinging a little in order to be ready for anything. He began to move, growling like a bear as he advanced and I transferred my weight a little to the left, while shifting my view from the blade to his eyes. "Watch your opponent's eyes," my instructor had said. "If you focus on the blade, you won't catch the sudden move..." But, dammit, I couldn't help glancing at the gleaming steel.

He feinted to the right and I shifted again, but moving too slow to adjust back to the other side when he reversed the move. I dropped and rolled, barely avoiding the lunge of the blade toward me. Springing back to my feet, I windmilled my arms, then ducked in low as he tried to avoid my flying swings. I brought up my right knee making a poor connection with his upper thigh, not the groin area that was my intended target. Without even a pause, he came back at me, ducking in with an arm to catch my right arm and twist it back. I went down hard on the mat and in less than two seconds, his knee ground into my torso with the cold press of metal at my throat. Training exercise or not, I felt my heart jump in terror at the feel of the blade.

"Enough," Arimoto called. "You lost focus, Gillian. You need to keep your attention on your attacker's face. If you don't, you will end up the victim."

I sat up as Gregory rolled off me. "It's hard to ignore the weapon, Ari." I pushed my hair back from my face and met his stern, dark eyes. He was not a man to accept excuses.

"You're not trusting that you'll be able to see what he's going to do in his face. When someone is going to change a position, he almost always telegraphs the change in his eyes. You need to learn to read those signals and react accordingly. On the positive side, you did go to drop and roll when you realized you'd made a mistake. Meditate on focus. That's it for today."

"Thanks, Greg," I said with a nod to my sparring partner, one of the nicest guys you could know even though he looked like the Hulk's cousin.

I glanced at the wall clock. Five-forty-two. I barely had time to grab a quick shower and get on the road. I needed to meet my band, Spicy Jam, at a club in Fallon for a gig at seven.

As I climbed into my Jeep and headed for the freeway, I reflected on today's lesson. I started coming to the self-defense class two weeks after Vincent Coblenzer, the so-called Holiday Killer, abducted me in February. The worst kind of monster, he preyed on young girls. I would have been dead if Egan and Hernandez, two detectives from the Sheriff's Department, hadn't shown up when they did. He almost raped me, stopping only because his usual prey tended to be much younger and he couldn't get hard with an adult. Nevertheless, the bastard planned to kill me.

Shortly after the hospital released me and I had time to come to terms with the whole situation, I swore that I wouldn't be a victim again. So, I decided that I would get into shape, learn how to defend myself, and carry a can of pepper spray with me at all times. I'd started going to a gymnasium to work out and found someone there who recommended Dae Arimoto as the kind of instructor who could help me.

I ran into heavy rain as I made my way across Reno on the I80 Freeway towards Fallon, a rural community about sixty miles from the dojo. I continued through Sparks and into the county without the downpour slacking any. Ahead, the highway paralleled a creek bed that snaked about fifteen feet below the road. Steep embankments, without railing, ran on both sides. I had never cared for this stretch, but it was a rural area with lots of open ground. Just after Lockwood, I noticed a dark blue SUV in the left lane as it sped past me and I got a glimpse of his plate, memorizing what I could see of it to report him for reckless driving. Hadn't that guy ever heard of hydroplaning?

People in a hurry, I thought as he zipped past the gray Camry in front of me. Then the SUV started to shift lanes too soon and cut sharply in front of the Camry. Tires squealing like a banshee, the gray car veered to the right and skidded on the wet surface toward the embankment. I slammed on my brakes just as the Camry started to career off and I barely avoided hitting the rear of the vehicle before it left the road, sliding down the muddy incline.

The Beast, as I'd nicknamed my Jeep, started to slide and I fought to control it, managing to stop in the nick of time before the back wheels followed the Camry's path. The skid left my vehicle angled into the right lane. Frightened, I looked toward the oncoming traffic and let out a sigh of relief as I watched the car a short distance behind me brake to a halt without incident.

Getting out, I hurried to the edge of the road and peered down to where the wet dirt showed the evidence of the descent. The vehicle had flipped as it rolled down and looked badly damaged. Running back to my Jeep, I grabbed my cell phone and called for help, giving the dispatcher a breathless account of what had happened. The driver behind me came over as I ended the call and asked if I was okay. I nodded, "Yeah, fine. Thanks. I just called 911. Help is coming soon."

Rain glistened on his nylon jacket as it ran down in thin rivulets. He looked to be in his mid-thirties, average height and from his build might have played football in school. He looked me up and down, no doubt seeing a smallish woman who looked like a drowned cat.

"Why don't you get back in your car and wait for help? I'll go down and see if I can do anything," he said as he turned and started down the embankment, sliding a little as he went.

Following his suggestion, I dashed back to the shelter of the Beast, then I dialed Ferris, my friend and bandmate. "Hey, Ferris. I'm delayed. There was an accident. I was right behind a car that went over the embankment and I barely managed to brake. I have to wait until the police arrive."

"Cripes. Are you all right?" he asked at once. "Where are you?"

"Yeah, I'm fine. Just a little shaken, but not hurt. I'm less than a mile beyond the Lockwood exit. I'm sorry, but I don't think I'll be there by seven."

"Don't worry about that. Digby and I can cover until you get here. Are you sure you're okay?"

I loved that he was concerned about me more than the gig. "Fine. Not hurt, no damage to the Beast. I'll call you when I get close."

After I hung up, I took several deep breaths to calm my shaky nerves, straightened the Jeep up a little, and pulled it off the highway, so no one would plow into it. Then I dug through the stuff in the glove compartment until I found a cheap plastic rain poncho, pulled it on, and went to look over the side of the road again.

I could see the man, his pants coated with mud, who'd gone down. The car had turned on its side and he'd climbed onto it and yanked at the driver's door, over and over, to try to pull it open. It didn't appear to budge, so I thought it might be crushed in. I shivered thinking about the poor driver.

I couldn't stand by while that man was trapped and maybe I could help get the door open. I started down the slope, sliding every few feet as my tennis shoes lacked the traction on wet vegetation. I'd almost reached the car when my right shoe shot out from under me and I landed on the muddy slope, sliding several feet before I plowed into a boulder that stopped me cold. Using the wet rock as a somewhat slippery support, I struggled to pull myself to my feet and staggered the remaining few feet to reach the Camry.

My heart fell as I saw crunched metal in so many places and the top caved in to where it almost sat on the top of the back seat. With the car reclining on the passenger side, the driver's door sat about four feet off the ground.

"What can I do?" I shouted to the man, who still struggled with the door.

"It's jammed," he called back.

I clambered up on the back wheel, using the door handle to haul myself up a little more to reach the back seat window. The opening was narrow with the top caved, but I thought it might be enough for me to reach the driver. I swung my left leg up to kick at the spider-web shattered window while I clung to the door handle. After three hard kicks, I broke through. I shoved glass out of the way and eased my body into the car while I kept my head low. A tight fit, I found it difficult to move without bumping my head or kneeling on glass. I hissed as I cut my knee, but managed to wriggle my way to the front seat.

The driver's upper body hunched over the steering wheel. The air bag hadn't deployed and the wheel was crushed into his chest. Blood streaked his face and dripped down his clothes. Swallowing my urge to puke, I pressed my fingers against his carotid artery to check for a pulse.

A groan startled me and I realized he was conscious. "Hey, stay with me. Help is coming," I said trying to put as much assurance into my voice as possible.

"My son," he gasped. He didn't try to turn his head toward me as he struggled to talk.

"Was he in the car?" I looked around to see if I had somehow missed a child in the backseat.

"No... student at UNR. Tell him..." He sucked in air as blood oozed out of his mouth. "Tell him... I... love him."

"You'll tell him yourself. Just hang on a little longer." I tried to be encouraging, but I could feel his soul slipping away. "No! Stay here. You have to hold tight." I slid my right hand into his, rubbing it, and feeling how cold it felt. His fingers tightened on mine in response as he drew a sharp breath of pain. I could smell the scent of the blood and something more, the odor of death on him. How did I know that? Why was I so certain he wouldn't make it?

I heard a siren approaching, alerting me that assistance was arriving. "Just a few more minutes and we'll have help. You have to hang on."

Within a few minutes that felt like hours, another face appeared beside the other driver's at the window. Then another climbed up to look. Sheriff's deputies. I recognized the uniforms. One had a crowbar and they began prying at the door, attempting to jimmy it open. It was like opening a tin can with a fingernail file. One of the officers got on his cellular phone to request more help. I hoped it was close.

I heard more sirens and glancing up through the back window, I could just see the white top of an ambulance arrive, then I heard the sound of a heavy truck and got a glimpse of dark yellow as an emergency vehicle arrived.

"More help," I said. "EMTs are here. Hold on." But I could see he'd lost consciousness. I held onto his hand and tried to will some of my strength to him.

About that time, one of the EMTs leaned his head in the back window and told me to crawl out, so he could get in. I wanted to stay, but there wasn't enough room for me to remain. I nodded, whispered to the dying man one more time, then crawled to the back window where the EMT helped to pull me through. I had blood all over me, all his, and two or three scratches from the glass that were barely noticeable. As I stood aside in the rain, letting the rushing drops wash the blood off as they would, I knew the driver wouldn't make it to the hospital. He was too badly injured and had lost too much blood. I felt helpless, knowing there was nothing I could do to help him except the task that would come in a few days.

I trudged back up the bank, sliding a little, and grabbing scrub bushes to pull myself up. Another sheriff's deputy caught my arm as I was almost to the top and pulled me the rest of the way. He led me to the ambulance where I could at least sit while he talked to the driver. The two of them found some gauze and the deputy wiped the blood from my hand and bandaged it while we waited for the experts to free the Camry's driver.

Patched up, I limped over to the Beast and climbed in to try to keep somewhat dry.

The newly arrived officers came over to talk to me, get my contact information, and a brief statement about what had happened. I related everything that I could recall. I described the SUV the best I could, a recent model dark blue Ford Explorer, four-door, Nevada license plate.

"Did you get the license number?" The officer who asked was partially bald and had identified himself as Deputy Miller.

"I saw a part of it, but couldn't get the whole thing. The last four read 2HJK. It was raining too hard to see more than that." I regretted I didn't get the whole plate.

They made notes and told me that I could leave, but a detective might be back in contact with me if there were more questions and Miller handed me a card in case I recalled anything else. I nodded, my eyes following as they hurried back to the SUV they'd parked near the embankment. On the highway, two more officers urged the evening rush traffic to continue without stopping to gawk. It felt a bit surreal, like being in the middle of a movie and seeing it from the inside out.

A chill rolled over me as I shut the door and started the engine. Below I could see that they had pried the door open and the EMTs were getting the driver on a stretcher. The other man who'd stopped was starting to climb back up to his car.

Feeling sad and drained, I glanced at the time on my smartphone and noted I was already an hour late for our gig. I still had about forty minutes to go to Fallon if the traffic kept moving. The gig seemed immaterial; the last thing I wanted to do right now, but I didn't want to disappoint the people who came to see our trio or let my bandmates down. The show must go on and all that.

You've done everything you can do here, I reasoned with myself, trying to pull my scattered emotions together and focus on what I needed to do next.

Before I pulled back on the road, I called Ferris to tell him the situation. His phone went to voice mail, so I figured they were on stage. "Hey, Ferris. It's about eight-ten and I'm just now leaving the accident and should be there in about forty minutes. I'm a mess, but I'll try to clean up once I get to the hall."

Reluctance tugging at my arms and heart, I pulled out onto the road, applying more care to my driving than usual. Aware of the traffic around me and the effects caused by too much speed in the rain, I drove with caution and applied defensive driving techniques with more diligence. Nothing like a fatal accident to turn you into a nervous driver.

By the time I arrived, my Jeep's heater had dried my hair quite a bit, but my clothes were still dirty with almost dry mud. I grabbed my gym bag and dashed into the club. I slipped into the women's room, pulled out a worn pair of jeans with holes in the knees and a dark gray sweatshirt then quickly changed. I brushed my hair out as much as I could, getting bits of dried mud out until it looked smooth.

I studied myself in the mirror, noting that the grungy look didn't seem all that bad for a casual club gig and at least I didn't look like I'd fallen down a muddy bank. My face looked paler than usual and the strain showed in the tired look around my eyes. I tried to repair my eye makeup and added a little face powder. That was the best I could do. Underneath the bandage on my hand, a little blood seeped through, but I could move it okay, so playing the keyboard, once I got it set up, wouldn't be a problem.

Shaking off the emotions of the past two hours, I grabbed my keyboard case and hurried to the stage. The club lighting was low, but not so dark I couldn't clamber up the side stairs in a run. Once I hit the stage, I turned on the show personality. If I learned one thing from doing theater in college, it was that whatever worries or problems plagued your daily life stayed behind once you hit the boards.

As Ferris glimpsed my arrival, he tapped a cymbal twice to alert Digby, who was at the front of the stage. The tall, lanky guitarist glanced over to give me a nod. In the middle of one of my songs, he finished the verse, then inserted an instrumental break to allow me time to get into place at the microphone. I scurried to my spot, flipped the mic to live, and picked up the song where he'd left off to take it to the end.

As I hastened to set up my keyboard, I apologized to the crowd. "Hey, guys! I'm so sorry that I was late to this party. I ran into problems on the way and was out in the rain and mud for a while. I may look a bit messy, but I'm ready to rock it tonight. Are you with me?" The crowd responded with cheers and we launched into the next song.

The gig went on for another hour before the club closed down for the night. As I put the keyboard away, Digby came over, looked me over, and commented, with his usual Aussie dryness, "You look a mite bedraggled. Are you okay?"

I nodded. "Yeah, a few cuts and a slightly sprained wrist. Minor stuff."

"Ferris said you weren't involved in the accident."

"I wasn't in it, but I was right behind the car and saw what happened. I climbed down the embankment to try to help the driver of the car that went off the road."

"You did what?" Ferris asked as he walked up at the end of that. A wrinkle of concern crossed his forehead.

"I tried to help him, but there was nothing I could do. I don't think he made it." My voice cracked as I said it, the pent-up emotion overwhelming me all at once.

A moment later, the comforting arms of my two bandmates cocooned me in a much-needed group hug. The boys insisted I sit as they broke down and loaded everything into their respective vehicles. We went down the street to a coffee shop where I ordered a bowl of soup and coffee to bolster me for the trip home, taking my time to eat it. My appetite waned but my stomach still growled. While the guys wolfed down burgers and fries, I told them the whole story and once again broke into tears as I described the dying man.

"But he was alive when you left?" Digby asked.

I nodded. "I think so. The EMTs didn't cover his head up when they brought him up."

"Then there's a chance he might make it."

"A chance," I answered, but a part of me knew he wouldn't.

Ferris insisted on driving me home, refusing to consider letting me make the drive back to Reno. "I'll bring you back for your car in the morning," he said.

I argued that it would be an extra trip for him, but he wouldn't give in. To be honest, I welcomed the offer. The stress of the whole evening hit me and I fell asleep with my head against the window before we'd left Fallon.

TWO

Janna and I bent over sideways, then back to upright, stretching our muscles to loosen them up before we started our morning run. Dressed in lightweight sweats against the chilly spring air, I bent down to tighten the laces on my new running shoes.

As part of my regimen to strengthen my body, I ran a mile at least three times a week. Since my best friend, Janna, lived and breathed physical fitness, she soon volunteered to be my training partner. After close to three months of this, I'd worked my way to keeping up with her. As a bonus, I'd trimmed down and gained more strength.

"I heard the guy died," Janna said, referring to the accident I'd witnessed. "That's a shame."

"Yeah, it is. I hope the police catch that jerk, who ran him off the road. It was a senseless accident and needn't have happened."

"Well, I'm sure glad you were clear of it." Janna pulled on her gloves, adjusted her pedometer, and gazed at me with a concerned look. "Are you doing okay, hunny?" She still used our teenage endearments even though we'd left those years behind almost a decade ago.

"I'm doing great. Why do you ask?" I clicked on my own tracker and smiled at her.

She shrugged. "You're just different after..."

Her voice trailed off and she turned her gaze toward Virginia Lake. I knew what she was asking.

"Look. It was a traumatic experience and a situation I never dreamed I would find myself in. But I'm coming to terms with it in my own way and I am stronger because of what happened. I mean, look at me. Slimmed down, running on a regular basis rather than just now and then. Learning to defend myself. You always wanted me to get into the fitness thing, so here I am."

"I know. I just think you're pushing yourself too hard sometimes. You seem restless, you look tired, and you're not eating as much. I guess I'm just a little worried that maybe you're still suffering from it."

"Thanks for the concern, but really, I'm doing fine. Let's run." I led off on the path around the lake and Janna soon fell into step beside me.

At first, I'd had trouble having adequate air to talk while we ran, but I'd built up enough now that we could carry on a conversation between breaths. Janna clearly had more on her mind as she asked, "So are you getting any odd dreams now?"

"You mean graveyard dreams? Not lately. Not since I accepted what I am. I guess they were all to prepare me for becoming a spirit escort to the transitional gate. I think of the graveyard as a waiting room to the next life or whatever is actually beyond that gate."

"'Spirit escort?' That's a good name for it. I take it you've accepted your gift and that it isn't you going nuts?"

"Love the way you put that. Nope, not nuts, but it still bothers me that I seem to have this peculiar gift and it's not my choice to use it or not use it. At least, every funeral doesn't turn into a crazy graveyard experience."

I picked up the pace a bit, not wanting to talk about this anymore. After I took a tumble and hit my head in the icy parking lot of the Sierra Towers Hotel, I'd experienced several dreams about a park that turned out to be an ethereal graveyard. Then, a woman asked me to sing for a funeral and the next thing I knew I started confronting the dearly departed in the graveyard from my dreams. In the beginning, I thought my mind must have been scrambled or plagued by a tumor, but it turned out I had become a funeral singer, someone who could sing confused or lost souls to the gate leading to the eternal light, or whatever the light tunnel was, beyond it. While it sounded insane when I tried to describe it, it seemed very real to me. My health was good, according to the two specialists I'd talked with about it. Of course, I hadn't told them the whole story, but enough that they confirmed I had no tumors, lesions, or other physical problems.

After we finished the run, Janna caught my arm, holding me back, and faced me. "You know, you could try to learn a little more about your gift. I know a psychic who might be able to help you. I mean, if you want to try to understand it more."

"A psychic? Are you kidding?"

"Well, no. You're still adjusting to all of this and I would think that you might have questions. I'm only suggesting that someone, who has experience with this kind of thing, might give you some insight."

I peered at her, looking for any sign of joking, still not certain she meant it, but then Janna had plunged into this stuff after she hit puberty and got caught up in "Buffy the Vampire Slayer". "Let me think about it, Janna. Maybe I might."

After the run, I drove back to my little house on a street just off Arlington Blvd. I rented the two-story, two-bedroom house that nestled about ten yards and a fence behind a larger red brick house. With its coziness and privacy, it suited me and my Himalayan cat, Nygard. However, lately, I hadn't felt as secure in it as I had before my abduction in February.

I hadn't been entirely candid with Janna. Sleep often evaded me; every little noise would wake me and I slept with a night light on. Her comment that I ate less hit the mark. My appetite had waned after I'd gotten out of the hospital and found I didn't care much if I ate or not. I threw myself into my job at the Pampered Pet Dog Grooming Salon and picked up as many singing gigs as I could. I figured that if I kept busy I wouldn't think about what had happened.

Facing the truth of it, I didn't know how to process it all. I had pursued a killer at the prodding of the ghost of an eleven-year-old child, but I hadn't expected to be abducted by the man and nearly raped and killed. It had shattered something in me and made me feel so ashamed that I'd ended up in that situation as if the fault originated with me. The counselor at the hospital had suggested I see a psychologist and talk to her about what had happened, but I couldn't bring myself to discuss it. Not even with my best friend. I'd never kept secrets from Janna before, but I couldn't tell her how horrible this made me feel.

I couldn't even talk to Mark, my current boyfriend, if I could call him that. As a second-year resident doctor at the hospital, he had less free time than I did, so we didn't see each other much. Meeting him had been the best thing to come from the emergency visit after the accident.

I grabbed a quick energy drink from the 'fridge, gave Nygard a few bites of leftover chicken, then dashed up to the shower. Hot water cleaned off the sweat and the icky feeling that plagued me every time I got hot and perspired too much. Enjoying the spray over my body, I turned to face the bathroom door to let it cascade over my back and a creepy feeling came over me. Something didn't feel right, almost as if I was being watched, but I couldn't pinpoint what it was. This, too, had been happening since the incident with Coblenzer.

Dressing in jeans and a sweatshirt, I hurried to get to work. Several dogs to bathe and groom filled my day's schedule and I wanted to do a little research on a dream I'd had the previous night. Not one of the graveyard dreams; I hadn't lied to Janna about that.

A more frightening one. In this nightmare, I struggled as a prisoner in a small, underground cell with no visible windows, yet there was enough light to discern it was a room and nothing more. Certain the dream's source grew from the fear of being tied down in the basement of Coblenzer's home, I thrashed in my sleep, twisting and turning. But the more intriguing part began when my vision closed in on one of the cell's walls where glowing silver lettering formed words in what looked like a Latin script. When I jerked awake, bed sheets tangled around my legs, I'd sat up and scribbled down the words the way I thought I'd seen them. Going to my computer, I tried to translate them and maybe I had it right, but I wanted to check the interpretation I'd pulled. I knew a professor at the University, who could verify what I had. At least, I hoped he could.

I greeted my boss Heenie Tuuta, a plump, transplanted Hawaiian woman, who owned the grooming shop, with a bright smile and a cheery good morning.

"Good run this morning? Another chilly one, I bet."

She was getting used to my perky attitude on mornings when I ran.

"Pretty crisp, but invigorating. At least, it's warming up some over last month." One of those places where winter liked to linger into spring, Reno could be hit or miss if you'd have a warm day or a freezing cold one. Today came in about the middle of that.

A glance at the schedule showed I had a toy poodle up first on the list. "I'll just get started on Gigi, okay?"

Heenie nodded as she clipped at a Border Collie. "Don't forget her mama likes the puppy cut."

Like I could forget it. I'd been clipping the small apricot-colored dog for over a year and she yipped with joy when she saw me. I greet her with a little song as I took her out of the cage and carried her to the table at my workstation.

I started the pre-groom before bathing when my phone, in my pocket, buzzed. Pulling it out, I balanced it between my chin and right shoulder to talk so I could continue combing Gigi's hair.

"Hello, Ms. Foster," a familiar woman's voice said. "This is Erin Jensen at the Hill View Cemetery. I've had a request for you to sing at a funeral here if you're available to do it."

"A request? Did someone ask for me specifically?"

"Yes, you were recommended."

"I see. When would this be? And who should I contact?"

I scribbled down the details of the service and got the name and phone number for someone called Celeste Hammond. I'd call later to discuss the music choice with her and went back to work on the dog.

During lunch, I called the number and a young-sounding man answered. He said Ms. Hammond had gone out for a bit and offered to take a message. As I explained that she'd requested my services as a singer, he replied that he knew about it. "My name is Thomas Willits," he said, his voice sounding strained. "My father passed away in a car accident over the weekend. My aunt thought that a couple of special songs for my dad would be appropriate at the service."

My stomach did an unexpected flip and I nearly dropped the phone. "I'm so sorry for your loss," I said as I made the connection that to the accident I'd witnessed. I hadn't contacted him yet, but I knew his name. "How about I call back later when your aunt is there and perhaps we can meet to discuss the music choices?"

He agreed and I added it to the appointment list on my smartphone. Since I had it out, I made a quick call to the professor I knew at the University of Nevada Reno, called UNR by most locals. He wasn't in his office, so I left a message to let him know I wanted to see him and I could be there around four-thirty.

About an hour later, I felt the phone buzz and checked to find a return text message confirming it.

After work, I drove across town to the University, dashed across the road, which was the only place that had any parking, and hurried through the campus to catch Professor Gavin Haines before he left for the day. Even though he expected me, he wasn't one to wait around if I was late. I strolled into his office as he clicked the locks on his briefcase.

In his early fifties, Haines remained a handsome man, even as smears of gray showed at the temples of his still-thick dark hair. He'd gained a slight paunch in the middle since I'd had an archeology period with him in my sophomore year. Like half the young women in the class, I took it while searching for my personal Indiana Jones. A little older now, Gavin still had that roguish, swarthy look that had attracted me to him.

After we'd exchanged greetings along with a hug, I told him that I'd stumbled across a curious phrase in an old handwritten book that I'd found and now I questioned if I'd translated it correctly.

He looked over the words I'd written down and the translation I'd made and frowned a bit. "You found this in an old book? It's a very old form of Latin, something no one's used for centuries. I would like to see this book."

"I don't actually have the book. I happened to find it in a bookstore, noticed the handwritten phrase inside, and copied it. Since I scribbled it in a hurry, I thought I might have written the words down wrong."

He stared at it for a few minutes as I sat and watched with my nerves on edge as if expected judgment for the quality of my work. My translation didn't exactly make sense to me, but it came out to, "a light illuminates dark." Given I was in a black hole in the dream, maybe it was a message.

He called up a reference on his computer and checked a couple of the words. "You're not far off, Gillian. It has more to do with the order of the words. 'In darkness, one light will illuminate.' Of course, other scholars may interpret the phrase differently, but putting it into English, that would be the closest. Do you have any idea what it means?"

"Other than the obvious?" I laughed as I said it. Was the whole message of my dream to turn on a light? "Is there any ancient proverb that might be a metaphor? I know there's 'a single light shines in the darkness' and things like that. I really hope there's more significance to it."

He arched an eyebrow at me in amusement. While Professor

Haines presented a scholarly-looking image with a usually serious expression and a no-nonsense manner during class, underneath that façade, he sometimes found his students to be a source of entertainment as he blasted preconceived notions. I recalled that he said the ancient texts recorded silly little phrases as he pointed out that they, too, were people with a sense of humor.

"There are many kinds of light, Gillian. And equally many references to darkness. The phrase can be a metaphor for any kind of dark times, whether they are physical or mental."

"Of course. Well, I thank you for your time and expertise."

"Anytime." He flashed a smile as he handed back my paper with his rephrasing scribbled on it.

As I headed back to my Jeep, I mulled over Gavin's words. Maybe my mind had attempted to link the dream to an insignificant message. I admitted that I'd had some oddball ones over the past few months and I needed to quit trying to turn them all into something prophetic.

Perhaps I should heed Janna's advice and talk to someone who understood the psychic world and could offer some guidance in this newfound unseen sphere of the spirit world. At least, a psychic might help me interpret the dreams I'd had.

Since I was at the University, I decided to call the son of the accident victim. When I'd talked to him earlier, Thomas Willits, a sophomore at UNR, told me he lived in a dorm near the campus, so I figured we might meet up if his aunt was available. The phone rang about four times and I almost gave up before he answered.

After confirming that I spoke to Thomas, I offered my sympathies before I explained why I'd called. "I know this is a difficult time for you. But if you have a few minutes to talk about the funeral service and what you would like me to sing to honor your father, I have some time now and I am on the campus. Can we meet at Pack Burgers a few blocks up Virginia?"

For a few moments, he didn't say anything and I thought this might be a bad time for them. I started to tell him that we could do it another time.

Then he said, "My aunt said you were recommended by a friend. I don't know what exactly you're wanting, but I can tell you a little about my dad and stuff he liked. But, maybe it would be better if Aunt Celeste comes along. She's in town now and I'll see if she can meet us in about fifteen minutes. Would that work?"

I agreed to it, although it meant a slightly longer wait. I went ahead to the burger joint, not the fanciest place, but more like a 50's 'teen shop with one of the best hamburgers in town. I figured it would be a relaxed setting to chat with Thomas, but maybe not so much for his aunt. Then again, the place held some good memories for me from my college days and it might be that his aunt had some also.

I ordered a diet soda and settled in a corner booth to wait. Pulling out my phone, I checked for any new messages, saw one from Janna, and one from Moss at the Sheriff's Department. I hadn't heard from him in several weeks although he had checked on me a couple of times shortly after the rescue. Curious, I phoned him back and got his voice mail. I didn't leave a message.

Right about that time, an average-looking young man, about five-foot-ten with light brown hair, and a college sweatshirt came in the door with an older woman in tow. The woman looked to be about fifty with dyed blond hair pulled back into a French twist, round glasses and a sternly set mouth that didn't show much expression. I guessed this was Thomas and his aunt. Standing I motioned to them, catching his eye at once. He came over, holding out a hand, "Miss Foster?"

"Yes. Call me Gillian, please. You are Thomas, I presume, and you're his Aunt Celeste?" I shook his hand, then offered mine to his aunt. Her eyes had reddish rims suggesting that she had been crying. Thomas just looked sad and a little lost. I motioned to the seats at the table. "I know this is an odd place to meet, but it was close. Can I get you a soda or something?"

Thomas accepted a cola drink while his aunt opted for hot tea. I came back in a few minutes with the drinks for them, then took my seat again. "I won't take too much of your time. I just wanted to talk a little to you both about what music you would like for the service. For instance, if your dad had a favorite song that you'd like sung? Something that is particularly meaningful to you and your dad, Thomas?"

Before the boy could say anything, his aunt spoke up, "When we were little, there was an old Civil War song that our father used to sing to us when he was telling stories. He said that his great-grandfather used to sing it to him as well. Emmett loved that song."

"Oh, I remember that one, Aunt Celie. Dad sang it to me also. It was called 'Two Brothers'. Do you know it, Ms. Foster?" His expression filled with hope and fond memories.

"It's an old folk song, isn't it? I don't know it right off, but I'm sure I can learn it before the service. I understand it's scheduled for this coming Friday morning. Is that correct?"

He nodded, as his aunt seemed to think about something. "We were kids in the seventies, Gillian. My brother was a big fan of Queen, Jethro Tull, and America. He was in love with Linda Ronstadt then. Maybe you could do something by one of them."

I made a note in my phone, thinking Ronstadt was a good choice. "Maybe 'Different Drum?'" I suggested.

"Yes! Dad still listened to that song a couple of times a week," Thomas said and his eyes glimmered with moisture.

"I am so sorry about your father," I said, reaching my hand to lay on top of his. "I was there when the accident happened. I wish I could have done something to save him."

Celeste sat forward in surprise, "You were there?"

I hesitated a moment, uncertain if I should say more at this time, but at their expectant looks, I plunged ahead. "I was in the car behind him and saw him start to slide. I slammed on my brakes and almost slid off the road as well. It was raining hard at the time and he just lost control. After I called 911, I went down to see if I could do anything. Another driver had also gone down, but we couldn't get to him. The door was stuck tight and the car was on its side, so it was resting on the passenger door. I broke in through the back window and was with him until the rescue people arrived." I paused as I thought about his father's last words. "Thomas, he asked me to tell you that he loved you... very much."

Thomas' eyes welled with tears as he bit back a sob. His voice was a strained whisper. "That's my dad. I'm glad you were with him before he died. That he wasn't alone."

"Did you see what happened with the other car?" Celeste asked. "How it caused the accident?"

"I did. The driver passed us both and cut sharply in front of your brother. That's when he hit the brakes and the car started to slide." As I saw her face, the thought occurred to me that I probably shouldn't have said anything. "Look, I really shouldn't talk about it since the police are still looking for the driver of that car and I was a witness. I just wanted to tell you how very sorry I am."

"Thank you, dear," Celeste said with genuine feeling. "We are grateful for all that you tried to do."

After an awkward pause when I felt uneasy saying anything else about the accident, I elected to move on with the planning. "All right, then, I think I have all I need to know. I can do the two songs during the service whenever you would like them. You can let the Funeral Director know and she'll fill me in on it when I get to the chapel. Is there a special hymn or inspirational piece that you'd like played?"

They looked at each other as if asking the same question, then Thomas said. "No, not really. My father quit going to church after my mother died, so I don't know if there is anything special he would have liked. It seems odd to talk about him in the past tense and realize that he's not here anymore."

"I know it sounds trite when people say it, but your father is always with you in your heart. You'll remember him often and there may be days when you feel he is very close to you. Don't ignore those moments. I think there is something beyond this life and those who went ahead of us do still keep an eye on us."

"That's a lovely thought," Celeste said. "My brother would probably pooh-pooh the thought of it, but there are times that I have felt he was near." She rose and offered her hand to me as she thanked me again. Thomas mouthed his thanks as he hurried to open the door for his aunt.

Good manners, I thought as I picked up my things and headed for the exit. *Something you don't see too often anymore.*

I spent the evening on the internet looking for the lyrics and music for "Two Brothers", a folk song that touched on the grief when two brothers from the same family went to fight on opposite sides of the War Between the States. Where the Willits had thought it was a song written at the time of the war, it turned out to be more contemporary than that having been written by Irving Gordon in the mid-1900s.

I was also able to find several recordings, including some rather lively ones that seemed totally wrong for the material. I settled on a moving version that almost brought me to tears while I listened and began picking out the melody on my piano. As I learned the lyrics, I grew more curious why this particular song was so dear to the Willits family. Maybe it had significance because of the Civil War and like many American families, one or more of their relatives had fought in that bloody conflict. I figured I would probably never know what it was that made Emmett Willits favor it.

On the other hand, "Different Drum" was a song that I performed often with Spicy Jam. Some songs from all eras of rock music stayed around and gained popularity with succeeding generations. This was one of them, but no one could quite rock it like Linda Ronstadt did, so that was the version I played with my own little special twists in it.

I thought about the upcoming funeral service. I had played at a couple over the past two months and both were quiet, normal services. I wasn't needed to escort the newly departed to the gate, which meant that they were prepared for death, I presumed, and could find it on their own. It's only when a soul didn't quite know where to go or didn't understand what had happened or flat out refused to go, as in the case of Marielle, that I found myself in the ethereal cemetery to guide them while singing praises for the mourners at the same time.

All in all, it was a peculiar and somewhat unsettling experience. I was understanding more about the process but knew nothing about the mechanics of it, other than I had no control over it when it happened. It was literally out of my hands. If there is an all-powerful being, then that entity certainly had a hand in my life with this. Given how Emmett Willits had died, I expected that I would meet him again on Friday.

THREE

My mouth dropped open as I got my first sight of the old house where Janna parked her car. A large sign in the front yard proclaimed:

Madame Astrid, Psychic and Seer, Learn your future. Let Madame lift the veil to your past, present, and future.

Couple that pronouncement with the brightly colored signage that included the moon, stars, an hourglass, a pyramid with the psychic eye in the middle, and assorted swirls and she might as well have screamed that a possibly insane woman lived here. I shot an accusing look at Janna that could only be interpreted as, *are you kidding me?*

"I know. She's a little flamboyant, but she knows her stuff. I promise you that," she said with a small imploring smile.

While I still had reservations about this plan, I'd agreed to pay a visit to Janna's psychic friend and she'd assured me that she was the real deal. "If anyone can offer advice, interpretation, or guidance about your 'gift', it's Madame Astrid," she'd said.

Ha! Madame Astrid. Now, that was a "professional" name if ever I heard one.

As she got out of the car and started toward the house, I followed with reluctant steps, asking myself for the umpteenth time why I let Janna talk me into this. *Because she'll keep at it until you try it*, my experienced-with-Janna voice answered.

She knocked on the door as a courtesy then walked into the house and I shuffled in behind her. Inside, it resembled a brightly decorated living room with pleasing colors of blue and pale yellow. Heavy, light-blocking drapes in shades of dark blue and green covered the three windows. A hefty, hexagon-shaped wooden table with a burgundy-colored fringed cloth over it squatted in the middle of the floor. I expected to see a crystal ball in the middle to complete the image, but nothing sat on it. A tall and wide oak bookcase claimed the wall next to a shut door. Books, notebooks and sculptures filled most of the shelves. In the middle shelf, a rough-looking, uncut lavender crystal that was about six inches across caught my eye. Next to it, a deep purple velvet drawstring bag bulged with something about four or five inches long.

Madame Astrid swept through the door and into the room as if she was making a stage entrance. She looked to be around sixty with long, graying hair hanging loose on her shoulders. She greeted Janna warmly before turning to scrutinize me.

"This is my friend, Gillian. I told you about her." Janna flashed an encouraging smile at me, followed by a don't-you-dare-embarrass-me glare.

"Oh, yes," Madame Astrid said, her lips splitting into a toothy grin that made me feel like prey. "It is my pleasure to make your acquaintance. Please sit down; be comfortable." I thought her accent sounded vaguely European or it could be phony. She motioned to the dark-blue overstuffed sofa on the long wall of the room. Janna and I sat as the psychic took the matching chair that sat at a ninety-degree angle to the couch.

I started to speak but she held up her hand. "No, allow me to concentrate for a few moments." She closed her eyes and hummed a little waltz-tempo tune to herself, swaying her head a little in time. Then she spoke, still keeping her eyes closed. "You are a talented musician as well as a gifted dog groomer. But I feel you are much more than that. You have recently acquired a unique gift that has proven to be uncomfortable for you, but you are coming to terms with it gradually. I sense that this ability allows you to see and talk to the dead, but I am not seeing the means of it too clearly. It appears that you visit them in parks?"

Eyebrows lowering, I glanced at Janna who stared at the psychic as if mesmerized by her words while I wondered just how much my friend had told her about me.

Madame Astrid continued. "It is interesting, Gillian, because you appear to be a skeptic, yet you can't explain what is happening to you. You have come here reluctantly. But that is all right." She opened her eyes, very wide pale blue ones, and peered directly into mine. "I want you to question everything, to disbelieve, so that when you accept it, it is because you have eliminated all other possibilities."

I admitted that this statement surprised me since I thought she would be expecting praise from me. She was correct that I was skeptical and not just about her, but about myself as well. I had more or less accepted my ability, although I wasn't convinced that it wasn't some weird hallucination. And I needed to find out how much Janna had actually told her.

Madame Astrid gave me a knowing look. "I don't blame you, Gillian. I happen to have a gift that allows me to have insight into people's psyche." She paused to pour cups of tea for us then leaned back into the chair. "I've told you what I can pick up easily from you, my dear. You are shielded, which is that you have your guard up. Since you distrust me, you're not that open and even a good psychic, such as myself, can only see so much in an unwilling client."

I had the good grace to at least gaze toward the paisley carpet and look a little chagrined. Her assessment landed right on the mark. I had come in completely defensive with a "show me what you can do" attitude. Even though I wanted her to help me, I didn't trust in her ability and wanted her to prove she wasn't a charlatan.

Madame Astrid continued, "Why don't you tell me about your gift and what I might do to help you?"

"I don't know how much Janna has told you, but let me start at the beginning." Before I said anything more, Madame held up her hand and both she and Janna started to speak at the same time.

"I didn't tell her anything—" Janna blurted.

"She only said that you had—" the psychic began and then both broke off. Madame Astrid took a deep breath before she continued. "Janna only told me that you had an accident that caused you to acquire an unusual psychic gift and that she thought that I might offer some insight. By all means, tell me as much about it as you care to."

I caught the quick nod of Janna's head and a raised eyebrow that, along with a lip pout, told me she was disappointed that I hadn't trusted her.

"You're right," I said. "I did come here with an attitude and suspicions. I apologize for that. Here's what has happened to me since a fall that caused my concussion last November."

I proceeded to tell her the pertinent details of the emergence of my ability to see and talk to dead people while simultaneously improvising lyrics to a tribute melody to honor the deceased and sing it for the mourners. I told her about Artesmia Maroudian, the former gypsy lady who first informed me of my new talent, as I preferred to call it, even before the accident happened. I also told her about the two subsequent visits from the woman, one in a dream and one at the old woman's funeral.

"I knew Artesmia," Madame Astrid said as I paused in my narrative. "She was still a gypsy, that does not go away. She also had a gift. She knew even before the accident that you had this ability?"

"It would seem so. I don't know if it was always in me, dormant, and waiting for something to activate it or if it was caused by the concussion." I ran my right hand across the side of my face as if I could erase it. "Have you ever heard of anything like this before?"

Taking a moment before answering, she sipped at her tea, then said, "Gifts that appear after a head injury? Yes, I have seen those. They happen now and then. One like yours? I haven't heard of it before. That does not mean that it hasn't happened, only that I haven't seen anything about it or anything like it."

I deflated a little, feeling that I wouldn't be getting any help here. At the same time, I felt surprised that I even thought I would. I hadn't told her about talking to Zak, the angel in my dream.

Janna nudged me in the ribs and mouthed his name silently, encouraging me to tell her. Reluctance held me back. Claiming to talk to an angel seemed an invitation to be called psychotic or at the least, too imaginative, even to someone who dealt with paranormal experiences.

Not seeming to notice this brief exchange, Madame continued, "You do not need to fear or be anxious about your gift, Gillian. It is not called a gift without good reason. Often people say that God works in mysterious ways and He has surely sent you a rare ability to help people who are lost after death. Sometimes souls don't know how to move on to the next plane, so they remain behind as ghosts or restless spirits. To be given such a gift is rare and you are blessed to have it. Trust in the Creator who gave it to you."

Part of me bristled and wanted to shout "Bullshit!" But how many times now had I been told it was a gift, unwanted though it was? Whether I believed in God or not, my experiences, hallucinations or otherwise, extended beyond the normal realm of this world.

Calming myself, I said, "That may be but this is all new to me. I'm starting to become accustomed to popping into an ethereal cemetery in a spirit form of myself, but I don't understand how it works and I still think I am hallucinating it. It defies a scientific explanation." My voice grew higher in pitch as I spoke, an indication of the anxiety building in me when I seriously considered the whole experience.

To my surprise, Madame barked out a short laugh. "I would say that is normal under the sudden event condition. Most of us with psychic abilities, whether to see the future, read the past, find missing objects, or read Tarot cards had these skills begin to develop when we were children. To be thrust into it all at once must be overwhelming and frightening. After a while, it will be as natural to you as any of your other senses. It may even expand gradually giving you more insight."

Oh, great. That was something I didn't need. But hadn't it

expanded already with me being able to "see" Marielle in places where she'd been as a projection from her spirit when I was trying to find her murderer? Would there be more to come? "How do I cope with the anxiety I feel about this?" I asked.

"Meditation is a good place to start. I can teach you a couple of simple breathing techniques that will open your psyche to learning more about your gift and its purpose. They will also help to center you and feel more comfortable with it. From what you say, you are still fighting the gift and denying it. Accepting and exploring will help you understand it more."

She got to her feet and took a few steps to the bookcase where she removed a candle on a small brass plate and set it in the middle of the table. She motioned for me to sit at the table and dimmed the lights in the room to very low, then lit the candle. The flame sprang to life and ascended into a teardrop shape of a rose-gold color.

"Now, Gillian, focus on the flame, clear your mind and breathe in slowly for a count of five," Madame Astrid instructed. "Good, now breathe it back out for five counts. Do it again. Inhale...three...four...five. Now exhale... good. Four...five. Repeat. Let your mind idle. Don't think of anything, just concentrate on the flame."

Following her instructions, I did this, repeating it over and over until I was feeling very relaxed and consumed in the even flickering of the flame.

After ten minutes of this, she added a stick of incense to the table, set it burning, and advised me to inhale, then hold my breath for five seconds before releasing the breath. I nearly choked on the smoky scent of something that smelled more like a forest fire than a pleasant garden by the time she ended the session ten minutes later. I coughed and reached for a tissue. "What was that odor?" I asked after I'd wiped my eyes and blown my nose.

"It was pine. You may have an allergy to the smoke so maybe a liquid scent would be more effective for you."

I nodded as she opened a cupboard door in the bottom of the bookcase and pulled out a small bottle.

"This is a lavender scent," she said. "It is a light fragrance and is very relaxing. Just put a drop in a small bowl with a teaspoon of warm water." She put one of the candles, a plate and the bottle of lavender oil into a little velvet bag and handed them to me. "Try doing this daily for two weeks and let me know how it goes or if anything changes. If you want additional techniques or want to discuss your gift's properties more, please come back and I will be honored to assist as you grow into it."

In a bit of a fog and feeling very relaxed, I took the offered bag and thanked her, then turned to go toward the door. I did glimpse Janna pressing some money into Madame's hand. Not a free consultation, I realized, knowing I hadn't thought about it until that moment.

As Janna dropped me off at my house, I managed a feeble apology. "I'm really sorry I didn't have more faith in you. In my heart, I know you wouldn't tell anyone my secrets and this whole seeing ghosts thing is something I don't want people to know. I'm over-sensitive to the possibility, I guess, thinking people would consider me a freak. So thanks for having my back on this. And for paying for that session. I'll pay you back."

"No, no, you won't. I insisted you go so it's my treat. I was disappointed that you thought I told Madame, but I do understand your worries. Honestly, Gilly, I don't think most people would give a hoot if you told them you saw ghosts. Those that make a big deal of it are not worth worrying about." She motioned me out of the car, then gave me a bright smile and a little wave through the car window before she pulled away from the curb.

FOUR

*M*ountain View Cemetery ranked as one of the nicest facilities in Reno, providing the traditional plots for caskets as well as a huge mausoleum and numerous vaults for cremated remains. Although being among them still made my skin itch, I coped with the uncomfortable feeling as I walked through the entrance and made my way to the chapel.

I had worked with Erin Jensen, the Funeral Director, before so she only had to fill me in on the plan for the service. I would play a hymn just before the service started then perform both songs, one after the other, after Thomas Willits spoke about his father.

As I sat at the piano to run through a sound check, I thought that possibly this might be just a simple service with no extraordinary happenings and Emmett Willits may have crossed into the light already.

The chapel began to fill as people arrived in twos and threes but it ended up about half-full. So far as family, it appeared to be only Thomas and his aunt. I guessed that the rest were likely friends and co-workers. A couple of kids looked around Thomas' age so I figured they were his college buddies.

As soon as I finished the last chord of the hymn, the minister stepped to the podium and began the service. It seemed clear that he didn't know the deceased but had based the sermon from talking to Celeste, whom he glanced toward several times as if for confirmation. It was short, about ten minutes, Biblical, and to the point. Then he summoned Thomas up to deliver the eulogy.

My heart went out to him as he nervously adjusted the microphone and began to speak with a waiver in his voice. Pulling himself together, Thomas talked about his family roots in northern Nevada beginning when his third great grandfather moved to the area after the Civil War, worked in the silver mines, then settled in

Reno. He praised his dad for his strength and love and spoke about his pride in his family.

After he finished, I took a moment to say, "Emmet Willits loved this song, one that he learned as a child. It's about two brothers who fought in the Civil War, one fighting on each side of the conflict. This is for Emmett and his family." Having heard Thomas talk about the Civil War connection, I felt the song even more as I performed it and to my relief, I stayed in the chapel, no sudden consciousness slip. Next, I introduced one of Emmet's favorite songs and started singing a slightly slower version of "Different Drum" and that's when it happened.

In a flash, I stood in the rich green gardens of the transitional cemetery. It looked spring-like with daffodils in full bloom while other small flowers were bursting out in clumps all over the open ground. The section where I stood sprouted numerous modest headstones from the lush grass. Most were marked, although a few were blank, waiting for the deceased names to be added at some point. I hadn't thought about it before, but it was curious that the headstones would have names on them and I wondered about it. The spirits had moved on, hadn't they? Or was it a reverse situation and the names would be removed when they departed from this cemetery? As I pondered this, I moved closer to one and read the name on it, Marion Wheeler Jones, along with a very old birth date and the equally distant date of the woman's death. Not erased then, so what purpose did they serve?

Ahead of me, the familiar silver path that led to the crossover gate sparkled in the morning light and not far away I spotted a man dressed in blue high-waisted slacks and a deep blue paisley shirt. Although he looked in his fifties, the clothes were straight out of the late 70s. Definitely not his funeral clothing. At the moment, he looked around the area with a confused expression on his face.

I started walking toward him, seeing the words in my mind

that praised Emmett's life. Words, that somehow, without any conscious thought on my part, were woven into the song I was singing back in the chapel. Words that somehow flowed into the music I played. This was the inexplicable gift that had been thrust upon me and now drew attention to my singing in a different way than I had ever anticipated.

I approached him, my voice still singing the song in the background of my mind but my attention now focused on the man before me. He looked worried, his eyes darting around the cemetery as if he was looking for something. Then he spotted me and his eyes widened.

"I know you! I saw you at the accident." He shouted the words as if I might not be able to hear.

"Yes, Emmett. I was there. I remember. Do you know where you are?"

"I believe so. I didn't live through the crash, did I? Is this Heaven? And you died also? I thought you were outside the car talking to me."

I understood his confusion. "No, I'm not dead. I've come to help you pass through the gate to your eternal home."

A look of joy filled his eyes. "Yes, I can go home. Back to my son. You can take me back." He misunderstood, confused by this turn of events.

"No, I'm sorry. I meant you can go through the light to your eternal home. To be with the Creator and your loved ones, who have gone before you."

His expression changed, worry bringing lines to his brow and a frown to his mouth. "But how can I leave? My son needs me. He's in college. He's going to be an ecologist. He wants to protect the environment. Save the planet. I have to help him finish. Just two more years, until he graduates. Can't you give me that?"

"Oh, Emmett, I have no power to change what happened. I'm just a guide, someone sent to help you find the way. I can't give you back your life on Earth." I felt so sad for him and what he had lost and must leave behind. "That journey is over now and you have to move to the next level."

He stepped back, moving away from the path and me. "I can't go through. I can't leave him alone. Not now. Doesn't someone have the power to send me back?"

I shrugged, feeling out of my element. "I'm afraid you're asking the wrong person. I don't know. On the other side of the gate is the light through to the next plane. Maybe over there someone can tell you, but I don't know."

"What if there's nothing? What of my son? I have failed him." He covered his face with his hands as his knees buckled and he dropped into a crouch of despair.

I knelt beside him, unable to actually touch him. "I have to believe that if we're experiencing this moment, this time where my spirit can meet yours in a place that doesn't physically exist, then there must be something more beyond that light. I think this is proof that people are more than just their physical bodies and there is a soul that moves on. Find your faith, Emmett."

He dropped his hands and gazed up at me. "But my boy, how will he get through?"

"I've met Thomas and your sister Celeste, as well. Thomas will be okay. He's coping very well although he misses you already." I told him this with conviction and hoped it would allay his concerns.

"He's not going to have enough money." Emmett wrung his hands. "I was his sole support and I didn't have anything to leave behind for him. I lost so much when the stock market crashed and I was putting most of the money toward his education. My savings are almost depleted. I didn't carry life insurance. How will he stay in school?"

His voice was the cry of a grieved man. He had nothing left to pass on to his son and I could see it was an obligation that he felt was left unfulfilled. "There are ways," I assured him. "He can apply for a scholarship. There are grants..."

Willits shook his head. "We tried already and he couldn't get one. I have to help him."

"How can you, Emmett? Your time on Earth is over. You can't help your son from here. Not in the way, you want. You can't earn money for him." I tried to reason with him.

"I have to do something. I promised him I would see him through college. Oh, why didn't I take out insurance?" He looked like he was about to cry, then a look of hope came into his eyes. "You can do it."

"What?"

"You're not dead, right? You're in Reno. You can help him."

Oh, no, I thought. "I can't help him. I can barely support myself."

"But you can help him get the funding, can't you? You must be able to do something." His eyes pleaded with me. "I know you have connections."

"Wait, no. I don't have connections. I'm just a musician and not exactly successful at it."

"But you're an angel, aren't you?"

"Hardly that." I'd been mistaken for one before. Just because I could wander in spirit form through an imagined graveyard didn't make me a heavenly denizen. "Trust me, I am just here to guide you to the gate and the light."

His face fell and guilt set in. Maybe I could do something; help Thomas find a scholarship. Shaking my head in disbelief that I was about to agree, I said, "Look, if I promise that I will help Thomas to continue to his graduation, will you cross over?"

He rose to his feet, uncertain if he could do it. But he nodded his head in agreement.

"Come on, walk with me now, and I'll take you to the gate." I motioned to him to step onto the path and he came forward with reluctance.

"I don't understand. Who or what are you?"

"I'm only a human, but I've been given the power to guide

souls to the light that lies just beyond the gate at the end of this path. It will take you to the next plane, to home. Your earthly concerns have ended now, Emmett, and it's time for you to let go."

He fell into step beside me, still talking about his worries for his son. Distressed as any father might be, except mine, at failing his child, he kept saying he needed to stay and help while I assured him that Thomas would be all right. He'd already done his job and raised the young man to be a decent, thoughtful citizen of the world.

For a moment, he paused and seemed to listen. "Ah, I recognize the song. Thank you. Perhaps it is prophetic in its own way. I guess we all travel to different drums, don't we?"

I saw the iron bars of the gate just ahead and it began to swing open. "We do, indeed. And now your travels will take you to a new path. Go home, Emmett. Follow your own drumbeat."

He looked where I pointed, smiled and, as I had seen before, the years and worries melted from his face and body and he was a young man again as he passed me to go through the gate. Before he stepped through, he turned to me and said, "Angel or not, I'm counting on you."

His step lightened and a glow of happiness filled his eyes as he passed into the light.

As I turned away, out of the corner of my eye, I got a glimpse of someone near the hedge of tall bushes that was about ten yards away. He was a young man, perhaps in his twenties, bearded, and with lamb chop sideburns. He wore a dark blue uniform of some sort and a cap on his head that looked like a military cadet's.

He stared at me for a few moments, long enough for me to know that he'd seen me, then vanished into the hedge just as I shifted from the vision and found myself back at the piano in the chapel.

As the last chord of my song died, I lowered my head. Emmett Willits had gone home, whatever that might look like. He hadn't been a very religious man, but he did believe in God. Was that enough? I hoped so. But who was the man by the hedge and why did I see him?

Following the service, I went over to speak to Thomas and offer a little encouragement without telling him about his father's concerns. "I could tell that you and your father were very close. I am sure he is still looking after you."

"Yes, we were," he replied, the sadness touching his eyes again and he forced a sad half-smile. "My dad was all I had and I'll miss him, even the nagging he sometimes did. My aunt is great, but she lives in Sacramento."

"I see. Well, at least, she isn't too far away. What about school? Are you set there?"

His lips turned down at the corners. "At least until the end of this semester, I'm okay. After that, I'm not sure yet. I don't know if Dad had any money left to carry me through another two years. I'm still trying to sort things out and I may have to sell the house. The last few years were a little rough for us."

"I'm so sorry, Thomas," I said. "I'm sure your dad would want you to continue. Maybe you can check out some scholarship funds?"

He gave me a curious look as if he was wondering what my interest might be. "Sure, that's something I can check into. Thank you again for singing. It was very special and the extra verses that fit my dad so well were amazing. It was as if you knew him."

"Sometimes I can be a bit intuitive when I get a sense of a person from the family. It just seems to come through to me. Take care and have faith everything will work out."

I left him to talk to other mourners and started to pack up my music case when I spotted Egan Moss at the back of the room. The Washoe County Sheriff's detective was wearing a dark brown suit, hands shoved in his pockets as he watched me. A sense of déjà vu hit me as I was reminded of Marielle's funeral and the first time I met him. This time; however, I knew the detective and was not a suspect in a crime he was trying to solve.

He strolled up to me, a smirk on his face. "We meet again at a funeral, Ms. Foster."

"What brings you here, Detective?" I snapped the case shut and set it on one of the chairs.

"You, of course."

"Me?" I arched a surprised eyebrow at him. All right, he'd left me a phone message and I still hadn't connected with him, but I hardly saw it as a reason to come to the funeral.

He nodded, rocked a little on his heels. He looked a little thinner than the last time I'd seen him. "This folder just landed on my desk yesterday evening. Hernandez and I are officially on the case of a hit-and-run vehicular homicide. Imagine my surprise to see your name listed as a witness."

"Oh," I said with a wise, knowing look. "So, if you saw my statement, then you know it wasn't exactly a hit-and-run, but a 'failure to yield the right of way' or the other driver cut Mr. Willits off causing him to lose control of his car."

"Yeah, I know. An H&R would be easier to pursue, but you and the other driver who stopped are both witnesses to the accident and that the SUV was speeding in poor weather conditions and cut into the lane too sharply nearly hitting Willits' car. So, that means that I'd like to chat with you a little about the accident. I didn't expect to see you here, but I just figured I'd stop by to talk to the family and introduce myself along with offering my condolences."

"I see. So that's what the phone call a couple of days ago was about. Do you want to talk now or can it wait? I have a gig to get to by six this evening."

"Actually, the call was about something else, but I'll tell you about it later. Give me about ten minutes to talk to Willits' son. How about I meet you at the Mexican restaurant at the bottom of the hill for a drink or lunch, if you haven't eaten?"

"You buying?"

"Are you kidding? It's supposed to be the other way around."

I laughed. "All right, Moss. I'll meet you there."

As I watched him turn and saunter over to talk to Thomas, I wondered what the other thing might be. Later on, there would be the trial coming up for Vincent Coblenzer and he had told me that I would likely be a witness for the prosecution. But plenty of time lay ahead before that and the DA would be talking to me about it in a month or so.

Making my way to my car, I thought about the trial. It was something that ate at me, little by little. If I had a choice, it wouldn't be to go in front of the court and talk about what had happened in that basement. If it meant convicting that bastard, I would do it, but it appeared that there was more than enough evidence from the three murders he'd committed to put him away for the rest of his sick, sordid life.

I got a table for two at the Mi Jardin Mexican Restaurant and ordered a soda and an order of nachos for myself as soon as I sat down. I hadn't eaten anything since my morning coffee and a breakfast bar after I'd come in from a twenty-minute run around the neighborhood and my stomach was more than ready for food.

Moss arrived about the time the nachos did and immediately swiped one off my plate.

"Hey," I objected. "Get your own."

He just shrugged, then ordered a soda and tacos for himself. "How are you doing, Gillian? You've lost weight. You look good."

"Thank you. You look trimmer also."

"I've been working out some. Got a punching bag in the office a few months ago and hitting it on a regular basis is paying off."

More seriously, he asked, "Are you having any nightmares from the ordeal with Coblenzer? I know the psych at the hospital recommended you see someone to talk about it."

My mouth tightened into a straight line and I averted my eyes. "No. Not that it's any of your business."

"You're right. It isn't. I just know that this kind of thing can really eat at you sometimes. Don't let it do it, okay?"

I nodded and popped another chip into my mouth. Why did everyone think I needed help?

"Right, so let's talk about the accident. We've been working on the license plate lead with the number and letters that you gave us and pulled up all the plates that matched. Then we eliminated any that didn't match the color and make of the SUV. We came up with nada."

"What? That isn't right."

"Are you sure you had the letters right? Maybe you misread one."

I felt confident that I'd gotten them right. I hadn't written them down, but I memorized them when he'd passed me thinking that I might file a report on the driver with the Highway Patrol. "I don't think so. It might be, but I'm pretty certain of them."

"It's okay. We'll try other combinations also to see if anything comes up matching the vehicle. Can you remember anything else about the accident? Anything that might not have been in the statement."

"I think I told the officer everything when he talked to me at the scene, but I'll go through it again with you. It's odd that sometimes something that happens so quickly plays out in slow motion in your mind, so I did recall a lot of detail."

I took the next ten minutes or so telling him everything I could recall from the time the SUV shot past me to seeing Emmett Willits lifted up the embankment on a stretcher.

He made notes and nodded his head but listened without interrupting. When I'd done, he cleared his throat and said, "Now, I'm not saying that I believe in this gift of yours totally, but I do know that you do get some insight from somewhere and since you were singing one of your deceased-custom songs today, I was wondering..."

His voice trailed off as his eyes asked the rest of the question.

"If I learned any more from Emmett Willits today. No, nothing about the accident other than he lost control. Mostly, he was concerned about his son."

"Of course. I see. Well, it doesn't hurt to ask."

He paused, sipped his soda, then cleared his throat again. "Since we're speaking about your insight, I have something to ask of you."

Puzzled, I bobbed my head in a shallow nod to encourage him to continue.

"I know that this doesn't have anything to do with you, but I thought maybe you might be able to help me out." He paused as if hesitant to say what he wanted.

"What is this about? Is it something more on Marielle Sanders?" I asked, referencing back to the little girl whose ghost had gotten me involved with Moss in the first place.

"No, it's an unsolved murder I've been working on for several months now that's going nowhere. I'm hoping that, with your unique skills, you might be able to provide some special details."

I got it now. He wanted me to try to talk to a spirit. "I can't just demand to know about someone or what happened to them. I sing at a funeral and I am transported to this sort of transitional cemetery where the deceased is in limbo until he goes through the gate." I saw the look of disappointment on Moss' face and felt bad that I couldn't do anything to help him.

"Are you sure there isn't something you can do? This case has been bugging me since last autumn and I just don't have any clues. A couple of kids found a homeless man, who had been murdered over by the 4th Street Bridge. If I could just get something, other than a tennis shoe with a hole in it, that might give me a direction, I might be able to find the killer. So far, Hernandez and I haven't been able to turn up anyone who saw or heard anything. I know it's a long shot. Hell, I wouldn't be asking you if I wasn't desperate."

I had to admit that it was a pretty big jump from Moss'

skepticism of what I told him when I explained my gift to coming here to ask me to try. Maybe I needed to be a little more open-minded with Madame Astrid.

"Look. A couple of times I was able to contact Marielle by singing at her grave, but I don't know. It might have been only because I had already made a connection with her." I tactfully didn't mention managing to contact Alicia Villanueva in the same way. Maybe it was possible and I was just learning to use my gift. "I guess I could try it with your homeless person. You do have a grave, don't you?"

He brightened up. "Oh, sure. Of course, there's a grave. You'll give it a try then?"

"When do you want to do it?"

"How's tomorrow morning for you?"

I sighed, thinking about the gig I had in a few hours that would likely turn into a late night. "Not before ten. Where should I meet you?"

Moss' expression grew sheepish as he pursed his lips in thought. "How about I give you a call later with the information?"

"You don't know," I said, amused as I accused him.

"Of course, I know. I've gotta check the records to see exactly where the county buried him."

*F*IVE

*A*s it turned out, unclaimed bodies; people who died with no relatives, no funeral arrangements or money, and no one to arrange for a final resting place ended up in a section of an older cemetery in Sun Valley. Most, Moss informed me, had been homeless.

I stood beside him in this bleak-looking sector without grave markers, just plot number cards in the ground, and a deep sadness welled in my heart. Forgotten in death, left to be buried in a nameless grave seemed to herald an empty life. Yet at some point, these people had hopes and ambitions, families and friends.

"Which plot?" I asked.

Moss checked his notes and pointed to a spot two markers to the right. Like most of these graves, the only identifier amounted to a number on an enclosed card on a metal rod. It looked temporary, like one the mortuaries used to mark a location until the headstone arrived.

I walked down and stood in front of it. "Do you know anything about him? A name?"

"The other homeless guys called him Jack from Modesto. No last name. We checked Modesto for missing persons and any other records, but couldn't find anyone to match. Nothing popped on the national database either. If nothing else, maybe you can learn his full name."

I gazed at the unadorned grave that barely had any grass growing on it. A single clump of purple-flowered redstem filaree weed grew along the right edge offering the only spot of color. Taking a deep breath, I began singing, "Be Thou My Vision", a traditional hymn I'd selected for this attempt. The song had a beautiful Irish melody I'd always loved, but I suspected the

English lyrics came much later. Perhaps it would have meaning to Jack, but I doubted this would work.

At first, nothing happened. I figured I'd give it to the second verse before abandoning the attempt. Then a graveyard image phased into my vision.

Familiar, yet different, it looked like a peaceful garden section of the cemetery that I usually saw in my visions except that the plain headstones here were unmarked, as devoid of names as the graves in the real cemetery. I looked around for the silver path and didn't spot it at first, then I glimpsed a slight glistening in the sunlight about twenty yards from where I stood.

"'Jack," I called out and waited a few moments, then called again. "Jack from Modesto? Are you here?"

A round little man came toward me from the bushes to the side. "Who are you?" His face wore a scowl and his loud voice bore an angry tone. "What do you want?"

"Are you Jack from Modesto?" I kept my voice calm and friendly, not wanting to add to his annoyance.

"I'm Jack. But I'm from Ely. Who wants to know?" His whole face wrinkled in the frown he cast at me.

"I'm sorry to have bothered you. My name is Gillian. I'm here looking for Jack from Modesto. Do you know him?"

"Know him? Do you think this is a social club, missy?"

"No, of course not. Why haven't you gone to the light?" Why was I confronted with this unhappy spirit? Maybe he needed guidance. More than that, where was the Jack that I sought?

At that point another man arrived, just seeming to appear.

"Did you call for me?" he asked. A very thin spirit, his ruddy-looking, wrinkled skin sagged around his cheeks and his eyes lacked any luster. I had the impression he'd starved to almost a skeleton before his death.

"Are you called Jack from Modesto?"

He shook his head. "No, I'm John Grant from Tulsa."

What was going on here? Why was I getting more than one person?

"There was another Jack, I think," John Grant went on. "But he didn't stay long. Don't know where he went."

"How many of you are there?" I asked as I realized that this might be a common grave with more than one person buried in it.

"None of your business," Jack from Ely growled.

"Look, both of you," I said in a firm, authoritative tone, then raised my voice in case there were more and pointed to the path. "And any others who might be hanging around here. You need to move on. All you have to do is follow that silver path over there. It leads to the gateway that takes you into the light. From there, you are with the Creator and you will be whole and mended."

"What path?" John Grant asked.

"Do you think you're some kind of angel?" The round Jack grumbled as he spoke.

With a flash of insight, I realized they couldn't see the path. "Follow me and I'll lead you to the gate." I turned and walked toward the path. Faint at first, it sparkled brighter as I drew closer.

I glanced back to see John Grant following me while the other spirit hung back, reluctant to leave. I halted and called to him. "Jack from Ely, come on. Is there something holding you back? Is there something unfinished? Did you leave relatives behind? Maybe I can let someone know what happened to you."

He shook his head violently. "No, quit meddling! You can't help."

I motioned for John to wait for me at the path and backtracked to face Jack. He looked as miserable as he did angry. "I can help. Tell me what's holding you back. When did you die, Jack?"

"I... I don't know. A few years ago, I guess." He paused, sighed, and looked away from me. His voice choked as he continued, "I had a baby daughter. I don't know what happened to her. I wasn't there..."

"Okay, Jack. I think I can help with this. Tell me your last name and your daughter's name. I have a friend who can find your daughter. We can tell her that you have passed to the next life and give her closure. Is there a message for her?"

His gaze swiveled to me, the anger in his face morphing into a mask of grief. "Her name is Amberlee Mitchell. I never married her mother. I'm Jack Ostero. Born in Ely, died in a cardboard box by the river."

"No one to miss you, Jack?"

Tears pooled in his eyes on the verge of spilling over. His voice strained. "No. No one. Just my baby girl. She barely knew me before I left her mother."

He looked so miserable that I ached to be able to comfort him, but I knew I couldn't touch him. Only my words could give him any solace. "It will be okay, Jack. Come to the gate with us. You will find forgiveness and understanding beyond. Have faith in that."

"Faith? I never had faith in anything. Why would there be anything for me?" His voice sounded hollow, a broken man with no reason to believe anything awaited him.

What could I tell him? My own faith was never that strong, but I couldn't deny that something was summoning me to this graveyard. Finding the words, I said, "There must be a God that believes in you, Jack Ostero, or I would not be talking to you. Some power in the Universe brings me here and it tells me to help you go home."

"You're nothing but a spirit! Or maybe my hallucination. There's no light for me and no forgiveness." With anguish in his expression, he turned away from me.

"I'm here in spirit form, but I am not dead! The Creator guides me and I believe that you will find peace and forgiveness beyond that gate. But you need to forgive yourself, now!"

I stepped back, stunned by the words I had spoken. I hadn't even thought them, but they had burst forth with the sharpness of a trumpet call ringing with Truth.

Jack bent over as if in pain and shook his head in denial.

As his shoulders shook with emotion, I whispered, "Believe in the Creator. He loves you and forgives you."

After a few moments, he straightened and turned toward me. I could see the shimmer of moisture on his cheeks and in his eyes. No anger showed, but he looked uncertain and fearful.

His feet shuffled in a reluctant step toward me. "Promise you will tell my daughter I'm sorry, so sorry, I failed her. That I wasn't a father to her."

"I promise." I hoped I could keep that promise. With his full name and the location, Moss should be able to contact his daughter and her mother.

With both of the spirits in tow, I led them down the path to the gate. In the quiet, I could hear my voice still singing and I thought that either I kept repeating the song or time moved at a different pace in this place. I'd have to ask Moss about it when I finished here.

Following a curve in the path, we came around it to where the gate, as beautiful as ever, loomed straight ahead of us. Beyond it the golden light glowed and shimmered, beckoning the spirits to it. It still amazed me. While it resembled the usual imagery of Heaven's Gate, its detail and simple design outshone any of the special effects or drawings I'd seen.

John halted in front of the gate, raised his rheumy eyes to the light and a look of reverence illuminated his face. In the space of a few breaths, his cares dropped away as his aspect reverted to a younger, more hopeful version of himself.

"Hallelujah!" he shouted, raising his arms to the sky, then he ran into the light like a child going home.

Less sure of his reception, Jack Ostero moved forward with uncertain, tiny steps. As the edges of the light touched him, his face grew gentler and relaxed as he, too, reverse-aged to a handsome young man a time before life had treated him poorly. Hope came into his face and straightening his shoulders, Jack walked almost into the light before he turned to me. "Remember your promise." I nodded and he stepped into the welcoming glow.

I sighed my relief that I'd gotten them through. I hadn't found Moss' John Doe, though. As I started to turn away, I noticed a dark spot in the center of the gate and I thought maybe a spirit was coming through it, but it didn't grow and after a minute, it vanished, then the golden light disappeared.

Odd. If my charges were through the light, I should no longer be here. Puzzled, I turned to walk back up the silver path thinking that another spirit must need an escort to the light. Or perhaps Jack from Modesto had heard my call.

Off to my right, the bushes appeared darker than earlier and I sensed something foreboding about them as if evil lurked there.

I recalled an early dream in the cemetery when I still thought it a garden, where the grounds gave way to dark bushes with thorns and thick running vines. Behind were grotesque-looking trees and I thought I'd seen someone running through them.

These didn't look as threatening, but I experienced the same feeling that they didn't belong.

I swallowed hard as an inexplicable fear touched me. I'd never felt unsafe in this place, but I did now. I was certain an evil entity lurked behind the bushes.

I needed to leave!

With the thought, I blinked and swayed, unbalanced a little, as I realized I stood at the unmarked plot in the Sun Valley cemetery. My voice broke on the last note I was singing.

I turned to face Moss, who watched me with a curious expression on his face.

"What happened?" he asked.

I held up my hand to indicate I needed a few moments, then

lurched back to the car to get a bottle of water I'd brought with me. I felt exhausted. Moss followed me over. After two big gulps, I asked, "How long was I singing?"

"About four minutes, I'd say. You really aren't aware of what you were doing?"

"No. It was a much longer time in the other cemetery. There were two spirits called Jack who answered my call. You didn't tell me this was a communal gravesite. Evidentially, there are quite a few people buried here."

"I also didn't tell you they were cremated. So, there are many boxes of ashes buried here. Did the right Jack talk to you?"

"No. He didn't respond." I saw the disappointment on his face. "Hey, I told you it was a long shot. But I did find two other men who need to be identified, I imagine, and I guided them to the light. I suspect your Jack had already gone through. Sorry."

Moss tapped his notebook and thought a bit. "I still don't understand what you do, but thanks. I really appreciate you trying to do this."

Still the doubt, I thought. Hard for me to believe, almost impossible for Moss.

I paused to drink more water before telling him about Jack Ostero and his request to notify his daughter. "Despite my lack of enthusiasm for doing this, I'm glad you're still working this case and maybe can provide closure for the relatives of the other two men. I did promise Jack from Ely you'd find his daughter and tell her about her dad."

"Yeah, about that... I don't know if I can do that. Besides, he wouldn't know if I didn't," Moss said.

"Yeah, he would," I answered. "And I don't want a ghost nagging at me because I hadn't kept my promise, so you'd better deliver, Detective." If Marielle had been able to contact me outside the graveyard, I expected the little man from Ely could manage as well.

He grinned, a little sparkle in his eyes. "I'll see what I can do."

As we started back to his car, Moss paused to take a phone call before getting in. A small smile lit his face as he started the car, then glanced at me. "My kid. He just got accepted on a Little League ball team. Had to tell me right away."

"Good for him. I didn't know you were a dad, Moss."

Apparently that opened a floodgate as he started chatting about his son and I learned he'd gone through a messy divorce eight months earlier. He added that the legal battle for joint-custody continued.

"It's hardest on my kid," he said. "Poor boy doesn't understand why Mom and Dad fight every time they get together. My ex thinks that I'm too busy with work to be a father, but when it comes to my son, I try to take as much time as I can to be with him. I do admit that my job demands a lot. Hers isn't much better. She works in Dispatch."

"I would imagine that being called out at any time does make parenting difficult," I commented. "But many other jobs put demands on a person's time and they just have to make adjustments where they can." I thought about Mark, who was in his second year of residency and always on call, or so it seemed. But then, being a part-time entertainer in addition to my day job put a lot of demands on my time as well.

"That's true. Being a parent isn't an easy job anyway. But I think it takes both parents working at it to be successful. I want to be a good dad, one that Garrett will look up to and be proud of as he grows up. Just because I'm not there every day doesn't mean that I don't love him and I want him to know that."

"I'm sure he knows it."

Moss grew quiet for a minute or so as he thought about his son. I could see that he missed him and wanted to be better for him.

"Have you thought about the trial?" he asked, changing the subject. "It's coming up in a couple of months and I'm pretty sure the DA is going to want you to testify."

"Yeah, I know. I try not to think about it too much. The thing is that I don't want to say anything that will relate to my ability to talk to dead people. I mean, people point and call you a freak or they crawl out of the woodwork asking you to talk to a relative or some other dead person—"

"Like I did?" he said, interrupting and shooting an apologetic look at me.

"Well, yeah, but at least you had a good reason. You know what I mean. This gig is hard enough to handle without any publicity attached to it calling me an alleged psychic."

"I do indeed know. Even from my standpoint, and my partner's, it's not a good thing for people to think we use a psychic or someone with an unusual extra-sensory gift to solve murders. It can put a bad spin on the Sheriff's Department. So we'd like to keep it out of the trial as well. But we all need to keep the explanation simple. Maybe you saw the perp loitering near the club downtown when you went in to ask about singing there. Or maybe we can just say that we got an anonymous tip."

"Well, I'm in favor of that so long as we're not perjuring ourselves." I didn't need to complicate my life with either option.

Moss pulled the car into the parking lot and stopped near my Jeep. "We'll talk again later about the trial," he said. "Try not to worry about it. We have a good case against that killer."

I nodded, then got out and unlocked my vehicle and slid behind the wheel, somehow glad that Moss waited until I was in the car and safely out of the spot before he parked. He was a good detective and a decent man, but he'd better come through on that promise I'd made to Jack Ostero.

SIX

I slept late on Sunday after a late night at an engagement party gig that went on longer than anticipated. But they paid us more for staying later and I couldn't say it wasn't a good time. Now, with my Sunday chores done, I cuddled on the couch with Nygard and I thought about the previous day's experience.

I hadn't expected to be able to contact anyone at the graveyard, so contacting two souls adrift, who had not yet crossed, surprised me. I regretted that I couldn't find the Jack that Moss wanted me to contact, but if he'd already crossed over, then I'd done all I could do. While it was true that I had talked to Alicia Villanueva, another little girl who had been a victim of the Holiday Killer, I believed it had been a fluke, a one-time connection. That I could connect with people I wasn't even looking for spooked me a little. What other things might I be able to do that I didn't yet know about?

While I was considering these encounters, I thought about the words I spoke to the spirits each time; words to assure them that life continues beyond the light, but how could I offer such promises when I doubted this outcome myself? In many ways, the words didn't come from me, not from my conscious self. Could I speak in a trance state and not really be in control of what I said or did? I recalled the words when I spoke them, but I couldn't say that anything I did or said in the transitional cemetery came from me. I shivered from a chill up my spine as I thought about it. The mere possibility that someone else, a spirit or God, might control my mind frightened me.

I scratched Nygard's ears, listening to the gentle rumble of his purr. "Wish I knew what you were thinking. Oh wait, I do. I'll bet you'd like a piece of chicken." He turned his head to gaze at me, his intent blue eyes making it clear that was acceptable.

Going to the 'fridge, I sliced off a piece of the chicken I'd roasted the day before and pulled it into pieces to feed to him. My veterinarian would have a fit if she knew how I indulged this cat.

My cell phone chimed a tune, a perky little ditty called "Busy Bee" that I'd assigned to Janna. Her voice matched the music.

"Hey, girlfriend. How about I bring a pizza over and we have an evening in?"

"Sounds great," I answered. "When will you be here?"

"Umm, less than a minute. I'm almost to your driveway."

Sure enough, I heard a honk and saw the front of her BMW coming up the drive.

"Pretty sure of yourself, weren't you?" I said as I opened the door to my little home.

With a big grin, she waved, climbed out, and brought in the pizza and a bottle of rose' wine. Clearly, she was looking forward to a chatty evening.

On-again, off-again with her boyfriend, she advised me she'd cooled it for a while. "He's getting too pushy and I need him to back off some." Since she worked with him, it made things awkward, but she managed.

"How are things with the dreamy doc?" she asked, picking up her third piece of pizza.

"Lukewarm," I replied and bit into my own slice.

Her eyebrows rose almost to her hairline. "Trouble?"

"No. Just not seeing much of him. I went to the hospital a couple of days ago for an exciting lunch in that little cubby they call a coffee shop. We spent about twenty minutes together before he had to go back to work."

With his insane schedule, free time was almost non-existent. I often wondered how working a resident for twelve to fourteen hours a day made for a competent doctor. For myself, I would prefer my doctor more alert than these tired interns were likely to be.

Being honest with myself, not seeing Mark didn't amount to

much of an issue at the moment. Still trying to shake off the dirty feeling from being with that monster Coblenzer, I didn't want to be cuddly with anyone just yet. Not my fault, I realized, but it didn't change how I felt about myself and what had happened.

"Let me tell you about the funeral I sang for Friday and what happened yesterday," I said to change the topic.

"You have got to be joking," she said after I filled her in on the latest spirit sightings. "You have to tell Madame Astrid about this. Your abilities are growing."

"You don't have to sound so happy about it," I groused. I wasn't all that sure that I was pleased with it. In fact, it troubled me more than it helped me. "I was hoping this would fade away."

"At least the spirits aren't asking you to do anything dangerous. How are the self-defense classes going?"

"Good. I'm getting better and quicker. I learned a new move the other night. Want me to show you?"

Pretty and slim, Janna was the kind of girl men noticed every time. With her working in a casino hotel, I often worried that my friend might be a target for some lowlife or an out-of-control drunk. While security in the hotel kept her safe, the walk to her car after her shift was another story. A few self-defense moves might help her fend off anyone who accosted her.

I urged her to her feet, then demonstrated a quick way a girl could efficiently disable an attacker long enough to get away. As I showed her, I explained, "Easy to do if you have a free arm, you only need to make a fist and jab hard with your knuckles to the attacker's eyes or nose." I punched my finger knuckles into my hand a few times to drive it home. "Most of us hesitate to punch anyone in the face, but it will slow or deter an attacker giving you time to run for help. And scream your head off if a security officer or anyone else might be nearby."

"I don't know about this. I don't think I could actually punch someone. Won't it just make him madder?"

"Possibly, but if you hit him hard enough, it will give you time to either follow up with another punch or to run back into the casino. I know you can run faster in heels than most people expect. I've seen you do it. And speaking of those heels, don't hesitate to use them against an attacker. Kick with them and step down hard on his foot or into his ankle."

Despite her misgivings, I encouraged her to go through it a few times with me. She began to feel comfortable with the move and reacted well when I attempted to grab her. Even expecting the blow, I didn't pull my head back enough to avoid her fist and it tapped my cheek hard enough that I stumbled back.

She gasped in surprise. "I'm sorry! Did I hurt you?"

She made a grab for me to see if I was bleeding, but I shook my head and held her away. "No, it's fine. You just caught the edge. But I think you have the idea."

"Can't I just stick with pepper spray or hair spray or something?" She looked unhappy about the idea of having to hit someone.

"Only if you have it in your hand or coat pocket every time you walk outside. You won't have time to find it in your purse, so it has to be handy." I rubbed at my cheek as I poured a little more wine for each of us.

"At least, keep it in mind as a possible defense," I said as I handed her the glass and dropped back to the sofa. "You never know when a threat might be serious."

"Would this have helped when you were attacked?" she asked. She sat down beside me, her eyes meeting mine with a searching gaze.

"No, not that move. He came from behind me and he was fast. If I'd had more training than an old self-defense class in college and had kept up with it, I might have been able to twist out of his grip before he drugged me."

Janna looked down as she sipped her wine, then cleared her throat. "Gilly, you haven't really talked about what happened other than you were abducted. I know the guy was the one who killed the children and that somehow he figured out that you knew about him, but how?"

I looked away, focusing on the fireplace at the end of the room and trying not to think about the incident, then answered, "I don't want to talk about it, girlfriend. It's something I want to erase from my mind."

"That's not healthy. It's changed you." She stressed the last with a slap of her hand on the coffee table. "Look at you. You're losing weight—too much of it and taking self-defense classes. To what purpose? Would it have helped?"

"I don't know!" I snapped my head back to her, my eyes narrowing with an irrational annoyance at her questions. I couldn't talk about it with anyone, not even my best friend, and I still feared I'd have to go into detail during the trial.

Janna looked disappointed and a little sad as she reached for her purse. "I'd better go. Let's get together for dinner next week, okay?"

I nodded. Then she left the house without as much as a hug.

However, she left behind a third of the pizza and Nygard begged a piece of the sausage. I gave him two, then wrapped up the rest and tucked it in the 'fridge before sitting down to finish my wine.

On Thursday afternoon, Mark finagled a whole three hours off, so we met for an early dinner at Sticks Restaurant near the Truckee River in the downtown area. An upscale place, it featured an assortment of chef-designed dishes that ranged from Cornish game hens to buffalo burgers and fresh salmon prepared in delicate sauces. The food tasted amazing, the price reflecting the quality, which meant I couldn't afford it.

When I arrived my typical few minutes late, I found Mark waiting at a table near the front windows. He looked as handsome and dashing as usual, in spite of constantly going with little sleep. He greeted me with a kiss on the cheek and a hug, then pulled the chair for me, reminding me why I liked him. His dark blond hair was a little disheveled, which only made him look cuter and sexier, and he cast a broad smile at me.

"You look great," he said right off, his eyes roving over my slimmer body. "Is everything good?"

"Yeah. I'm doing terrific. And you?" Typical small talk to get things going. He knew a little of what had happened although I hadn't told him the whole story. Not Janna; not him. Not even Egan Moss, who was there and wrote the police report.

Mark was considerate and understanding, showing that he would be a great doctor. He didn't press me for details at the time. Even though he knew I had issues after my head injury, I wasn't his patient when I'd been brought in after the ordeal with the Holiday Killer and he only knew what I told him.

I also hadn't told him that I could talk to dead people. I felt a little like that kid in "The Sixth Sense" and I didn't want him to think I was delusional, something I still questioned myself.

"I'm good. I had something a little weird happen in ER Saturday, a week ago, but I'll tell you after we order. I am so ready for a break."

"Any chance of that happening?"

"Not for a couple of weeks, then I might get a whole day off. You go into medicine knowing that your residency is going to be a non-stop work-a-thon, but actually doing it really begins to wear on you. I'll have a whole week off coming up in about two months. Maybe we could do something. Go to the coast for a couple of days. What do you think?" He looked hopeful as he said it.

We'd been dating for about three months, but in real dates, it amounted to about five with another four quick lunches or dinners. To go off with him for a solid forty-eight hours would be exciting and a real breakthrough in our relationship. It also meant a closeness that we hadn't had before. That worried me and I didn't know if I could face it yet.

"That would be awesome," I replied, putting on a big smile and sounding more enthusiastic than I felt.

We paused to order dinner. Mark ordered crab cakes for an appetizer, then a New York steak while I chose the salmon teriyaki salad.

"You mentioned something happened on Saturday. To me, too. Last week. I witnessed an accident that almost creamed me as well. A car cut off the driver in front of me, who braked and lost control and just missed taking me with him," I said.

"My God! Thank goodness, you're safe. I think the victim might have been the man that was brought into ER Saturday evening. He was about fifty; had head injuries, and a punctured lung and fractures from a car accident. He died shortly after we got him, and we were doing everything we could to revive him. He came back for a just a few seconds; I really thought we were going to be able to keep him. But he just mumbled a few words. 'Lost... graveyard, Tommy, and great-great-grandfather.' Then we lost him again. It was really strange."

"It sounds like it was the same man."

The words may not have made much sense to Mark, but they did to me. Willits had already gone to the graveyard and wandered around in confusion. He showed concern for his son, but I wondered about the remark relating to his great-great-grandfather? Could the other man in the cemetery be his ancestor? Did that mean that the elder Willits hadn't crossed over or had he come for Emmett?

Hesitating a moment, Mark dipped his head once in agreement. Was he violating a patient confidentiality by telling me?

"I didn't think he would survive. The car flipped a couple of times down the embankment. I tried to help, but the door was stuck and it took the emergency crew to get it pried open."

Mark slid his hand on top of mine and squeezed it a little to offer reassurance. "I know you did all you could. I'm just glad it wasn't you that came into Emergency."

"Me, too. I've been there enough for the year already. Anyway, in an odd coincidence, I sang for his funeral on Friday."

"You're still singing for funerals? That seems odd. Not that you would sing, but that people would hire a singer for a funeral."

"A little unusual," I agreed. "But sometimes people want a favorite song or a special hymn to be sung live to honor the deceased or to assuage their own grief with the familiar words or music. It's actually a pretty rewarding moment in the service."

He arched an eyebrow and gave me a small grin. "If you say so."

Then we changed subjects and talked about a movie that we both wanted to see if he could eke out the time. The crab cakes arrived and he urged me to try them. With reluctance, I took one and nibbled at it. While it tasted good, crab didn't rank on my favorite foods list, so I left the other three for him and sipped on my iced tea.

After we ate, we still had about an hour before Mark needed to get back to the hospital, so we decided to stroll along the Truckee River, which flowed past at a fair clip. The city had revitalized the downtown River Walk area to make it a pleasant and inviting zone for shoppers and visitors.

Although the day was sunny and I'd worn a heavy sweater, I felt chilled. Mark noticed when I folded my arms across my chest to try to add more warmth, then he put his arm around me, pulling me closer to him to share his body heat, and I snuggled into the embrace. Why did it seem like men always radiate more heat than a woman?

We found a vacant bench to sit and Mark continued to hold me close, his arm completely encircling my shoulders and urging me against him. He lifted his free hand to my face to caress my cheeks before leaning in to place a light kiss on my lips. I melted a little more into him, enjoying the touch, but at the same time, nervous about it. I hadn't been close with him since the abduction. I think he sensed the tension and he pulled back.

"You okay?" he asked.

I swallowed my nervous lump. "Yeah. Just a little tense. It's been a busy week."

"Doggies giving you trouble?" He said it with a teasing tone, but I thought he worried that it involved more than I wanted to say.

"Something like that. Lots of dogs to groom and the not-so-good gig last week after the accident. Plus the funeral. I think I'm just keyed up a bit."

His breath whooshed out. "I wish we had time to do something about that tension, but—"

"You need to get back, I know. You warned me."

He grinned, then kissed me again, deepening it, but still not demanding any more than a simple kiss. Getting to his feet, he pulled me beside him and guided us back toward our cars.

I felt relieved and disappointed at the same time.

SEVEN

"**I** think you know that my student apartment is near the Hillside Cemetery?" Thomas Willits asked with a touch of excitement in his voice.

"Catty-corner, if I recall," I answered. He'd left a message on my home phone saying something odd had happened and I might be interested to hear about it. Maybe I could explain it, he added. Admitting that it piqued my curiosity, I called him back.

"That's right. I live in that building. Well, something really weird and hard to explain happened last night. I had a few friends over for pizza, beer, and a movie. Now, there's been a long-running rumor that the cemetery is haunted, but most of us haven't paid any attention to that."

He paused to compose his thoughts or give a more dramatic effect. I wasn't sure which, but I gave him an encouraging, "Uh huh."

"So, last night, a couple of my friends went outside to smoke and they crossed over the road to get away from the building. They saw a man in the cemetery and he appeared to glow with an eerie white light and moved around without making any noise. Robbie called out to him, but he didn't respond, just kept moving through the grounds as if he was looking for something. Then both of them yelled at him. Finally, the man turned to look at them and... Poof! Gone! He disappeared. They ran over to the fence surrounding the graveyard, but they could see nothing of the man and they couldn't spot a way he could get in or out without being noticed."

Goosebumps cascaded down my arms. "That does sound like a ghost sighting. I've heard about at least one woman who has made frequent appearances in the cemetery and there may be others. But why do you think this might interest me? Do I look like a ghostbuster?"

He chuckled a bit, then hesitated and I heard him draw an uncertain breath. "When we talked at my dad's funeral, you said that you had a feeling that he would be near and keeping an eye on me. So, I thought that maybe it could be my dad in the graveyard. Maybe he wanted to be close."

"I get it. You think it's your father?"

"Maybe. I mean, it could be possible, couldn't it?"

"I don't think so, Thomas. I think he wouldn't be in the cemetery if he wanted to keep an eye on you, and I don't know that he would be visible to you. You might sense him more in things around you. Maybe something moved to a new location in the house. Or something that connects with your father being called to your attention somehow. From what I've read about it, the spirits communicate with loved ones in subtle ways."

"So it wouldn't be anything so obvious?" he asked. I could hear the disappointment in his voice.

"Not likely. But you have gotten my interest, so how about if I come by in a couple of hours and we can take a walk over to the cemetery? Maybe we'll see something or maybe it was just a fluke of the lights."

A fluke of the lights? I gave myself a mental slap.

There were no lights near the cemetery, I noted as I parked my car across the street from it. A large white marker facing the road caught my eye and I crossed to get a better look. A chain link fence surrounded the cemetery, but I could just make out the large sign, thanks to the white background on it. I switched on a lantern-style flashlight that I'd brought with me.

Mounted on a metal mesh frame shaped like Nevada, the sign declared the area as a Civil War plot and the official state seal below marked it a historic site. As I ran the light over the words, I learned it was the final resting place for Union soldiers from a Nevada regiment.

Okay, so maybe a restless spirit wandered in the cemetery, but if he hadn't crossed over, then it meant he must have haunted it for close to sixty or seventy years or even more.

While I wasn't afraid of the graveyard, I hurried away from it with a twitch of unease. I sprinted across the street, bounded up the steps to Thomas' door, and knocked. He answered almost immediately.

"Hey! Thanks for coming," he said as he stepped back, opening the door wide.

I stepped into an apartment that seemed a comfortable, if not extravagant, size. Judging from the doors off the living room area, I guessed it had two bedrooms and one bath. A small table with two chairs created a division in front of the kitchenette. Overall, it resembled a motel room with cheap furniture.

Thomas watched me assess the place and said, "It's not fancy but the rent is cheap. For student housing, it's not too bad and I have a roommate, so that helps keep the costs down."

I thought about the nice little apartment I'd had when I attended the university and it barely stacked up to this, but in my mind, it rocked. "It's a good little place. But I'm not seeing much in the way of personal items that make it feel lived-in, if you know what I mean."

He looked puzzled a moment, then he got the idea. "I don't have a lot here. Most of my stuff is still at my dad's house in Fallon. I have a few pictures in my bedroom though - family photos and stuff that my aunt dropped off   and I have my laptop and tablet in there. I usually do my studying at the library or in my bedroom."

"Sounds about right." I faced him. "I stopped by the cemetery before I came in and I had a thought about it. There's a section that's for Civil War veterans. If I recall from the funeral, you said that your great-great-great grandfather fought in the War Between the States. Is that right?"

"Yes. For the Union. He was a sergeant; got wounded at Shiloh and left the Army shortly after that. He limped the rest of his life from the damage to his left leg."

This confirmed something I had begun to suspect. "Was he buried in that cemetery across the street?"

Thomas thought for a bit. "You know, I think he might have been. When I was little, I went there once with my dad and grandfather. Why?"

"I have a theory that if - and that's a big if - a ghost there has an interest in you, it might be your Civil War great grandfather. Shall we take a walk over there and see if we spot anything tonight?"

Without hesitation, he grabbed a sweater and opened the door for me.

We hurried across the street to another fenced cemetery on the other side of a dirt road from the one where I'd seen the Civil War section. As I turned to go toward the plot I'd seen earlier, Thomas caught my arm and pointed up the road. "Robbie saw the ghost up this way."

Off to the left, below the grounds, the city lights glowed in the distance. Could that have contributed to the sighting? Perhaps his friend did see a reflection of those lights and not a ghost, but then a reflection wouldn't turn toward you.

"He saw the ghost here? Not in the Civil War plot?"

"Yeah. If it was him, my triple-great grandfather wouldn't have been buried over there. I was young when we came to the grave and this was all open land then, but I'm pretty sure it was on this side. I remember thinking that you could see the entire city from up here."

"Oh, I just thought he'd be over there." I focused away from the city view and looked toward the darker area that was the old graveyard. I didn't see anyone, but a whitish glow hovered around one of the gravestones.

"Do you recall about where he's buried?" I asked.

Thomas gazed at the various markers in this part of the graveyard as he tried to recall where he might have been. With the fencing around it, we couldn't actually get into the area to look.

Finally, he shook his head. "I was about five and it was in this section and toward the middle. But I don't know exactly which one."

"That's okay. Do you see anything going on now? Anything unusual around the graves?"

"Not exactly, but there seems to be a shadow on one of them and there's nothing to do it."

Earlier clouds had blocked any illumination from the partial moon, but they'd cleared, giving us enough light to see the light-stoned grave markers.

"Where do you see it?" I asked, peering in the direction he looked.

He pointed. "Over there next to that taller stone."

I shifted my glance that direction and spotted the dark patch that he had noticed, but I didn't suspect anything unusual about it. If a spirit lingered by it, I expected to discern some movement.

I returned my gaze to a lighter stone I'd noted where a glow seemed to come off it, but nothing emerged. On an off chance, I started humming a tune called "Buttermilk Hill". I recalled from earlier music classes that this old American folk song went back to the Revolutionary War, although I thought it might be one that had come over with the British, mostly from the Irish and Scottish military. But the song had been around for ages, so I thought it very likely that any Civil War soldier would know it.

Thomas froze beside me, listening to the melody. "I know that song."

I nodded, still humming it.

I saw the figure materialize out of nowhere. One moment he wasn't in sight and the next, he stood alongside the glowing tombstone gazing at me, a scowl on his face. The sensation felt different from being in the ethereal cemetery and I shivered as if it had suddenly grown colder.

Here I stood, outside in a physical graveyard in the real world, and I saw a ghost, who could, it seems, see me as well.

Definitely a Civil War soldier, he wore the blue of the North with one of the caps on his head. It looked very much like the man who had been in the graveyard with Emmett Willits a few days ago.

I nudged Thomas and whispered, "Do you see anything?"

He didn't answer, but he stared where the man stood unmoving next to the grave.

"Do you see him?" I asked.

"I see a whitish glow, like a mist above the stone. Are you seeing it also?"

"Yes." I didn't tell him I saw the man in detail, almost as if he stood there in the flesh. He looked about twenty-five, handsome with the mustache and mutton-chop sideburns people considered so fashionable in the eighteen hundreds. He made no move toward me, but his light-colored eyes, either blue or gray, seemed to pierce me with his gaze.

"You were in the pretty cemetery," he said. His voice was like a whisper in my head rather than an actual sound. "With my great-great-grandson when he crossed through that gate."

"And you watched him go. And you're...?" I wasn't sure if I spoke it or if this was the internal conversation that I often experienced. If I'd said it out loud, then I might have to explain this to Thomas.

"I am Emmett Willits, ma'am. I do not believe that I know you. But then, after all these years, there are not many people that I do know. I have watched most of them pass through to their next destination." His voice had a southern drawl to it and a gentleness that spoke of the family that raised him and the courtesy of the south.

"Why haven't you gone through?" He knew about it so something had to be holding him back.

"I cannot," he said sadly. "There are things in my life that prevent my passage. But that young lad there..." He gestured with his head toward Thomas. "I might be able to help him. I know that his father left him very little when he was killed and I had some resources when I lived that may help him out."

Resources? That confused me some, but I felt compelled to help both Thomas and this Emmett. If I could persuade him to cross as well as learn what resources he mentioned, I needed to do it. Not here, though; not with Thomas to witness any more of this bizarre conversation or my trance state, whichever condition prevailed.

"Emmett, I want to talk to you more and I think I can help you as well. Is it possible to meet in the other place?"

He moved forward then, almost to the fence surrounding the graveyard. I noted a slight limp as he walked. "Maybe. If you can do whatever it was that you did to get there and summon me, I might be able to go there again. Come back."

With that, he vanished and the glow of the headstone ceased as well. Fingers pressed against my arm and I jumped at the unexpected touch. My heart pounded and I looked around wide-eyed, then I realized Thomas had nudged me.

"Look over there," he said.

My eyes followed the direction he pointed to see an almost transparent woman walking, although her feet didn't seem to touch the ground, on the far side of the cemetery. At once, I thought about the famous ghost that many had sighted here. She continued around that section of the graveyard in a big circle before returning to a grave. I presumed it was hers.

"She's gone. I think that's the resident ghost here. Or at least one of them. She's been spotted a few times over the years. Let's go back to your apartment. I have a few questions."

As we walked back, Thomas cleared his throat and said, "Were you talking to a ghost? I heard you mumbling something and it sounded like you said, 'Emmett'. Was it my dad?"

I glanced down, trying to decide how much to tell him. "No, not your father. But I think it was a relative. I'll tell you what I saw."

Back in his apartment, I waited while he made instant coffee for both of us and we sat on his couch sipping it.

I spoke first. "Before I tell you anything, tell me what you actually saw in the cemetery."

"I saw that dark spot, but I guess that was nothing. Then I saw a white mist above a grave after you started humming that song. It kind of hovered around that grave, then moved toward the fence. Then it sounded like you were talking to someone, but it was a low mutter and I couldn't hear much."

"But you never saw anything more clearly?"

"No. I did see more of a shape on the second ghost, if that's what it was. It seemed bigger and rounder, but I couldn't see any details."

"Okay. You did see indicators of the ghosts. I have a small gift and I can see them in more detail. I think the man I spoke with was your triple-great-grandfather. Tell me what you can about him, please. You wouldn't happen to have a photo, would you?"

I thought that might be a long shot, but I hoped to distract him. I wanted to downplay my gift as much as I could. At least, he hadn't heard the entire, seemingly one-sided, conversation.

"Wait," he said, then slipped off to his bedroom. A few moments later, I heard a drawer being opened, then some other sounds of things being moved around. He returned with an old, sepia-toned photograph in a paper frame, which he handed to me. Two men, who looked very much alike, stood ramrod straight in the photo, arms at their sides, as many of the photos from the era showed. Slower exposures meant holding still longer so they tended to be pose-and-hold looks. I studied the faces. Brothers. If you didn't know which was which you might have trouble identifying them.

"Emmett was the younger brother," Thomas said. "The older one was Menafee Thomas. I was named after him. He fought for the South and was killed at the Shiloh battle."

"They looked like twins," I commented, not sure I could have distinguished the difference between the two at an older age. "I'm amazed that you even have a photo of them."

"My dad got a lot of the stuff from his father. Both of them had been very proud that they'd had a Civil War connection. My dad used to be part of a recreation group and he had a uniform, rifle, and everything. My aunt brought all of those things he'd accumulated to me from the house just before the funeral, in case I wanted to use any of it in the service."

I was impressed. I didn't know anything about my family beyond my mother's mother and even then, I'd only seen her a few times before she died. We'd never talked much about her family. And my dad never mentioned his parents or any siblings. I didn't even know if he had any.

"So, tell me about them," I said.

"They were almost two years apart and very close when they grew up, from what I was told. They disagreed when the Civil War started. It wasn't that Menafee didn't think that the slaves should be freed, but he resented being forced by the northerners. He thought that in due time, the southern plantation owners would come to it on their own. Many were giving their slaves more privileges and some were releasing them. But my grandpa said it was a complicated issue. Emmett felt that they needed to be pushed toward it more. From what he said, I don't think that anyone who went into it thought that the war would last as long as it did or be as devastating."

"The bloodiest war on American soil," I murmured, recalling what little I'd learned of the War Between the States when I was in school. Family against family, fathers against sons, and brothers against brothers. Here was a classic example of how emotionally wrought that battle was. "So what happened with Emmett?"

"As I said earlier, he was wounded at Shiloh and almost lost a leg and it took a long time to heal. Once it did, he'd had enough of the fighting and everything around him reminded him of the war and his brother's death, so he packed his few belongings and moved west, coming to Nevada to make his fortune in the silver mines."

"Did he have any luck with that?" I asked.

"He did pretty well, I guess. He made enough to build a nice house, get married, and have two kids. I don't think he ever made enough to say he was rich, but he wasn't totally broke. My grandfather once passed down a family story that Grandpa Emmett always hunted for the mother lode, but he never found it."

I handed the picture back and he stared at it for a moment or two before he rose to return it to his bedroom.

He seemed sadder when he returned carrying a little wooden box. He set it on the coffee table and removed several objects. I recognized two old buttons, a small, broken wooden bowl that appeared to be from a tobacco pipe, and a square belt buckle. From his jeans pocket, he pulled out two lumps of metal that looked like pointed balls and a short piece of braid. "These were all objects from the war that Grampa Emmett brought with him when he moved west. We always meant to frame them in a shadow box as a memorial, but granddad never got it done and neither did my dad."

"May I touch them?" I asked. I wanted to examine them more and touch the surfaces. They were pieces of history. One thing I learned in that semester of archeology was that artifacts were links to the past and should be revered.

Okay, those were Gavin Haines' words and I hung on almost everything he said as if it were gospel.

"Of course. More coffee?" He pointed to my almost empty cup. I shook my head.

"Beer?"

I declined.

He went to the kitchenette and pulled a beer out of the 'fridge before he sat down again. "That's about all I really know about him. And these things. I took them to school once for a show and tell."

"I'll bet that was a hit," I said and a small smile tugged at my mouth as I thought about being a kid with a prize to show the class.

I picked up the belt buckle and admired the detailing on the brass object. About three inches across and two and a half in height, an American eagle cast into the metal's center identified it. The Union army had the eagle, so Emmett's, I assumed. I turned it over to examine the bar on the back and saw a casting date of 1862 scratched into it along the edge near the metal loop for the leather belt to go through.

The pipe bowl, darkened from frequent use, still smelled of tobacco, even after all this time. It looked like a hand-carved bowl, but the stem had broken off at some point. I could almost picture Emmett sitting by a campfire with the pipe in his hand, taking a few minutes to savor the quiet of the night when the next day might bring death. My throat tightened with the emotion of the thought and I set the object back down.

Next, I picked up one of the buttons. Like the buckle, it bore the image of the eagle cast into the brass. As I rubbed my finger over the bird's image, feeling the detail in it, I felt a sense of déjà vu, as if it spoke to me. Compelled to ask, I gazed at Thomas and said, "Would you mind if I hold onto this button for a while? I know this sounds strange, but I feel a connection with it."

He shot a puzzled look at me, but he nodded. "Sure. It's not worth much except sentimental value, but if you can use it, go ahead."

"Thanks," I said as I slipped it into my pocket. "But you might be undervaluing these items. They could sell for enough money to buy you another year of college. The belt buckle is in perfect shape, just needs a little polishing, and it has a story behind it, so that makes it valuable to collectors. The more you know about an object, the more it's worth. Since you know these belonged to your Civil War great grandfather and he was at the Battle of Shiloh, it gains value."

"Really? I never thought of that. But, naw. I couldn't part with any of them. They're my family's history and about all I have of it now." His eyes grew misty as he gazed at the objects on the table. I couldn't blame him for not wanting to sell them, but it wouldn't hurt to know what they might fetch if he needed money.

"Tell me about the braid," I said as I picked up the almost two-inch long piece of woven threads.

"It came off his hat, I think. At least that's the story my granddad told me. Although it could have been off Menafee's hat. Granddad wasn't entirely sure." He looked up at me and smiled.

At that moment, I was struck by how much he resembled his ancestor. The shape of his face and the nose were almost identical. Strong genes on that side of the family.

"How are you doing, Thomas? I know this is a difficult time for you."

"I'm okay. There are bad moments when it really hits me that he's gone. And other times, I feel overwhelmed by everything. You know, the disposition of what little property my dad had, the lack of funds to continue my schooling, and having to try to get loans or scholarships. Even trying to find out if my dad's insurance is going to cover all the funeral costs." He sat with his hands clasped, rubbing at his knuckles.

"This is a difficult time," I commiserated. "But it will get better. Don't let it get you down too much, but you also need to take the time to grieve."

He looked up at me, a curious expression on his face. "You're an unusual person. I thought you were different when you sang for the funeral. The lyrics you sang seemed so personal and geared toward my dad as if you knew him. That's why I called you about this ghost sighting. I thought that if anyone could see a ghost, it would be you. I admit that I was kind of hoping that it might be my father's spirit and I'm a little disappointed that it wasn't. But I'm also excited that you've contacted my Grandpa Emmett."

"Well, it's good and bad," I said, trying to talk kindly to him. "It's good because I can see him and talk to him so there might be some more I can add to the family history. But it's bad because it means that he has not crossed over to the next plane that the soul is destined to reach."

Thomas' look turned to surprise and a glint sparked in his eyes. "Do you really believe that?"

A bit amused myself, I laughed and said, "You know a year ago I would have said no, that I didn't believe any of it. But some things have happened in the past few months that have made me question my beliefs. Things, like what we saw tonight, have forced me to open my eyes and look at possibilities that I didn't believe could be real. Ghosts, spirits, soul survival. I don't have the same conviction that they are fantasy as I did before I started seeing them. Now? I think there is something there. What it is, I can't say, but I do believe in a powerful force in the Universe and for now, let's call it God."

His expression grew more serious and a frown creased his forehead. "I'm not too sure either. I used to believe more before Mom died. Then I had to question it all and now Dad is gone. But then, seeing those ghosts tonight... It changes everything and I'm more confused than ever."

Rising, I turned to him. "Keep an open mind, Thomas. It isn't as simple as we might think and it's probably not as complicated either. I need to be going, but I'll let you know if something else turns up."

The encounter with Emmett gave me quite a bit to ponder as I returned home. Considering the possibilities, I concluded the best course might be to contact the Hillside Cemetery, see if they had any records, then go right to his grave there and sing. Given the success I'd had at contacting him, I felt the chances leaned toward meeting him in the transitional cemetery again. Perhaps I could learn more about him, then persuade him to move on.

I heard my own thoughts and broke out into a giggle. In my own way, I was becoming a ghostbuster. Maybe I should watch the movie again for a few tips.

EIGHT

On Thursday morning, I geared up for a solo run at Virginia Lake before work. I enjoyed the mile-long path around the water and not that many people used it at the time I ran. Most runners were early birds, getting a run in before work, so by the time I got there for a run they were gone. One of the perks of having a job that started at nine instead of eight.

Positioning my earbuds, I selected my favorite jogging playlist on my old MP3 player and set off on the path at a comfortable pace. Warm enough now for shorts, I'd worn my knee length ones and a light knit blouse.

For the most part, the pathway stayed a few feet from the shoreline but in a few places, it got very close to the edge. Although a shallow shelf of submerged land edged much of the lake, people couldn't swim or wade along it.

Familiar with the close spots by now, I kept my pace when I came up to one and only cast a brief glance at the water. In that split second, I glimpsed a figure behind me, felt a sudden jar, and the next thing I knew I floundered in the lake, arms flailing around as I tried to get above the surface. Once I got my bearings, I broke through in a couple of kicks and gasped for oxygen. Twisting my head to see the shoreline, I looked for the person who'd bumped me. Although it couldn't have been more than a half-minute since I went in the water, I couldn't see anyone in the vicinity.

Shaking my wet hair out of my face, I swam the three or four feet to the shoreline and climbed onto the dirt. The water felt slimy on my skin and who knows what had been in it recently. Fish, for certain, and some ducks or even gulls often landed and searched for food in the water. The scent was not fresh and clean for all that it was spring. Like a wet dog, I shook myself off as best I could and started jogging back to my car. My MP3 player, a relic from my university days, now resided somewhere in the lake along with my ear buds.

What the heck had that been about? Who had run into me and why? I didn't think it was an accident, not as hard as he'd plowed into me. My bad. If I hadn't been listening to my music, I would have heard him coming up behind me. The more I thought about it, replaying the quick view I'd had before flying into the lake, the more convinced I became that the man had bumped me on purpose.

He wore a dark-colored jogging suit with a hoodie and although I couldn't see his face, I had an impression of something red under the hood. He seemed about medium height and build, but I couldn't recall any more about him. As to why he'd knocked me into the lake, I had no clue. For now, I needed to get home, shower, and get to work.

On my day off, I attempted to find a phone number for the Old Hillside Cemetery without much success. When I looked it up on the internet, I found an article that said four cemeteries were in the area. Pulling up a map of the area showed three in what I'd thought constituted one graveyard. The Old Hillside was the bigger one where I'd found Emmett, but the Civil War one actually bore the name of Grand Army of the Republic Cemetery. The third one belonged to the Knights of Pythias, a national fraternal organization.

More than that, I discovered that the university now owned the one I needed to access. I called UNR's office and after explaining that I wanted to go onto the graveyard grounds for a genealogical research project, the admin clerk I spoke to told me she couldn't find out anything about it.

Frustrated, I decided to go in person and an hour later, I stood in the administration office and explained my purpose again. As the clerk, likely a student intern, started to tell me again that the University had no connection with the cemetery, an older woman looked up from her desk and said, "Wait. We did own it for a while, but we sold it in 1996."

She rose and came over to talk to me. "I can find the name of the company that owns it now, if that would help."

"Thank you," I replied. "Actually, I just need to know how to gain entry into the cemetery. There's a gate and I would like to go inside to research a death date."

The woman nodded, scribbled down a name and phone number on a piece of paper and handed it to me. I glanced at it and thanked her.

As soon as I was out of the office, I called the number and a man answered. I repeated my research story and asked about access to the graveyard.

Surprised by the question, he said, "It's open. The gate is accessed from Tenth Street."

"Oh, I thought there was a lock." I felt somewhat dumb. I hadn't even checked and had just assumed it was locked.

"Not at this time, although we may have to consider it at some point. Just be careful when you go inside. There are a lot of loose stones and broken markers."

"I will," I assured him, then before he hung up, I asked, "Do you happen to have a list of everyone buried there?"

He hesitated a moment, then I heard the clicking sound as he pressed a few computer keys. "Not completely. We're still hoping to identify more."

"It would make it easier to find the grave I'm seeking if he's on your list," I added and put a pleading tone in my voice.

"What's the name?"

"Willits. Emmett Willits."

After a short search, he said, "I show a Charles Emmett Willits, died June 11, 1908. Is that the one?"

"Yes," I answered, while an ornery part of me wanted to ask if he showed more than one.

"Do you have GPS on your phone?"

I replied that I did and he gave me the coordinates.

"That will take you to the location. It's about mid-way down the dirt road from University Terrace and about twenty feet in. Not many of the graves have headstones left, so you might not find much there."

Happy, I thanked him twice over and started on my quest. I hoped to find a marker, but if not, at least I had a location for his bones.

As I came out the door and started around a corner, I ran into Gavin Haines, literally. I had been distracted by entering the coordinates, so I wasn't paying attention to anyone around me and I smacked right into him.

The paper flew from my left hand, but I managed to hang onto my phone as I stumbled back from the impact.

"So sorry," I said before I even registered who'd I'd hit.

"Same old Gillian," he answered as he grabbed at the folders he carried, but not before one escaped. "You always were a little distracted when you hurried across the campus. What brings you here today?"

He bent to retrieve his folder, reaching for the paper I'd dropped along with it. I knelt to reach for it at the same time, but he'd already snagged it. He glanced at it, then handed it to me.

"GPS coordinates? Are you going treasure hunting?"

I laughed. "Nothing so adventurous. I'm doing some research for a friend. It's the location of a grave in the Hillside Cemetery, a few blocks from here."

His mouth twitched up into an attractive little smirk that reminded me why I'd had a crush on him.

"Ah, yes, the school's white elephant."

At my confused look, he clarified. "They were 'gifted' the property some years ago and thought they'd relocate the remains and build university housing there. Until they learned how many were buried in it that would need to be reinterred and markers set up and that shot the whole plan to hell. So they sold it and the new owners cleaned it up and put a fence around it. Now, it just sits there untended. A shame, really."

"You're kidding," I said. "I wondered how the school ended up with a cemetery."

"You know, I've been wanting to take a look at that place myself. I might go over with you if you can wait..." He paused to glance at his watch. "About an hour. I have a class to teach as soon as I drop these folders off at my office, then I could meet you there."

"That sounds great," I answered. He'd caught me off guard and while I loved the idea of exploring the cemetery with him, I needed to be alone to talk to Emmett. An hour should be enough, though. "I'll see you there then. I'll be inside."

He grinned, gave me a little one-fingered salute, with his index finger, not the bird one, and resumed his course to his office. *Nice coincidence running into him,* I thought.

It took about ten minutes to go the full block to the opposite end of the road from where I'd parked across from Thomas' apartment. I located the gate and noted it just latched shut. Note to self, always check before causing yourself extra time and work.

Pulling out my phone, I checked the coordinates on the GPS and followed it to the location pinpointed. If anything, the cemetery looked more bleak in daylight. Very few headstones even showed, although here and there, a couple of recent additions stuck out like neon lights on a wedding chapel. I paused to look at one of the newer ones and amended that view to replacements. The person in the grave had died in 1902. Very little vegetation pushed its way through the ground and the few that made it were weeds.

Although a waist-high monument stood near the location where Emmett's grave should be, I saw little to indicate anyone was buried there until I glimpsed a piece of stone poking out of the dry ground. Using my hand, I began trying to shovel the dirt away from the cracked stone. It emerged slowly and after ten minutes, I could just make out the faded letters on the stone. I ran my fingers across them to feel the edges of the carving. I just made out his name   C.E. Willits   and his rank of sergeant. There had been more, but time and the weather had worn it off.

I twitched as a chill crossed my arms and shoulders making me wonder if Emmett passed by there. I'd heard that the temperature drops in the presence of ghosts.

I straightened my back and prepared to sing, hoping that I'd end up in the transitional graveyard. I'd chosen an early American folk song, one of the most beautiful ones I knew, and I felt confident that Willits would recognize it and respond. Called "Shenandoah", the song wove a tale about the beautiful daughter of an Indian Chief along the Missouri River and it spoke of the unrequited love of a sailor for the chief's daughter. Most likely a sea-shanty that sailors sang when they worked, it nonetheless bore a haunting melody.

Halfway through the first verse, the setting shifted.

I stood in a cemetery, but it didn't look like the one I usually visited. Here, the surrounding bushes appeared darker with deeper blue-green tones and I could see only a few gravestones. A carpet of rich bluegrass covered the ground while yellow and white flowers bloomed profusely on the shrubs. Low hills, looking purplish-blue, rose gradually in the distance. Peaceful, yet it disturbed me as I felt unsettled souls lingering in this valley.

Out of nowhere, Emmett came toward me, not limping, but walking briskly as a young military man would. He stopped a few feet from me, took off his hat, and bent in a half bow.

"Ma'am. You have a strong power to be able to bring me to a place like this. It is far from the graveyard where I have been for many years now."

"I didn't select it," I answered. "But it's where the Creator has chosen to place us. My name is Gillian. I hope that we can help each other."

"That would be my wish also, Miss Gillian. You have an exquisite voice and I would truly love to listen to it longer, but I think we had best get to business. Tell me about my descendant. He seems a fine young man, like his father. I would like to help him if I can."

A large boulder nearby afforded seating, so I walked over to sit on it, and he followed, standing comfortably a few feet away. I told him all I knew about Thomas and about his concerns for the future. Emmett listened attentively, occasionally nodding his head, until I finished.

"As I indicated the other night, I think I may have some help for him. I was neither rich nor poor, but I hoped to become more wealthy and to be able to build a legacy for my family. I had quite a lot of money from silver mining in Virginia City and I was able to build a fine house before I married my beautiful Gwennet, but it was not enough for us to live well. I kept bringing in a fair amount and it provided enough to get us by, but only a little remained for any luxuries.

"Miners came down from the Sierras where they said they had found gold just lying around in the streams in the mountains. I decided to try my hand at it. So, I headed off with my pan and high hopes, ma'am. At times, it proved frustrating and often very cold. Eventually, I turned up a section of a creek that yielded a few gold nuggets. I could guess at the weight of my stones being about six ounces, so I took them into Truckee to be assayed. It was almost pure and worth a lot of money then, almost one hundred twenty dollars."

"That would be quite valuable." I shifted on the rock and leaned closer, intrigued by this story.

"Unfortunately, where there is gold, you will also find thieves. A pair of them followed me out of the office and even though they didn't make their move in town, they continued to follow me as I headed back toward my claim. To cut a long tale short, I will just say that I thought that I had evaded them, but to be safe, I did not

return to the location where I had panned the gold. I went to a different area and they caught up with me, beat me up, and stole my gold."

"Then what happened?" I prompted when he paused to think.

"I went back a few weeks later to the creek. It was not an easy place to find so I was confident that it had not been plundered and I was correct. I panned as much gold as I could carry in my pack. I would guess it weighed about twenty pounds. Then I climbed back up the hill and walked to where I'd left my horse. I rode back to Truckee where I kept out of sight. I was worried about the gold I carried and I didn't let anyone know I had found anything." I could see his clear light blue eyes as he gazed up at the sky, a smile on his face at the memory.

"I had enough gold to take care of my wife and ensure that my daughter found a good husband and still have plenty left to carry us for several years. I was thinking on that when I left town the next day heading down the trail toward Reno. About mid-way down, in the late afternoon, I became aware I was being followed again. I knew it was a possibility and I had a plan. I was close to the railroad tracks and the flume that ran nearby. Underneath, there was a section where I could slip out of view of anyone following me and climb into a small cave where some supplies had been stored when they were building the railroad.

"I went in, hid the gold in a recess in the back of the cave, and moved a heavy rock in front of it. Unless you knew to look for it, you wouldn't find it. I figured it would be safe until I could come back with my son and claim it. I stayed in the cave a while, ate a bit of my food, then when I came out, I started back toward Reno. I expected I would get into town just after dark. It was a good plan, I thought, but the same two men caught up with me and stole everything I had, including my horse.

"They were angry that I didn't have any gold in my bags. I did have my gun on me though and when one of them tried to take it from me, I pulled it on him and shot him in the chest, but I was

not fast enough to get the second man. He shot me, then took my horse and rode off, leaving me and his cohort for dead. It wasn't long before we were. I got the man's name, Frederick Holstein, before he died. I tried to get to a house but I didn't make it more than a hundred feet."

"So no one knew where the gold was? And you think it's still there?"

His head dipped in an affirmative. "Yes, Miss Gillian, I most certainly do believe that to be the case. Do you think twenty pounds of gold might serve young Thomas well?"

I couldn't quite believe what I had heard, but if the gold remained in the cave, it would be worth much more now than then. Well, not really worth more, but it would have appreciated well with the current market prices, even though the value of money had depreciated. What was a fortune in 1890 would be worth less in buying power now, but still enough money to get Thomas through school and set him up for a few years, I felt certain.

"Why do I have a feeling there's a catch attached to this revelation?" I said, getting to my feet.

"There is a little bit of one," he replied. He gazed down at the ground, then looked around the lush, fragrant graveyard. "Are all the resting places on this side as beautiful as this one?"

I shrugged. "I don't know. I have seen a sinister one that was frightening and dark, but the one I see most often is quite beautiful. This one is not a place that I've been before. Judging from the look of it and the bluegrass, I think it is more from the Appalachian area than the Reno area. Would this be more like your home?"

"It is. Mid-Tennessee is very close to the mountains. My family had a farm a little northeast of Clarksville."

"It must have been hard to leave your family and move west," I said.

"It was. But staying there would have been even harder. The

war left such destruction and hardship behind. If I wanted a future, I thought that it would be on the west coast and Nevada was known for its silver strike. It seemed a good place to start anew."

I strolled past him, my eyes scanning the unmarked stones that lay flat to the grass here. It appeared that no one rested in the graves, yet at least twenty headstones were visible. He fell into step beside me.

"You said that you might be able to help me. What I need is for you to do something for me. It may take a little time and possibly even a little money, but it is important to me."

"What do you need?" I asked as I turned my head to face him, just catching an anguished expression before it fled. Something in his past haunted him.

"I left behind a dead brother on the battlefield. Worse, he had a wife and a daughter. I was there when he died and I couldn't stop what happened. He was the enemy..."

"You killed him?" My voice carried my shock and disbelief.

"No, not I. I would have saved him if I could. But I was not alone when we encountered him and one of my fellow soldiers shot him before I could even shout a warning. I was wounded myself and I don't know what happened to his body. I never returned to my parents' home and I broke contact with them completely."

He looked away for a moment, then turned back to me, the pain of this incident still in his eyes, and he said, "I would like to know what happened to his family. Please find out what you can. If there are descendants from his little girl, then I would like to make sure they are doing well."

"You're asking me to be a detective? To hunt down information about your brother's wife and daughter and find out if they still have descendants alive?"

"That is exactly it," he replied. "When you have done this, I will tell you where to find the gold and you will be rewarded."

"Unbelievable."

I considered his request for a few moments. I admit it intrigued me, but could I do it? Research tools could help me find his family and it might be interesting. I'd promised Thomas' father I'd do what I could to help him.

"I will try to do it for Thomas' sake," I replied. "As for you, this may clear your conscience, but you need to cross over. It's time for you to move on. Once I find out the information you want, you will do it. Is that an agreement?"

He hesitated, a nervous tic showing at his right eyelid, but at last he said, "Agreed. I look forward to when I will see you again, ma'am." He bowed to me again, then walked toward the bushes, vanishing before he reached them.

Behind where he'd been, I glimpsed a dark shape and an impression of movement. I thought it might be another spirit and I called out to it. The bushes around it shook and the noises of branch hitting branch carried to my ears as I crossed the open ground toward it.

"Hello. Is someone there? Maybe I can help you."

Without warning, a black blur of energy rushed me, knocking me back as it plunged into me and I screamed out in shock and an odd sensation of pain. I stumbled, trying to avoid a fall, reaching out to steady myself...

And my hand gripped the rough surface of the tall headstone near Emmett's as tears leaked down my cheeks. I let out a breath and felt an ache in my stomach where the dark spirit had struck me. I shook with the shock and fear at this unexpected occurrence and my stomach felt queasy, threatening to vomit. Taking a deep, unsteady breath, I leaned against the tall stone and closed my eyes.

"Are you okay?"

Gavin's voice startled me and I jerked my head up, whipping it toward him. "Fine. I just got a little dizzy."

His appraising gaze swept over me and I guess he deemed me okay as he offered his bottle of water. "Take a couple of sips. Maybe you're a bit dehydrated."

As I swallowed down a gulp or two, I did begin to feel better. Handing the bottle back, I thanked him and added, "So, what exactly did you want to see over here?"

"Nothing specific, just take a look around. I didn't have the opportunity when the University first acquired it. You know me, I like to see what treasures might be hidden in a place like this." He grinned. "Are you up to exploring it?"

"Sure," I answered, although I would have preferred to hop in my car and leave at that point. I felt off-balance and weary after my recent experience, but I didn't want to turn down the chance to spend a little time with Gavin. He still managed to make my heart flutter.

What constitutes a treasure for one man, such as Emmett, is entirely different for another. Gavin led the way through the stones, pausing at several to study the carvings and some of the stonework on the battered monuments. He snapped a few pictures along the way and even asked me to pose next to a couple. For a height indicator, he claimed.

Based on the headstones we could read, it seemed the burials dated from the 1880's to the early 1900's. I think Emmett might have been one of the last interred there.

"Now, tell me what you were really doing here," he said as we turned to walk back to the exit.

"I told you. Researching a grave for a friend. His triple-great grandfather is buried in here and I thought maybe a few details might be on his burial stone." I kept my eyes forward, not looking at him in case he might somehow detect the half-truth in my face.

"Did you find anything?"

"Not much," I admitted. "The headstone has been badly damaged and is barely readable. It just had his name and his rank in the Union Army."

Gavin picked up on my slip right away. "Union? He served in the Civil War?"

I nodded.

"Do you know where? I've always had an interest in that era, so I might be able to locate some information if you'll give me his name and where he served."

The offer surprised me. Gavin had never been overtly helpful to his students in the research area, but maybe, since I no longer studied under him, he didn't mind offering his expertise. Still, it wasn't my information to share without checking with Thomas.

"Thanks for the offer, but I would need to okay it with my client."

"No problem. How long have you been doing genealogical research?"

We'd reached the gate and I stepped through, waiting for Gavin to clear before I pulled it shut, turned, and offered a big smile. "I don't do it. I'm just helping out a friend."

Gavin's eyes showed amusement and I felt certain he didn't believe me, but he only said, "I see. Well, if you change your mind and you'd like a little help, give me a call."

"Where's your car?" I asked as I looked down the dirt road to the end where I'd parked the Beast.

He pointed the opposite direction. "I parked up near the Pythians' Lodge. Thanks for letting me tag along."

He winked at me, then turned and started walking toward the west.

What was that wink about? Had he just flirted with me? A wry smile crossed my lips. Eight years ago, I would have been thrilled, but now? Not so much.

I spun around and started toward my car, my pace picking up as I neared the mid-point of the road near Emmett's grave. A chill touched me, as if something opened a freezer door and blew cold air out of it.

Hairs on the back of my neck rising, I turned to look behind me, half-expecting to see the dark spirit, if that's what it was, following me.

I broke into a jog the rest of the way back to my car. I may not fear any ghosts, but *that specter* was a completely different issue.

NINE

*T*hat afternoon, I did something that I never thought I would do. I visited a firearms shop I'd spotted a few weeks earlier and inquired about a small handgun. Between my growing anxiety and the possible attack earlier in the week, my fear of being in a dangerous situation prompted me to take more action to secure my life.

Nevada laws on firearms are simple. You pick out a gun, fill out a form, pay a fee to verify you're eligible, wait for the background check, and take your new security companion home. Unless you live in Clark County the Las Vegas area where additional steps need to be completed before you get your weapon. It surprised me that I could obtain a gun so easily.

I found a nice, small firearm at the second shop I visited. The first had recommended the same model the clerk now showed me, but that shop didn't have it in stock. More helpful than the first one, this man happily showed me how the gun worked, how to load it, and pointed out the instructions for safety and cleaning. If I bought it, he also strongly advised me to take a course on how to handle the weapon, clean it, and fire it safely.

"Seriously, miss. This little beauty will offer some protection, but you need to feel comfortable with it. A course isn't too expensive and it is worth it to learn how to use the gun properly. I have a card here for a shooting range that is really good, so you check it out, okay?"

"Sure," I agreed without hesitation. But I did balk at paying the asking price. The cost ran higher than I anticipated and I told him I needed to think about it.

A few hours later, I sat at my dining table with my new-to-me purchase on the table and stared at it. I'd found the pistol at almost half the cost that the firearms shops priced them at a pawnshop downtown. Even then it'd cost more money than I'd wanted to spare. My income tax refund covered most of it, but the rest came out of the recording fund.

All three dealers I'd talked to agreed that the weapon, a Ruger LC9 Muddy Girl model, would be a practical size for a woman to carry. One even pointed out that if I wanted to carry it in my purse or concealed on my body, I would need to get a concealed weapon permit.

I picked the gun up, admiring the colorful pink and black camouflage finish on the grip. It settled into my hand comfortably, not too large or heavy for me to handle. But I needed to practice with it. Just as I regularly attended the self-defense classes, I would need to start going to the range at least once a week. It wouldn't do me any good if I couldn't hit a barn at fifty feet.

I packed the gun up in a kitchen cloth then took it upstairs where I put it into a small chest that I could lock as soon as I located the key. For now, it would be close to me at night, but not in an obvious spot. Until I felt comfortable using it, I didn't want the weapon too accessible. An indication of my state of mind, I perversely didn't approve of guns, yet felt compelled to have one in my house for protection.

I set the business card for the shooting range on my desk and told myself I'd schedule a session for my next day off.

Somewhere in the night, I slipped into a dream in the transitional cemetery that I usually saw. Unlike my other dreams, this didn't lead me on a path to a new section; instead, it replayed my encounter with Thomas' father from the funeral. I saw it as if I watched a movie rather than through my own eyes. I could see myself talking to Willits. In the background, near the bushes stood the younger version of Charles Emmett Willits in his blue Union Army uniform, watching us. He moved forward a few feet from the hedge as if to hear better, but his eyes focused on me more than on his relative.

Then I saw something else back behind the soldier, a dark man-shaped shadow lingering next to the hedge, not moving forward and it appeared to be watching me.

At least, it watched the vision-me who conversed with the recently deceased Emmett and encouraged him to move through the gate. As the song became clearer and we followed the path to the gate, so, too, did the other two spirits. The soldier one didn't come onto the path but marched alongside, following to see where we were going. The dark-shaped spirit stayed well away but followed us nonetheless.

I couldn't see any details or features on the black spirit, but even my dream state, he disturbed me, creating a sense of foreboding. When Thomas' father stepped into the light, I turned to face the spirit of the other Emmett and he retreated from me. At some point between my seeing the recently deceased off and turning to face the other, the black spirit disappeared. No sign of him that I could see.

When I woke, the dream details remained vivid in my mind. Sitting up, I pulled on my robe and started downstairs to make coffee and wondered about the significance of the dream. Who or what was the faceless black spirit and what did it have to do with me? I shuddered with the remembered image and feelings about the inky blob that seemed more interested in me than in the man I escorted. Besides that, given the perspective of that dream, who sent it to me? It sure as heck didn't come from my subconscious. I had that feeling you sometimes get when you think someone is watching you and the hair on the back of your neck trembles. A tremor of concern ran through me.

Nygard cut in front of me without warning and I jumped in surprise and fear before I identified the shape as my cat. My over-stimulated nerves had me looking for ghosts.

Janna and I met on Saturday, a warm spring morning, for a jog around the lake at Idlewild Park. I loved it when the temperatures felt like the season rather than lingering winter or premature summer, so it felt invigorating to get out and breathe the fresh air. A zephyr carried the delicate sweetness of freshly mowed grass that delighted my senses, making me feel exhilarated. We kept a moderate pace making it an easy run to the mid-point of the perimeter where we stopped for a breather.

For Janna, that meant stretching exercises and I joined in with her while we talked.

"Why did you want to run here today? Janna asked. "You usually try to avoid too many people and the weekend is family-invasion time at this park."

"Yeah, I know. But something happened a couple of days ago at Virginia Lake and I thought a little more company might be good. And these duck ponds are shallower than the lake."

She shot a questioning look at me.

"A guy bumped me on the running path and knocked me into the lake."

"Omigosh! Into the lake?"

I nodded.

"Deeper water? What was his excuse? Did he at least help you out and apologize?"

"Nope, he didn't hang out. He'd gone before I even surfaced again. The thing is why would he run into me? The path is wide enough that he could have passed me."

"Wait, you think this guy intentionally knocked you into the lake?"

"Seems like it."

"Why?"

Her confused expression reflected my own feelings about the incident.

I shrugged. "Wish I knew. Let me tell you what happened yesterday." I hadn't told her about the ghost visit at the Hillside Cemetery so I brought her up to date on all that had happened, including the whole story with Emmett Willits, the Civil War ghost.

"Oh wow. So, do you really believe there might still be hidden treasure under an old flume?"

I shrugged and reached my arms to the sky in alternating stretches. "I don't know. I think it's a possibility. If it's well hidden and no one discovered it, then it could still be there. But I also think it's a long shot. Aren't you intrigued, though?"

"Of course, I am. Do I want to go hiking through the hills on possibly unstable ground? Not really." She changed the exercise to toe touches.

"Where's your sense of adventure?" I teased.

"Not tumbling down a hill," she said as she shot back up in an upswing.

As I rolled my shoulders, I said, "How about if we just take a little drive to Truckee, do a little shopping at the outlet stores, then kind of take a look at the hills below the flume to see if we can spot the place where he might have cached the gold? It would be fun and if we can spot it, then it probably wasn't safe."

"When do you want to do this?"

"Are you doing anything this afternoon?"

Her face scrunched into an exasperated look, but she muttered, "Why not?"

Shortly after noon, we zipped over Highway 80 in my Jeep, through the Sierra Nevada Mountains, bound for the little town of Truckee in California. Originally a railroad town and a frequent stop for travelers before going across the higher elevation around Donner Lake, the city had grown some over the years but remained a small mountain community of about ten thousand residents. The California Zephyr, a train that ran between the San Francisco Bay Area through to Chicago in Illinois, still came through twice a day, once for each direction. Although it was the only passenger train that made the trip across the Sierras, a few freight trains used the tracks daily.

Once we reached Truckee, which took us about an hour from Reno, we grabbed lunch at a café near the outlet mall. The shopping area consisted of about a dozen businesses that represented some major companies. In theory, and to varying degrees, the outlet stores offered lower prices on goods carried by the stores in regular malls.

Over our chicken fajita salads, Janna filled me in on her latest infatuation. An auditor guy had come from the casino's main office in Ohio a few months ago that she'd liked quite a bit. Now he'd come back for a couple of weeks and she was smitten with him. That was the only word for it. Of course, it was a doomed relationship unless one of them decided to move.

Once we'd covered that, I tossed out something that I'd had on my mind during the drive up. "You know, the best way to investigate what happened to Willits' brother and his family would be to go to Tennessee and see what might be in the records there. Possibly I could go to the graves and maybe learn something."

She blinked at me, surprised. "Are you serious? Will you get paid to do this?"

"I don't know. Willits said that I would be rewarded. But I don't know what he meant by that. If it could help out Thomas, then it would be worth it. I could come out a financial loser on the deal; I admit it. Still, I am curious and I haven't had a vacation in a long time." My face assumed my best pleading expression as an invitation for her to join me.

"Me, neither." Janna scrubbed her teeth against her lower lip as she thought. "You know we would probably have to fly into Memphis and rent a car to drive across the state. I always wanted to go to Graceland."

I grinned, "Me, too. After all, the King once lived there."

A frown creased her forehead. "Weren't you going to be working in the studio on that album you've been planning for months?"

I gritted my teeth in a grimace. "Yeah. I'd probably have to use some of the money for the trip, so that would set the album back a little."

"That won't please Ferris and Digby," she pronounced.

I had to agree on that. The album was a project we'd been planning for over a year now. I had hoped to record it in the early part of the year, but we hadn't earned enough money to make it. Now, we were almost there; however, if I took out the expenses for a trip to Tennessee, it would probably take another three months to replace it. Did I dare do that?

After lunch, we shopped. I wanted to check out one store that had sweaters on sale and Janna was looking for new boots. End of the season is always the best time to find winter clothing.

We stopped in at the bookstore to browse for about an hour, before piling back into the Jeep around four o'clock to start back down the hill.

We soon came along a stretch of road where we could easily see the flumes that transported logs down the mountain. I slowed some and even pulled over to the side a few times to see if we could get an indication of the area where Willits might have stashed the gold.

At one promising point, I pulled my binoculars out of the Beast's storage compartment. Old, but serviceable, they had belonged to my dad, one of many items he'd left behind when he moved across the world. Climbing out, I focused them on one of the more promising locations and tried to see if anything lay beyond the scrub brush screens across the way. In the few places where I could see a break in the foliage and branches, most of the background looked like dirt, although a couple of darker spots could indicate a hole or deeper cut into the cliff. If Willits came through on this, I hoped he could give clear directions or I'd be going down a trail without a compass.

The results of this excursion had been inconclusive, I decided as we neared the city again. No areas jumped out at me as a likely hidey-hole location and heavy vegetation obscured many spots that might have potential. The land below either belonged to the government or the railroad, but it didn't look like anything, such as fencing or barriers, restricted people from using it.

"Just finding the cave might be a challenge," I said as we drove past the Gold Ranch exit. I made a mental note since it seemed like the only point I'd seen where we might be able to access the road that ran near the flumes.

"If it's still there, it could be home to a mountain lion or a bear," Janna, ever the optimist, commented.

As I pulled into a gas station to refill, Janna stood leaning against the Jeep while I pumped gas and said, "You know, I've been thinking about the trip. I have enough air miles for a free ticket, so why don't you use that so you don't have to dip into your album money?"

"I can't do that, Janna. You should use it. I'll save up enough for the album in a couple of months."

She shook her head. "No, you use it. You have a birthday coming up soon, so let's just call it an early birthday present. Now, let's see if we can both get the time off to go."

Within a short time, we had planned the trip out, tentatively setting it up to go in two weeks for only four days. We'd go over the weekend, so we could leave Thursday after work, provided we could find a flight, stay until Monday morning, and fly back. I'd only need to get the Monday off, and I could negotiate with Heeni for that. Janna had time coming from her job and the only problem would be if they didn't have enough coverage for her. Although she managed the front desk staff at one of the big casinos in town, there were others who could work her shifts.

While honestly intrigued by Emmett's story and wanting to know more, I admitted I felt pretty jazzed about going to the heart of rock 'n' roll, rhythm and blues, and great BBQ. I needed a vacation and even a mini one like this promised to be a fun break with Janna along.

With a gig scheduled for Saturday night, it seemed like a good time to tell my bandmates that I planned to do this trip. We'd have to reschedule a rehearsal for the album material, but I figured it wouldn't be a big deal. You would have thought I'd dropped a bomb on them.

"What? You've up and decided you're going out of town for a few days and it had to be at the same time we're trying to finally get this album together?" Ferris said, his voice rising with his irritation.

"Aw, c'mon. It's only one rehearsal and we don't have any gigs that weekend. I need to do this, Ferris." Boy, what would it have been like if I'd told him I had to use some of the album money and the session would be delayed?

"Something's happening with you," Digby said as he flipped the straps to his bass over his shoulders. "You seem distracted these days, not as focused on the music as you used to be. What's going on?"

As with Mark, I hadn't said anything to my bandmates about my new gift, not at all certain that they would understand it or believe that it was real. All they knew was that I had started singing at funerals and had somehow gotten mixed up in a murder that had resulted with me being abducted. But I knew they were concerned about my welfare and were curious.

"I'll only be gone four days and I need to have a break. I know it seems like I'm distracted, but I think it will help and I'll come back raring to go on the album. Really, I will. Trust me?"

Ferris frowned at me, but his expression softened. "Okay, babe. But we hit rehearsals hard when you come back. We have a lot of work to do to get these songs down just right and we need to work with Rob and Dana on their parts more."

He meant Rob Triana and Dana Capraru, a couple of friends and local musicians, who would be adding more instrumentation to the album. They'd agreed to play on ours if we reciprocated when, or if, they made albums. Rob played guitar and bouzouki while Dana worked with the local symphony as a featured violinist but she also rated as a top-notch fiddler when she hit a country music, bluegrass or Celtic festival.

"Agreed. You schedule the rehearsals and I'll be there."

The intense look, with his eyebrows lowered, informed me that I'd better not miss any. When did I lose control of my band?

The gig was at a dance club, one of the few we played now and then. Most of the time they used a deejay, but for this special occasion of their five-year anniversary, the owners wanted a live band so we were thrilled to do it.

Not strictly a rock band, we made the effort to look a little more rocker for the evening, although the music choices covered tunes from the seventies and the eighties.

Ferris wore black; black jeans, black shirt, black vest and a black and white bandana around his head that kept his hair out of his face while he played. More flamboyant, Digby wore tight-fitting blue bell-bottoms with knee-high inserts in a chartreuse paisley fabric that matched his slim fit shirt. Where the heck he'd found those, I couldn't say, but the look screamed sexy-hot and hands-off-gay at the same time.

I'd opted for a blue suede mini-skirt with a cap-sleeved crimson jersey crop top and short suede boots with two-inch heels. I'd borrowed the skirt from Janna and it snuggled my hips a little more than I liked, but between grumbles, Ferris assured me I looked fine.

From the opening chord on, our band grabbed the crowd and didn't let go, pulling them along note by note. They danced, clapped and shouted, bouncing up and down, and bumping into each other on the crowded floor. The drinks probably helped, but I thought we sounded fantastic. I didn't know what Ferris worried about so much, but, then again, we planned new, original material on the album so that did require extra rehearsals.

Looking forward to the Tennessee trip elevated my mood, so I rocked the music hard, pulling off a few vocal-chord challenging runs. Still, it bothered me that I couldn't tell the guys the real reason I needed to make this trip.

During the break, I plowed my way to the bar to get a glass of wine, the only one of the night I planned to drink. Behind me, I heard a voice that sounded familiar, although I didn't place it until I turned to face the man and recognized Roger, the guy I'd met at the wedding back in November. He'd asked me out a couple of times, but we never connected. I didn't really know him other than having danced with him the one night, but then the accident had happened and I met Dr. Gorgeous. It did surprise me to see him here, though.

He appeared to be alone as he ordered a beer and greeted me. "How ya' doing, Gillian Foster?"

"I'm good. How about you?"

"Fine. Still hoping for that coffee date sometime." He took a sip of the beer, then leaned forward looking directly into my eyes. Talk about an uncomfortable situation.

"Oh, yeah. About that, I don't think it's going to happen, Roger. Nothing against you. You seem like an all right guy, but I have a boyfriend."

His eyes fell. "Oh, I see. So, we can't be friends?"

How the heck could I soften this? "I don't think it's a good idea right now. I'm glad to see you at gigs, but even a coffee meet up would feel like cheating on my guy. I'm sorry."

He sucked at a cheek and his fingers drummed on the edge of his beer glass. "I understand. I just hoped we could be more than casual bar encounters and snippets of chat. You know..."

I nodded and gave him another "I'm sorry" look, then skittered away heading back to the band. I had a feeling that I hadn't seen the last of Roger. He kept turning up at my gigs and I suspected he would continue to do so. I'd just thought he was a fan, but now I was beginning to think he might be more of a stalker. Harmless, maybe. At least I hoped that was the case.

Mark had said he might try to get by the club for a little while and I hoped that he would make it. It would make it clear to Roger that I wasn't available. But it didn't look like this was one of those nights the doctor could get even an hour off from work. Maybe next time, I thought.

TEN

I'd made another appointment with Madame Astrid to see if I could connect with her better and if she could shed some light on this latest development with the unexpected ghost. I had been practicing the meditation sporadically since I last saw her, as in only three times. With my busy schedule, I tried to squeeze it in, but it didn't feel like I benefitted much from her advice. Not that I planned to tell her that.

"Good afternoon, Gillian," she said as she swept through the curtains to greet me. "It's good to see you again. Sit, please."

She peered at me as if I was a small, weird bird in a nest and she was thinking about dissecting me. In other words, she made me uncomfortable.

"You're troubled by something," she said as she arrived at her conclusion. "Have you been meditating daily?"

"Not exactly," I replied, trying to hedge my answer. "A lot has been happening lately."

"I see." She squinted, her eyes narrowing into thin slits and she shifted her head back and forth as she scanned me. "Your aura is disturbed. The colors appear muddled with streaks of brownish-yellow in it. You've met someone that has confused you or is upsetting you. Tell me about it."

She poured a cup of tea for each of us, then sat back to listen.

"I've encountered an old ghost," I started, then explained about Thomas' ancestor and described my meeting with him at the small cemetery with unmarked graves. I said nothing about the gold or the request he had for me.

Her eyes grew wider as I spoke. When I'd finished, she set the cup down and sat quietly, her gaze focused on a framed mandala print on the wall. "I have nothing," she finally said. "What you are experiencing is something that I have no connection with. I cannot see anything relating to it. I believe that this gift is for you alone. You have whatever resources you need within you to resolve the situation. This, I believe. From what you've said, it appears that your old ghost fears something that keeps him bound to this plane. He is afraid to go to the next level. You must find what that is and help him resolve it so that he can be free. He asked you to do something for him, didn't he?"

"He did. He wanted me to find out what happened to his brother's family after the war. He seemed very concerned about it."

"Then whatever he fears may be tied to the fate of his relatives. If he fled to the West, then he may just feel guilty and ashamed to have left them behind." She relaxed then, leaning back in her chair again. "I wish I could guide you more, but all I can say is not to fear what is presented to you and meditate on it. It will help clear your mind and allow answers to come to you."

Right. I drew the word out as I thought it. Meditate on it. It sounds so easy to do until you try to sit in front of a candle or other object and empty your mind only to have it flooded with a dozen other non-relevant thoughts, like which bills you need to pay, where you left your sunglasses, and other trivial worries. Sometimes my mind filled with random song lyrics, which I then needed to write down before they fled again.

"It takes practice," Madam said as if she could read my mind.

"One other thing happened," I said, speaking the words slowly as I tried to describe the black spirit that had attacked me. "I encountered a spirit, a thing, or some force in that graveyard. It appeared like a blackish, smoky man shape and it rushed me, hitting me in my stomach."

Astrid came to alert. "Where? Show me where it impacted."

I pointed to the center part of my torso, curious about her question.

"Your solar plexus," she said in a low, mysterious voice as if I should understand the significance. She read the uncomprehending look on my face with ease. "It's the center of your stomach where many nerves radiate out from the central core. A blow here can incapacitate the body and make you feel like the air was forced out. When this spirit hit you, did you feel it? Were you dizzy?"

I recalled reaching for something to grab for support and the feeling of weakness along with pain and described it to the psychic. "I didn't think any spirit could touch me or harm me on the other side," I said as I concluded the story. "I thought it was all illusion."

Astrid's eyes opened wide, very wide, as she peered at me. "Where did you get that idea? The soul is a powerful energy source. I thought you realized that. It is energy in its purest form, able to affect what the spirit wills. Objects can move, sounds can be created, and pure force can attack another spirit in any form."

I squirmed in discomfort. Of course, I hadn't realized it. No one told me about it. "So the blackish figure was another spirit who had a bone to pick with me?"

"I would venture to guess it was an evil entity of some sort. Where there is light, there is also dark. For those with tortured souls, guilt so deep that they can't see redemption, dark spirits can claim them."

"Demons from Hell?" Panic swept over me. Damn, if I had drawn the attention of a demon, what would it mean?

"No, Hell isn't a real construct. Neither is Heaven in the sense people and religions imagine it. But demons or shades are dark spirits and they can latch onto damaged souls."

"And they can hurt the living?" My voice wavered as I asked.

"They can, if you are not prepared and don't take defensive measures."

"What kind of defensive measures?" I leaned forward, my body at the edge of the seat, worry nipping at my voice so that it sounded scratchy.

"At the very least, throw a protective prayer out to the Universe," she answered. She shifted her weight a little, peering at me, or maybe her eyes focused more to my right. She tapped the fingers of her left hand on the edge of the table in rotation, as she seemed to think about something.

"I have a little book here that I can give you with chants or incantations for protection. Learn a couple of appropriate ones for spirit travel before you start to sing at the graves and they might offer some protection against the evil spirits. There may be some other things that can help, but I'll need to do some research."

She turned and thumbed through the books on her shelves until she found a small, no more than six inches high, thin book that she handed to me. I glanced at the cover, "Incantations for Wiccans".

"Witches?" I asked.

"No. Although some practitioners may be. This book is more a distillation of the Druidic wisdom and the prayers they used. It doesn't involve using any creepy items like bat's blood or eye of newt, as if you could lay your hands on them easily. No, this is simple, straight forward prayer to the Creator."

"I see." I gave the book a doubtful look and didn't see at all how this would help. What was I getting into here?

Madame eased back in her chair and poured us each more tea.

Feeling more relaxed with Astrid now and wanting to direct the conversation elsewhere, I asked the question that had lurked in the back of my mind ever since I'd seen her building. "You're the real deal, Madam. So, why the gaudy signage out front? It almost shouts 'scammer here'."

She snorted out a laugh, almost spewing tea out her nose. As she wiped at her face, she said, "Perhaps it does, but about fifty percent of my business is walk-ins and skeptics. It's often something one does on the spur of the moment, intrigued by the idea, but thinking it an entertainment. Most leave here convinced and about half of those come back for readings and advice. Unlike you, I earn a living from my gift while I help people with guidance."

I ignored the jibe. "But all the symbols and hocus pocus?"

"Is expected. People who don't know about it expect the symbols and the trappings. Do I need a parlor that looks like a gypsy tearoom? No, of course not. But it goes with the territory and I enjoy playing the part."

"Oh. That makes sense, I suppose. It does seem so theatrical, not that you did any of that with me."

Her eyes twinkled with amusement. "It is, my dear. It is. You should see me during a séance. It's all performance. I don't need the drama to connect to my spirit guide, but people expect it."

"A spirit guide. What's that?"

"Ah, it's just as it sounds. I have a spirit on the other side that I can contact. His name is Elias. When I need to learn something about someone who has passed, Elias helps me by trying to connect with the person on the other side."

Shocked and, yes, a little disbelieving, I said, "You can just ask? You don't have to go into a trance or anything?"

"It's not quite that easy. I do have to prepare myself and often I need some basic information on the person my client wants me to contact. Of course, not all attempts to connect are successful. If the spirit doesn't wish to come, he won't."

She regarded me with curiosity etched on her face. "Have you encountered a helper on the other side?"

"A helper?" I felt stupid. I'd only encountered Zac in my dreams and assumed, by his appearance and words, that he manifested as an angel, sans wings. Maybe I misunderstood; he never said it, but he did imply as much. Could he be a spirit guide instead?

I shook my head. "Not that I know about. I talk to spirits in the graveyard, but not to anyone guiding me. I mean, Artesmia Maroudian gave me guidance before she passed and in a dream afterward, but no one has helped me during the graveyard phase."

"Interesting... Your gift is unique and perhaps it has different limits on it. And not everyone who has a gift has a spirit guide." She put her cup down and rose to clear the pot, signaling the end of the session.

I paid her consulting fee and a small amount for the book; she'd only charged half her normal rate since she felt she hadn't been able to help me. As I drove home, I mulled the session over in my thoughts and realized she'd told me more than I had expected. I needed to talk to Zak and commanding the angel or spirit, or whatever, to my dreams didn't work.

In a burst of frustration, I slapped my right hand on the steering wheel and called out, "Dammit, Zak! I need guidance. If you're my guide, then help me... Please."

Once through the door at home, I picked up my own meditation object, Nygard. Nothing soothed me as much as his rugged little purrs as he accepted the stroking and scratching behind the ears with enthusiasm and rumbling through his body. Nonetheless, I resolved to be more diligent about the candle and incense meditation practice starting this evening.

Following a semi-successful mediation, meaning that I managed to keep my mind from wandering more than two or three times in the half hour I allotted to it, I was more than ready for bed. Before I turned off the lights, except for my nightlight that glowed at the end of the walkway to the bathroom, I offered a quick prayer and once again asked Zak to come to me.

Although I dreamed that night, it didn't seem like the kind that came from my gift, but more like a normal dream relating to something that happened during the day. I'd misplaced a pair of scissors at work and had trouble finding them. A Yorkie dog, wearing a holding collar, crouched down on the grooming table, waiting while I searched for them. In my dream, I turned to assure him it would only be a few minutes and the dog's mouth seemed to form words as he said, "Remember. You promised you would help me."

The voice snapped me out of the dream, pulling me awake as I realized it sounded very much like Jack from Ely's voice. Damn, I needed to follow up with Moss on that search for Jack's daughter. I scribbled a note on the pad I had by my bedside before dropping back on the pillow to sleep again.

ELEVEN

*H*eavy rain and chilly breezes pelted us as Janna and I exited the main airport terminal and sprinted, luggage in tow, across the open breezeway to the rental car parking. We battled our way through traffic and construction to a downtown hotel near Beale Street. By taking an extra day off work, we arrived in Memphis at a decent hour, giving us more play time in the city.

While the hotel seemed fine, clean, and not too pricey, we soon learned about Memphis time. Janna shot impatient glances my way and rolled her eyes as the check-in clerk performed her job in slow motion. "That wouldn't cut it in Reno or Vegas," she said once we were a few feet from the desk.

We loved the view from our room on the third floor where we could see the riverfront and a couple of paddle wheelers tied at the dock. After a quick glance at the area map the hotel provided, we headed out to catch the trolley to Beale Street for a meal of fabulous Memphis barbecue and some soulful music. Although the rain had slowed to a light sprinkle, we took along rain bonnets, just in case.

Eateries lined the street and the enticing aromas of spices and cooking meat as we passed made my mouth water in anticipation. Soulful sounds of the blues poured out the doors like a smooth glass of Southern Comfort.

With a mini-skirt that highlighted her long legs, Janna caught whistles and catcalls all up the street. I wore plain old jeans and a lightweight sweater, so I didn't draw as much attention, but there were a few aimed at me as we went along. I didn't mind and thought it flattering. Being able to draw any attention away from the bombshell that was Janna Lewis constituted a major accomplishment.

Of course, my friend downplayed it when I said something. "It's the long, naked legs. They always attract attention. But if you were to open your mouth and sing 'Summertime", they'd be eating out of your hands."

We paused at an establishment that had the most wonderful scent of spices and meat pouring out the door and, deciding we'd found our dinner spot, stepped inside. The down-home place went by the not-too-unique name of Bubba's BBQ and we settled into a wooden booth to get a taste of the best barbecue in the city, or so their menu informed us.

True or not, just the scent of the sauce suggested it would be great but deciding between chicken, pork, or beef proved impossible. I ordered a sampler plate with a baked potato, loaded. Janna went for the pork on a bun along with fries. Beers for both of us, even though I rarely drank it, but it somehow went with this type of food. I admitted after the first few bites that the victuals lived up to their claim.

After we ate, Janna and I moseyed down the street checking out the venues as we went. At a club called The Midnight Masque, a low, alto voice drew my attention. It could wrench your soul out and send it on a journey of pain, joy, and pure love. Lured in, we shoved our way through a blockade of people who stood just inside the door. I had to admit our lily-white-skin-tones stood out in the room, but a few other folks of a similar shade occupied scattered seats at cocktail tables. I felt a little uncomfortable at first, but they paid no attention to us, so I began to relax.

A stunning woman with tobacco-colored skin and green eyes fronted a piano player and a guitarist. While I appreciated her exquisite beauty, what mattered came in that silky, husky voice that transformed the lyrics into sweet honey cakes. If you combined Eartha Kitt with Peggy Lee, you might produce this mesmerizing sound. In awe, I listened and little bumps of amazement skittered up my arms. She made me feel like I could barely carry a tune and I both envied and admired her.

We sat through two sets and drank a little more than we should have of a sweet brandied brew that went down too easy. Maybe it was Picon Punch or something similar.

Ambling back toward the hotel, our spirits soared as high as the drinks as we giggled and struggled to walk a semi-straight path. Janna swerved the wrong way and bumped into a big truck driver-type, who caught her when she tripped, but seemed reluctant to let her go. She jerked back from him, but he kept a firm grip on her right arm and yanked her toward him again.

"Let go of me," Janna yelled at him as she pounded her free fist against his arm. He tightened his grip, pulling her closer, clearly going in for a kiss on her lips.

For a few moments, a wave of fear raced through me, turning my body to jelly that didn't want to stand on its own. Then the anger cut in as I recalled that I didn't plan to be a victim again and I would not let my best friend be one either.

"Let her go!" I yelled as I jumped for the man's shoulders from behind him, flinging my arms around his neck and wrapping my legs around his waist. I slid my right hand under his chin and jerked it upward while I clung like a monkey with my left hand and arm.

"Nose! Janna, nose!" I shouted as I pulled my hand into a fist and swung it at him as his head pivoted toward me. I caught him between the eyes and he staggered back, letting go of my friend's arm.

Freed, Janna turned and kicked as hard as she could, connecting with his right knee. She stumbled to one side, off-balance from the impact, but the action brought the dude to his knees as he cursed and growled. I slid off his shoulders and landed a solid kick to his back, right at kidney level, and a whoomph sound burst from him as he pitched forward.

"Let's go!" I caught Janna's arm, pulling her away.

Before we could run, a bouncer from one of the clubs seemed to jump out on the sidewalk. *Oh, great,* I thought. *Now I have to defend us against this big, burly guy?*

He looked at the trucker dude, who struggled to get to his feet, and turned to us. "This guy giving you trouble, ladies?"

"Not anymore," I shot back, feeling a sense of confidence flow over me that the self-defense classes might be paying off if I could bring down a big bruiser like that. Never mind that he was probably as soused as we were.

The bouncer grinned at me, then grabbed the dude by the arm and hauled him in the other direction.

I deflated as quickly as I'd reacted as the adrenalin wore off leaving me weak-kneed. The light mood had vanished in the altercation and stone cold sober, Janna and I, arms around each other's waist, dragged ourselves back toward the trolley. I remained watchful all the way, but no one else bothered us.

Come morning, we drank enough coffee to grant us status as major consumers and downed a few aspirins to ease the headaches and other minor pains from our previous night's outing. On the road about two hours later than planned, we pointed the car east toward Clarksville. I took the first driving shift, taking us out through Germantown.

As I glanced at my right hand on the steering wheel, I noticed the bruising where I'd pounded the ape the previous night. Although it still hurt a bit, I counted it worth it to have won that battle.

While I drove, Janna studied the map. "You know, I think we should go to the Shiloh battlefield first, Gilly. It's only a little jog southeast and we'd have to backtrack to it anyway."

"You could be right." I programmed it into the car's navigation unit and noted the more-than-a-little jog to take us to the battlefield. "It might be better to see it first to get a sense of Menafee."

"That's an odd name, isn't it? Wonder where it came from?"

"I'm thinking it had to be a family name." An unusual one, I conceded. "Maybe it's from an Indian word. Chief Menafee, I can hear it in my head."

Janna laughed, but it became a bit of a joke as we drove through the rich green fields and forests of Tennessee. We stopped at a store to grab some water and sodas, plus a bag of chips and a couple of apples to augment the large coffees we'd bought at a fast food place.

The turn for Shiloh came up a little over two hours after we'd left Germantown and Highway 22 took us right into the National Park where we turned onto Pittsburg Landing Road to go to the visitor's center. My eyes drank in the rich shades of green of the fields and woods. Even though I knew it was a national cemetery as well as a park, nothing prepared me for the sheer beauty of the setting.

One of the bloodiest battles of the War Between the States, Shiloh played out in one the most beautiful locations in the country. Trees lined the road and the woods extended for quite a distance, then there would be a break to an open green field. I wondered how much it had changed since the mid-eighteen hundreds.

We pulled into the visitor center and went inside to learn a little about the battle and which way to go to find the Confederate graves. I didn't know for certain if Menafee's remains stayed at Shiloh, but I knew many soldiers had been buried here.

As we walked in, an older gentleman with thinning gray hair greeted me and offered a map to the park. He explained that a self-guided drive, following markers, would take us through the various locations of the battles in the park or we could hike the entire seventeen-mile route.

"We also have Indian mounds on the site," he added as he pointed out the various roads on the map.

"Burial mounds?" I asked, thinking about the possibility of any spirits lingering around there.

"No. Archeologists believe they were foundation mounds for the important buildings of the town. But they don't know much about the people who lived there."

"Oh, that's interesting. So where are the Confederate graves located?"

His eyebrows went up in surprise. "Darlin', the Union soldiers are interred in the cemetery," he said in his lingering drawl. "The Rebel dead are buried in trenches."

"Trenches?" My mouth felt dry suddenly. They dumped them all in trenches? No proper burial? "Is there any way to know where a specific Confederate soldier is buried? Is there a list of names?"

"Oh, no. No one knows who all is in them. There are five mass burial sites marked in the park and there are probably more that haven't been found. The survivors buried them on the battlefield where they fell. There might even be a few single graves out there. We just don't know. I'm sorry. Are you looking for an ancestor?"

"For a friend's," I said, the sheer magnitude of the number of soldiers who could still be spirit-bound left me feeling drained.

"Might I suggest you watch the film about the encounter? It provides the details of the battle and gives you a good foundation before starting the tour. If you know which regiment he served with, it might help you locate the area where he's likely to be buried. The next showing will begin in thirty minutes."

I thanked him and took my map to a display where Janna stared at a detailed map of the battleground sites.

"Finding Menafee Willits in here could be next to impossible," I told her and explained the problem. "Let's go grab a soda and figure out a game plan."

We sat in the car and considered the options as a refreshing breeze blew through the open doors. It lifted Janna's bangs, pushing them to one side to reveal a tiny scar just below her hairline where she'd fallen and hit a barrier at the skating rink when we were thirteen. Barely noticeable now, it had been ugly when it happened.

"Well, if there are five identified sites, maybe you could sing at each of them and see if anyone contacts you," she said.

I glared at her. "I don't think it works like that."

"Hey, you managed to conjure up two homeless Jacks at a multiple burial site in Reno. How is this different? And it isn't likely there would be more than one Menafee in the whole park."

She had me there. *The whole park.* It was a memorial cemetery. Perhaps I didn't have to visit each grave but simply sing to make contact with the spirit I sought. And maybe all of them had gone to the next plane by now and there would be no answer at all. Bolstered by this thought, I finished my soda and rose to my feet.

"You may be right. Time to get on with it," I said. "Let's go watch the video, then find out if I can reach this soldier."

As the video wrapped up, I wiped the tears away from my eyes and considered the number of Civil War soldiers who lay buried under the beautiful green fields of Shiloh. Over three thousand Union soldiers alone rested in the cemetery that overlooked the Tennessee River. Half that many Confederates shared the common graves on the property. All that from a war that should never have happened. Of course, I knew about the Civil War and the reasons for it, but to see this story told through the words of the survivors of one of the first major battles of the war brought home that neighbor fought against neighbor, family against family, for something that should have been negotiated.

I turned my gaze to Janna and saw the tears glistening on her cheeks. The story affected her as much as it did me. Now I needed to go out into the fields to try to contact a spirit that died, along with thousands of others, in 1862. I shuddered at the prospect.

I noted the location of the only listed Confederate burial trench on the map, marked stop eleven. We backtracked down the road we'd come in, turning left at the first marker, then to the right on Jones Field Road where the trench would be coming up on the left.

The road ran through woods of hickory, oak, and other hardwood trees, that even in spring, cast a lot of shade on the road. Dampness from an earlier rain gave a fresh, earthy scent to the woods.

As we came around a curve, a marker alongside the road indicated the burial trench. I pulled the car to the side into a designated parking area and climbed out, pausing to gaze at the serene-looking location. Situated toward the back of the open area, the burial trench rose a few inches above the ground, a long rectangular grave outlined with a brick border. A larger marker in front read:

To the Confederate dead in the trenches.

Erected by Tenn. Division

I took a deep breath, taking in the scent of the magnolia trees that had burst into blossoms in recent days. Trees of all sorts bordered on the curved field dominated by the mass grave. An impression of the serenity and sheer beauty of the surroundings settled on me. So much death happened here. All of Shiloh served as a cemetery and war memorial, yet the very word meant peace in Yiddish. If nothing else, the victors of the battle had given these poor souls a serene resting place. Perhaps it provided enough to allow them to have crossed over and I wouldn't find the soldier I sought.

And perhaps not.

Without singing a single note, I could sense unrest in the area and the hairs on the back of my neck rose. Nearby, the twittering chirp of a song sparrow challenged me with his song.

A hand touched my shoulder and I nearly jumped with fright until I realized it was Janna.

"It's daunting," she said in a low voice, the kind of respectful voice you use in church. "You can do this, Gilly. I know you're strong enough to handle however many may be here. Just focus on finding Menafee Willits."

I swallowed hard, then went back to the car to get a bottle of water. My throat felt dry and my lips stuck to my teeth. Dang, singing in front of a large crowd bothered me less than doing it here. Since these men had died over a century ago, most of them had probably moved on and had found peace somewhere. Nevertheless, if a few remained, could I see or help them? And what if Menafee had moved on? Would I have any way of knowing?

Steeling myself for this, I faced the grave and started singing an old song called "Shule Aroon" or "Siúil A Rún" in Gaelic, an ancient Irish song that had made its way to Appalachia. I learned it back in grade school as an American folk song called "Buttermilk Hill" but discovered its history later on as I researched Celtic songs. Typical of Irish ballads, the haunting melody thrives in the minor key that touches the heart's harp.

In the quiet afternoon, I gave thanks that more tourists weren't stopping by to look at the gravesite and take pictures, then I realized my mind buzzed too much with these thoughts. I needed to clear them in order to allow the vision happen. Always easier said than done, but I focused in on the rhythm and melody of the song, letting my mind drift. When I started the second chorus, I almost decided I'd failed to connect.

At that instant, I transitioned to the cemetery where I'd talked to Emmett, or at least, it looked like the same place. Now that I'd seen Shiloh, it appeared similar to this area but the hills still seemed more like Kentucky or Virginia.

However, my attention focused on thirteen men dressed in gray and off-color yellowish uniforms, even one with dark blue pants. Uneven in color and style, most wore a coarse gray jacket and a French-style cap. Many bore splotches of very wet-looking blood. The soldiers didn't move from their positions, seeming to either not see me or respond to my presence.

With a catch of hesitation in my voice, I called out, "Menafee Willits, are you here? I need to speak to Menafee Willits."

I saw a few heads tilt as if they were listening, but no one answered at first. Then one of the men came toward me. I could tell immediately that this wasn't Willits.

The very thin young man stood about five-foot-eight and looked like he might have been all of eighteen when he died. His chin sprouted a very light fuzzy beard and a hint of a mustache crossed his upper lip. He came to within three feet and stopped to gape at me. Confusion swirled in his light brown eyes as he peered at me as if a strange creature had arrived in his world. Most disconcerting, though, his bloody left arm hung like a useless club from his badly torn shoulder by just a thin tendon and splintered bone.

A cannonball victim, my inner voice supplied, as I reeled at the horror of what had happened to him. And he was still here. He hadn't crossed over.

"Hello. I'm looking for someone. Do you know Menafee Willits?" I managed to ask. I put his tragic appearance aside as I'd already resolved to help him.

He shook his head in a slow back and forth movement and his young, high-pitched voice asked, "Are you an angel?"

How did I answer this? "No, not an angel, but I am here to help you find your way to the Creator. He has given me the ability to see and talk to you and the others."

"Others?" His eyes took on a worried look as his face scrunched up in puzzlement. "What others?"

"You don't see anyone else?" I looked beyond him to see the rest of the ghosts still waiting where they were. Could they not see each other?

"No. Just you. I haven't seen anyone since the battle..." His voice trailed off and tears glistened in his eyes as he cast a sorrow-filled look at the useless arm. "It was terrible. Horrible. All the blood and cries and noise." His voice had a soft drawl and a gentleness that belied the violence he'd experienced.

"It's all right. It's all over now. What is your name?"

His head dipped, a little shaky, and he replied, "Seth Harper. I was known as Seth Harper."

"Good, Seth. I'm Gillian and I will try to help you. Where are

you from?"

"Georgia. I came with my company from Atlanta. No offense, ma'am, but how can you help me? I fear my soul is lost." His voice carried such sadness that it made my heart ache. He'd been just a kid and had probably been religious. He shouldn't still be here in this purgatory of a graveyard.

"I will help you get home, Seth." As I said it, I hoped that I could find the path to the gate or the light in this place. I gazed around the open field, looking for an indicator, worried that I wouldn't find it; that helping him cross exceeded my mission. Then I glimpsed a sparkle off to the left, leading into the first line of trees. "Walk with me, please." I pointed to the direction we needed to go.

Although he seemed uncertain, he followed. Moving slowly with a limp, he stepped beside me as I set an easy pace toward the very faint path. When I came closer, I began to see words before me; no book as I sometimes saw, but the words that would praise Seth's life and I sang them to him. Just ahead, only a few yards away, a glowing circle formed in the air and I knew that he would be able to cross.

I turned to face him. "Do you see that light ahead, Seth?"

He gazed over my shoulder. "Yes, ma'am, I do."

"It has come for you. Don't be afraid, but walk into it in joy. Your Father is waiting to welcome you home."

His face reflected the happiness that awaited him as he thanked me. He'd already begun to transform, the weariness and pain lifting from his young face and the injuries to his arm vanishing in the healing light. Then he stepped forward with pride as a hopeful young soldier and marched into the light.

After he stepped through, the light remained so I knew others waited, who would be able to cross now. Addressing the glowing opening, I called out, "I'm looking for Menafee Willits. If he has passed here, please let him speak to me. His brother Emmett sent me to find him."

No answering spirit arrived, but I had deemed it worth the try. I retraced my steps back to the other spirits and called out again. "Do you know Menafee Willits? Menafee Thomas Willits, please come to me."

Another ghost approached, a big man about six feet tall, with broad shoulders, golden brown hair, and deep blue eyes. He looked me over and said, "I knew Willits. I dinna see him after the battle... not after I died. For a while, we could see one another then the spirits began to fade. I dinna ken where they went and now there is only me."

I detected a Scottish burr in his voice and caught the words dinna ken, which meant did not know. "You came from Scotland, didn't you?"

"Aye, I did. From Dunbar. I came to America almost ten years afore this war started. I am Hamish McAlester. I had hoped to build a new life here."

"I am sorry." What more could I say to a man who had died in 1862? "When you last saw Willits, was he around here? Did he fight alongside you?"

"Aye, we started out together, but we were separated. Willits did some scouting on the first day and saw a few of the enemy blue towards the old church and went to ground, hoping to confront them without being seen. I parted from my unit after we attacked and ended up down here at this field where we ran into the enemy. I dinna ken whether he survived."

"Thank you for that information, Hamish. I am Gillian and I will guide you to the path that will lead you to the other side. Will you follow me?"

He nodded and I repeated the walk as I sang the praises of the Scotsman who'd come to America looking for a better life and lost his in this terrible war.

And so it went. After I showed McAlester to the light, another ghost soon took his place and I guided him to the light. I got names, ranks, and place of birth for most of them. How I could *possibly update their family records with the information, I had no idea, but at least I would know who they were and that they had a name as they went across.*

I guided eight of the ghosts across that afternoon, learning a little about each of them and always asking if they knew Menafee. I had pretty much decided that he didn't lie among those here in this trench and if he could hear me from the other side, he'd not come back.

After the eighth one passed through the portal, the light grew brighter for a moment giving me hope Menafee might step out, then it winked out. As I turned back, the woods seemed to darken and a foreboding settled on me. The path had vanished with the light and I hoped I headed in the right direction, but it all seemed different. A black form materialized a few feet in front of me, taking on the aspect of a shadowed man with crimson, glowing eyes. Fear touching me like a tangible hand, I shrieked and jumped back. The figure seemed to laugh, if that's what the sound bursting in my head could be called.

Then it hissed, "I know you now, Gillian Foster, and I have marked you. You will not take those who are mine."

"Who are you?" I barely managed to form the words let alone say them aloud. But it heard anyway.

"You will learn." A cackle of sound erupted in my mind as the figure vanished. Terror washed over me and I cried out, "No!"

In the next instant, I knelt on the damp grass in front of the mass grave, tears streaming down my face and arms hugged around myself as I cried out, "no," over and over again. I must have yelled when I came back to my body because Janna knelt beside me, an arm around my shoulders as she offered me a tissue to wipe my eyes.

Worse, a man, who appeared to be about thirty, dressed in a Confederate uniform, looked down at me from a couple of feet away. My muddled mind couldn't grasp it. He didn't look like a ghost and I didn't think one had followed me back.

"Is your friend all right?" he said, addressing Janna.

"I believe so. She gets very emotional around graves," Janna said. "She's an empath, so she picks up on the emotions of the event."

I could tell she was trying to explain my distraught state. I had no idea when the man had arrived, but I guessed it was within the last few minutes. Was he the reason I'd been pulled away from that demonic shadow? I grabbed control of my emotions and yanked myself to my feet. I wiped at my eyes as I faced the newcomer.

"I'm sorry about that. I do get a little overwrought when confronted with such a sad event. So much grief and pain here..." My voice broke and I hoped my story sounded convincing.

"I understand, ma'am. I'm Robert Harding, one of the volunteers here at Shiloh. Pleased to meet you." He offered his hand in greeting.

Relieved, I shook it and forced a small smile at him. "This is the first trench I saw marked on the map. Where are the others?"

He barked a laugh at that. "Are you sure you want to see the others? This one seemed to have caused a lot of stress."

"Yes, it did. I guess when I say I soak up history, it takes on new meaning." I tried to make light of it even though my voice sounded weak and harsh. Janna handed me a bottled water and I swallowed down a large gulp.

Harding proved to be helpful and knowledgeable, showing us on a larger map where the other four graves were. He pointed at the area called the Hornet's Nest, then moved his finger up to the Shiloh Church and on to a left turn where a marker indicated a burial trench. The largest in the park, he told us. "No one knows for sure," he said, "but they believe there are seven hundred Rebels buried there. There are a few single graves but they aren't marked. I'm pretty sure there's a couple by the Hornet's Nest."

"Are there ghosts in the park?" Janna asked. "We've heard

rumors."

"Well, there have been those who say that there are. Me, personally, I haven't witnessed any. But I've done the recreations of the battles here and sometimes, it feels like someone is right behind me when I go charging in. You could be stepping on graves anywhere in the place and that alone is kind of spooky."

"You do battles here?" Janna queried before I could.

"Yep. It's too bad you ladies weren't here two weeks ago when we did our annual recreations on the anniversary weekend of the battles. It's quite a sight to see and just makes you completely aware of the chaos of the war."

He paused and glanced around the area as if he expected a spirit to step out. It had gone oddly silent, no birds chirping or even leaves rustling, I noticed and I wondered if the dark spirit could come into this world. Nearby, I heard a distinct whooing call of an owl. That would be why the birds weren't making noises and were likely hiding.

"Something woke that owl," Harding commented. "Probably a great horned one. They show up around here often. I gotta get going now. The park closes in about fifteen minutes."

Then he wished us a good day and went on.

"When did he get here?" I asked as soon as he was out of hearing range.

"About five minutes or so before you came back," Janna said. "I was getting worried since you were at it so long."

"How long?"

"Twenty-seven minutes. What happened? Did you find Menafee?"

"No." I sighed and looked out over the field. "So many dead. But eight of them have now moved on. Sometimes I wonder if I'm doing them a favor or not. In spite of all of this, I don't know what's beyond that light and I can only hope that it's what is promised."

She pulled me into a hug. "It is. I'm sure of it. You were *not* given this gift for evil. Your gift comes from love. If you can't trust God, then trust me."

I laughed at that. "I always have, my friend. I always will. If you say so, I believe you."

"Do we try another spot?" she asked.

"No, I'm beat and the park is closing soon. Let's get a room for the night, then come back in the morning."

TWELVE

"**Y**ou're being quiet," Janna said as we ate dinner.

"Just tired." I'd felt so drained after the afternoon's experience that she drove us to the nearby town of Savannah while I dozed. She'd located a nice, inexpensive hotel not too far from the main drag. After I'd grabbed a cup of coffee, we walked a few blocks to a local restaurant that the hotel manager recommended. A nice mix of comfort food and Cajun, it satisfied the taste buds and filled our stomachs. Although I figured I had room enough left for a piece of pecan pie with ice cream.

The twenty-seven minutes bothered me. Before, when I'd spent a lot of time in the transitional cemetery, not that much time had passed in reality. It worried me that I functioned in this trance-like state that long. "I have to ask, did I sing the whole time?" Boy, that sounded really weird to say.

Janna shook her head as she bit into a hush puppy. "No, you went through the song, started it again, then your voice just faded out and you knelt on the grass, humming and rocking from side to side. I thought you'd pull out of it then, but you still seemed..." Her voice trailed off as she sought the words to describe it.

"In a trance," I supplied.

"Kinda, yeah. Or maybe deep meditation."

"That about what it feels like. I don't seem to be totally in control and although I remember everything I see, say, and do, it doesn't feel like I'm controlling it. You know what I mean?"

Her mouth lifted up on one side into a semblance of a shrug. "Not really, but I get the idea. You're on auto-pilot."

"Close enough. This whole session seemed more strange than usual and I don't quite understand why, but the spirits were unaware of each other. I counted thirteen of them standing in that clearing, but when I spoke to them, they all said they didn't see any others. Although the Scottish guy did say that he saw the others at first, but over time they faded."

She shuddered a little, then said, "I dunno. But you said you showed eight over. What about the other five?"

"Not their time, I guess. The portal closed. So let's get back over there around nine-thirty tomorrow and see if we can find Menafee Willits. If he was near the Shiloh church, maybe he's buried in that area."

"I think that if he's already crossed over, there's a real possibility that you won't be able to contact him."

"I know. However, I have contacted people who've crossed, twice now. Madame Astrid said it's more of a question of if they want to respond."

Then our pies arrived and we dropped our conversation in favor of savoring the richness of the pecans and brown sugar custard.

While an early shower the previous day had made Shiloh smell fresh and given a deeper color to it, the heavy clouds of the morning promised more rain soon. I pulled my heavy sweater closer to my body as Janna and I stopped at a memorial to the Confederate soldiers. They had won on the first day of the battle, only to lose terribly to the Union forces under the command of Ulysses S. Grant the next day.

The monument I gazed at with a mixture of awe and sadness had to be one of the largest memorials in the park. The sets of figures were mounted on a platform rising in steps to the raised ledges where the bronze figures dominated. The central figures on it bore the descriptive name of *Death Overcomes Victory.* It depicted the beautiful woman, Victory, who represented the South, being overcome by two hooded figures, Night and Death. According to my guide description, the Death figure referred to the demise of Confederate General Albert Sidney Johnston, a West Point Graduate, who some considered the best commander in the country, north or south. Suffering an injury during a battle on the first day, he died from it, which dealt a terrible blow to the southern forces. Then night came and the Northern troops gained reinforcements and were able to rally to defeat the rebels on the second day of fighting. Thus, Victory had been snatched from the South.

Facing the monument, the figures on the left depicted two Confederate soldiers, a cavalryman and an officer, with their heads lowered in defeat. On the right side, the figures, artillerist and infantryman, looked up as they headed to battle with hope in their hearts. Between them, two friezes showed soldiers' heads bowed on the left side and raised on the right side.

My eyes filled with tears as I gazed at the memorial, understanding what it represented. Two opposing points of view and so much sacrifice for what each side believed to be right. Thomas said that the war hadn't been just about slavery; that it was more complex. Were the principles of the war right or wrong?

However, standing here now, I could only feel that the cost of the war had exceeded what anyone anticipated. Some battles must be fought with guns and bombs, but most should be addressed with words and negotiations.

Janna's arms wrapped around my shoulders as she leaned her head against me. "Such a beautiful piece of art and so sad." Her voice caught with emotion. "Are you going to try here?"

I closed my eyes for a few moments to concentrate on my surroundings. I heard the soft plop of the light rain coming down and a slight rustle from the nearby trees, but I didn't sense any kind of presence in the area. "No. I don't think this is where he might have been. Let's go on up to the large trench that Hastings told us about yesterday."

We continued up the road that went past the Sunken Road, an offshoot dirt by-way that didn't look all that much lower than the ground around it, then we drove by Shiloh Cemetery, just before we came to the church that gave the battleground its name. Several cars occupied spots in the small lot near it and a few others parked in front of the newer, and still active, Methodist church nearby. I wanted to stop here also, but not with so many people around.

We took the turn-off to the left at Peabody Road then pulled over at the marked area for Rhea Springs. This parking lot overlooked a creek that ran alongside an open field bordered by trees. Through the gaps in the woods, I glimpsed the bricks of the new church and realized how close it sat to this area that had been a battlefield.

Across the creek from us, the ground rose in a shallow hill where a monument, flanked by two cannons, commanded it. I nudged Janna and pointed, "Shall we check that out? See what the monument says?"

She nodded and pulled her rain hood over her head.

Steps led down to the creek where a wooden footbridge crossed it, then we started up the hillside. I paused a few times, listening to the sounds and trying to detect anything unusual in the area, but nothing struck me. Where had the trench been placed? Was it beyond the monument? In a few minutes, we came close enough to read the inscription saying it honored the Illinois Battery of the Army of the Tennessee, General Sherman's regiment.

"Union Army," I said to Janna. "I don't see anything else here that would be the trench."

"No, I don't either. And these woods look pretty thick through here."

Disappointed, I turned and we started back down the hill. For a moment, I glimpsed something in the woods, a shadow that shouldn't be there, but it skittered by so quickly that it might have been my imagination. I knew stories of ghosts in Shiloh were plentiful; I'd read a few accounts that had been posted on the web. After the events of the previous day, I could verify that unsettled spirits lingered here.

As we almost reached the creek, I saw the figure again. This time, he paused between two trees for several seconds and stared at me. A young, dark-skinned man, he wore the uniform of a Union soldier and even from where I stood, I could see his wide, frightened eyes. A freed slave serving in the Union army? Or had he been a northern freeman who'd joined up? I started to take a step toward him, but he vanished. I stopped.

"Did you see that man?" I asked Janna.

"What?"

"Over between the trees. A man darted between them."

Wide-eyed and a little spooked, she answered. "No. I didn't see anything." She shivered and pulled her sweater closer as she picked up her pace back to the parking area.

Gazing back at the trees, I waited a minute or so longer to see if he would appear again, then resumed the trek to the creek. I felt uneasy as if something watched me and I continued to glance toward the trees on my right.

Back at the parking lot, I gazed around the area, turning to take in the full scope. I noted a bronze group statue on a pedestal depicting three men with a flag raised above them, carried by the central figure, which appeared to be falling. My eyes moved down to read Mississippi inscribed in the granite pedestal. Another work of art that stunned with its beauty while honoring those who died there.

Just behind the statue, I saw a sign for the burial trench across the road. I nudged Janna and started across. Rhea Field stretched out on a rise of land with a few steps leading up to the level. Another rectangular monument, about a quarter of a mile distant, drew my eyes and, beyond it, I could just make out the cannonball-lined trench.

I barely paused as I reached the monument to Indiana, going directly to the mass grave instead. I paced off the length to about forty feet and the width to ten, give or take a few inches. Seven hundred soldiers buried here, Hastings had said. Would one of them be Menafee?

I shivered in anticipation or possibly from the damp. Thus far, the rain kept to a light sprinkle, but even at that, my plastic poncho allowed water to leak down my neck, chilling me a little.

I hoped not to encounter as many restless spirits as I had the day before, but I braced for it as I began to sing "Shenandoah". I freed my mind to accept what would happen.

Faster than the previous day, I projected to another section of the cemetery, one that mirrored the area where I stood so I felt confused as I saw several soldiers on the field. Some sat moaning while others moved around within a small area as if seeking something. For now, I ignored them and called out to Menafee Willits. I waited and called again two more times with no response.

One of the soldiers approached me, peering intently as he did.

"Menafee?" I asked, hope rising that I might have contacted him. A closer look as he drew nearer told me Willits hadn't come this time either.

"No, ma'am. Who might you be?"

With that, the whole process began again with me telling him my purpose and getting details of his life. He said he was Charles Layton from Mississippi and had died on the field.

"Did a circle of light appear for you?" I asked, curious why he and the others didn't cross over at the time.

"No," he said at first, then added, "Maybe. I was confused. I didn't know what happened. I saw my comrades and there were so many of us. I didn't know I had died. Even now, it's confusing. It seems like a bad dream. One that keeps repeating."

"And you've not seen a glowing tunnel of light in all this time?"

"How long?" he asked, a look of confusion drawing down over his forehead and eyes.

"Over one hundred and fifty years."

I looked around now for the silver path or a welcoming glow. I didn't see the path anywhere, but just a short distance into the woods and near a blooming dogwood tree filled with fragrant pink blossoms, a golden glimmer pulsed behind the branches.

"It can't be. It's only been a short time."

"It is true, I promise, Charles. Look, your door to the next level is open. Go through it to your future." I pointed toward the vibrant glow where an oval opening, barely visible through the branches, beckoned.

He stood rock-still, not moving, fear coming to his eyes. "I cannot. My soul is unclean; my sins sullying it."

"Trust me, if the Creator sent me to show you the way, He will not forsake or reject you. The light calls you home. Go now."

He shook his head. "I have not been a good Christian. I have broken God's laws. There is no place for me."

"The Creator forgives us our weaknesses," I said as if I knew what I was talking about. "Have that much faith."

When he looked about to reject my words again, I saw a gleam of joy come into his face and turned my head toward the light. Standing just in front, a woman dressed in a long nineteenth-century dress reached her arms out to him.

"Amelia," he said in an exhaled breath.

"Go to her." I hardly needed to say it as he started toward the waiting spirit. In two shakes of a lamb's tail, they were gone.

As soon as I looked back, another soldier, broken and battered, limped before me and I asked his name and heard his story. Again, I watched him become whole as he went through the light.

I repeated this process another four times with a man stepping forward, each one joyful to go through. After the last, I turned back and faced the dark face and wide brown eyes of the man I'd seen across the road.

"Is there hope for me, ma'am?" he asked in the deep drawl of the south.

He couldn't have been more than sixteen, very slim and as lost as the rest of these spirits. Tears touched my eyes as I answered. "Of course, there is. What is your name?"

"Lucius, ma'am. They call me Lucius."

"Do you use a last name?" I knew that slaves frequently bore their owner's last name.

"Ledbedder. From Tuscaloosa."

"Alabama?"

He nodded, still looking fearful.

"How old are you?"

"Coming up on sixteen summers, ma'am. I'se been here a long time but time don't pass." He looked nervously at the ground, worried that I might not believe him.

"I know. But you will be welcome beyond that light. Will you tell me your story before you go?"

He shuffled his feet. "Not much to tell. I be sold when I'se ten and my new owner, he live in northern Tennessee. When Union soldiers took Fort Donelson, they freed all us slaves and I joined up." He told a sad tale, one of gaining hope and losing it. As he talked, I walked with him until we stood in front of the glowing circle.

"This it? I just walk through it and I be safe?"

I nodded, hoping that I told him the truth. As I watched him step into the light, I heard a voice shriek. "Not that one! That one is mine!"

I whirled toward the voice and saw a furious-looking bat-shaped creature with burning red eyes. Wings sprouted from his back and he hissed like a serpent.

"Too late," I yelled back at him, unaware of even choosing to say it. "He's safely through."

I glanced back at the light where no sign of Lucius remained and a moment later, the portal winked out. Whatever existed on the other side of it had to be better than this creature that hovered a mere ten feet or so from me.

"Who are you?" I asked.

If the creature answered, it went unheard as it dived toward me and...

I pitched forward grabbing at the burial monument for support. I'd returned, shaken and more frightened than I'd ever been. Dizzy and gasping, I clung to the rock for support.

"Gillian!" Janna called.

The alarm in her voice rang in my brain as I lifted my buzzing head to gaze at her.

Her frightened wide eyes and open mouth conveyed her alarm. "Are you all right, Gilly?" she asked, an edge of panic in her voice. "You screamed out."

"I'm okay," I managed to say, although I didn't feel it. My hands shook and my heart pounded as hard as it would if I had run a hundred yard dash. Determined, I pushed myself to my feet, wobbling a little, but settling back into my body. "Let's get away from here."

She nodded, grabbed my left arm to help support me, and we hurried down the slope, half-running to the car. I went for the water as soon as we got in and swallowed half a bottle without hesitation.

What the hell was that thing? Could it be related to the last dark spirit I'd seen? Was it Satan? I shivered. Between the rain and the fear, I felt frozen.

"What happened? You're as white as a sack of flour." Janna started the car and turned on the heater.

I took a few deep breaths and shook my head. "I'll tell you later. Let's backtrack to the church now. Maybe the crowd will be gone."

Janna frowned at me, her lower lip twitching in annoyance.

I would tell her about it later, but for now, I wanted to think about what had occurred and try to apply some logic to it. I couldn't even begin to describe the creature let alone define it.

She started the car and pulled out of the parking area a little faster than necessary. Her way of letting me know she was annoyed that I hadn't offered an explanation.

Only one other car sat in the wide lot when we got back to the church. Luck, maybe, but more likely the heavy rain contributed to the lack of tourists.

Plain and small, the church looked like nothing more than a cabin about the size of a modern living room. A small community Methodist congregation, it reminded me that those surrounding fields, where battles had raged, had been farms at the time. While the church hadn't been touched, heavy fighting had broken out all around it.

According to the guidebook, the Union army had camped nearby when the Confederates attacked them. The church survived the attack and found use as a hospital, but it collapsed a few days later. This building, a rebuilt replica of the old log cabin one, stood in place of the original, possibly on the same foundation.

Mounting the few old steps at the front, we went inside, getting out of the rain for a bit, and looked around. Even the benches - two aisles of them, five rows - and the pulpit had been faithfully reproduced. With only the light from the windows on this gloomy day, the room seemed even darker without candles to light it. I wondered at the people who had worshipped here, and how much the events of April 6, 1862, had changed their lives.

The rain let up a little, so I stepped outside to look at the building and the surroundings. A chill breeze touched me and I shoved my hands into the pockets of my sweater. My fingers landed on a round object in my right pocket and I explored it, feeling the raised emblem on top.

Emmett's button.

The one Thomas had loaned to me. A little smile tweaked at my lips with the odd thought that this button had been here at this very location over one hundred and fifty years earlier. I wrapped it in my hand and pulled it out.

I looked around, recalling that the Scotsman had said Menafee had been here, but didn't necessarily die in the area since little fighting had occurred in the vicinity of the church. I turned to say as much to Janna when I saw two men dressed in Civil War uniforms, one dark blue and one gray, standing by the back edge of the building.

Like watching a movie shown without a screen, the images appeared transparent and overlaid the background of trees without obscuring them. Just a few feet from each other, they talked with animation, their hands gesturing with the conversation, but they seemed to be friends. They stood about the same height and as I focused in, I knew I watched the Willits brothers. They looked so much alike that it made it difficult to tell them apart, but I knew the one in gray was Menafee.

Suddenly, Menafee pushed his brother away, hand gestures urging him to leave. He raised his rifle and pointed it at Emmett. In a few moments, I saw why as two more Confederate soldiers emerged from the trees and came forward with their rifles raised. I thought Menafee tried to urge his brother to flee. Emmett's gun came up and he fired at one of the approaching Rebels as he sprinted away. Menafee fired his rifle, but the bullet missed his brother. I knew for certain that he'd planned to miss. The other soldier paused at his fallen comrade, so he didn't get a shot off in time before Emmett made it to the safety of the woods.

Not the moment of Menafee's death then, but it showed me what had happened leading up to it. I caught my breath, amazed by this vision. Who had sent it? I didn't get the sense of seeing through someone's eyes as I'd gotten from Marielle, but it appeared that someone wanted me to see it.

I turned to Janna. "Did you see anything just now?"

At her blank look, I gave her a quick rundown of what I'd seen.

"Wait a minute. This wasn't one of your transported to the graveyard trances? You weren't actually there?"

"That's right," I said as I pulled my hand out of my pocket and the button tumbled out, dropping to the ground.

Janna spotted it and bent to pick it up. "What's this?" she asked as she looked at the brass object.

"It's a button from Emmett's jacket." I told her about Thomas letting me take it and I'd forgotten I had it in my sweater until I'd touched it.

"It could be worth a pretty penny," she said handing it back.

I nodded and put the button back in my pocket. "I think we're done here. One last stop where Willits might have been, if the Scot was right."

We backtracked down the road, past the Water Oaks Pond to the tree-surrounded area called the Hornet's Nest. Referred to at the time as a bramble, a wooded area next to the road, it gained the name Hornet's Nest as one report said that the bullets firing back and forth sounded like hornets. This area had been held by the Union Army until Confederate guns and a line of cannons that now sat across the field from the wooded area had doomed them, but I had a feeling that something remained of either Menafee or Emmett here.

Janna and I walked around the area wondering if the trees were thicker then than they were now. I thought it might be the case as I couldn't see the location being all that valuable to the north. As I crossed over a section of the ground, I got a tingling sensation. I remembered my mother saying when you got that reaction that you'd stepped on someone's grave. I believed that quite literally, I had.

I stepped to one side and stared at the ground below me, singing softly. Unplanned, but appropriate, the song "When Johnny Comes Marching Home" flowed from me. Another old song that predated the Civil War, it spoke of the good times ahead when the war ended and the people the soldier left behind could celebrate his return.

In an instant, a man stood before me in ghostly form and I knew at once that I'd contacted Menafee Willits, only he wore dark blue trousers, not gray. In contrast, his torn coat appeared to be gray and seemed a little too large on him. His steady gaze at me made it clear that he saw me.

"Menafee Willits?" I asked.

"No, not my brother. I am Emmett Willits. I heard your call for my brother."

My mouth fell open in surprise and it was a moment or two before I could speak. "Emmett? Then if you're here, the man in Reno is..." I must have sounded stupid to him.

"Menafee."

"I don't understand." I had trouble accepting the obvious.

"My brother and I confronted each other twice on the battlefield. The first time I escaped when his comrades showed up, but the second time, I could not get away in time. I argued with Menafee, trying to get him to flee the battle. Neither of us wanted to hurt the other, but he was stubborn.

"The South had the advantage then, you see. The battle was going poorly for the Union and we were struggling to hold the line. When our paths crossed the second time, Menafee flat out told me to desert, that there would not be a third time. He was my older brother and I loved him, but I could not listen to him tell me that. Before I could get away, more Confederate soldiers came toward the Hornet's Nest and some of my unit opened fire on them. Menafee was wounded and went down and when I bent to help him, one of the Rebels shot me. It was over in less than a minute." He paused in his story, looking around him as if seeing the setting for the first time.

"I came to awareness in a graveyard, one that looked very much like one near our home. When I realized what had happened, I began exploring the area and found the way to the light tunnel. I was not there long. I had nothing to tie me to this place."

"I know your brother will be glad to hear that." At least, I thought he would.

"I have not seen him on this side, but surely he has passed on. It has been many years, has it not?"

"It has," I said as I studied the face of this man who resembled his brother so closely. I could see that he was at ease with his

death. *Was this what had tied Em – No, Menafee! I had to get used to that - to this earth?* "Your brother is in a graveyard in Reno, Nevada. He took your identity and moved west after he recuperated from his injuries. But I think he blames himself for what happened."

"What of his wife and daughter?" Emmett asked, a frown on his handsome face.

Wife and daughter? My mind stumbled on it. Menafee had a wife and daughter he'd left in Tennessee? Of course, he did. He'd told me as much, but I hadn't connected it.

I answered Emmett, "I regret to say that I believe he left them behind. He sent me here to learn what had happened to 'his brother's family', when in fact, it seems it was his own family he was worried about. I had no idea..."

Eyes widening with surprise, he said, "Nor I. I cannot believe he would do such a thing. His daughter was only two years old when the war started. Emily left for a widow. I am shocked."

Upset, he vanished then, without another word. I still felt a little numb myself. I hadn't even guessed at this.

Thunder rumbled across the hills, threatening a heavier downpour. Janna called to me from the car and I hurried to get in before the rain grew heavier. The engine roared to life and she turned toward the park exit.

"Let's head toward Pittsburgh Landing and see more of the monuments before we go," I said. We'd come this far and I thought I'd like to at least see as much of Shiloh as we could. Another hour would still give us time to find the Willits' past in Clarksville.

"What happened?" Janna asked as we went past Ruggles Battery again to connect to Highway 22 to the north.

"This story took an interesting twist."

"Did you see someone? Menafee?"

"Oh, it's better than that. I talked to Emmett."

"He was here or did you pick up on the Reno site?" Janna asked, clearly confused by this.

"Nope. Emmett was the one who died at Shiloh."

"What ?." She stretched the word out as she thought. "So, the ghost in Reno is really Menafee?"

"You got it. Quicker than I did. Boy, do I have some words for that ghost when we get home. After we're done here, let's find a place for lunch and I'll tell you everything I've learned."

*T*HIRTEEN

*W*e ended up at a little diner just off the freeway toward Nashville, one of the few places that actually seemed to be in business. The food tasted okay but nothing to write a review about. I filled Janna in on everything that had happened at both burial trenches, including the threatening bat-like thing that still made me shudder when I thought about it.

Janna's face registered alarm and concern, "Oh, that doesn't sound good. This gift of yours seems to have added danger. I don't like it."

"Well, I'm not crazy about it either, but it seems to come with the territory. I just want to know what the heck it is and what to do about it. I didn't think anything could harm me in the trance state, but the one in Reno bruised me and this one threatened."

"Ask Zak," she said as if I could summon my angel or guide, or whatever he might be, whenever I wanted.

"I've tried," I hissed back, keeping my voice low. "He isn't responding and it's not like I can call him on the phone or send an email."

"Oh, I guess not." Her head dropped to an apologetic dip. "This is so out of my league."

Mine, too, I thought as I finished my coffee.

As we moved further north, the rain dissipated, although thick clouds still hung above us like a bad omen. The actual travel time slowed as the roads weren't as nice as we'd thought they'd be, much of it being two lane roads that dropped speed even more as we passed through towns and offered very few passing lanes.

By late afternoon, we were getting close to the city when we saw the sign for twenty more miles to Clarksville. In unison, we broke into song with "Last Train to Clarksville". As we laughed, the somber cloud we'd felt between us lifted. This spirit-chasing business tended to put a damper on our usual camaraderie.

Our road into Clarksville took us alongside the Cumberland River and we pulled into a motel near the junction that would take us back to Memphis. After we took our things into the room, I consulted the local area map on my tablet.

"Fort Defiance is nearby. It was a Civil War fort. We still have a couple of hours of daylight left; let's check it out."

With a groan, Janna grabbed her sweater and followed me out to the car. It turned out to be very close, just across the river with a left turn through a residential area and up a road that led to a bluff overlooking the water.

The fort didn't exist anymore. Pieces of lumber and other items that might have been part of the building lay in piles on the ground where a marker indicated its placement on the top of a hillock. I turned around the area thinking it might have offered a good panorama of the river during the war, but now trees blocked the view and I couldn't even glimpse the Cumberland. Even though a cannon had greeted us at the entrance, the city had converted the whole area into a park with a few informative signs and a pathway down to the water.

The modern-looking building that perched next to the parking lot housed an interpretive center that explained the fort's function and recounted life in Clarksville during the war.

Started by the Confederates in 1861 to control the river traffic, it soon surrendered to the Federal troops, who expanded it. It changed hands again in August 1862 until the Union again claimed it in September and retained control during the rest of the war. Being far north in Tennessee and near the Kentucky border, it appeared that the city went with the flow of whoever held it and life went on somewhat peacefully. Had the Willits brothers remained in Clarksville, Emmett wouldn't have been killed and Menafee probably wouldn't have fled west.

"Do you feel anything on the grounds around here?" Janna

asked as we came out of the center to gaze at the tree-filled city from this height. Unlike most western cities, many trees towered above the buildings and woods surrounded it, giving it a lush, gentle appearance.

"No, there's no vibe of any sort in the fort area. I don't think it saw much fighting if any. Shiloh had a charged energy feel from the moment we got close to it. This place is calm and it's not a burial ground."

"Thank goodness," she replied.

I shot a questioning look at her, then we both started laughing for no reason except relief.

As I fell asleep in our motel room in Clarksville, my mind rehashed the events and discoveries of the last two days. As surprised as I'd felt that the Reno Willits had failed to disclose the truth to me, more distressing proved to be the thought of all those souls I'd seen in the graveyard who had not moved to the next plane. No wonder people saw ghosts at the memorials. I closed my eyes and I still saw the face of Seth, the first soldier I'd spoken with and felt sadness for how young he'd been. Then there was Lucius, a frightened kid.

As a race, we had learned nothing. We still sent our young men, and women now, off to war. What senseless tragedy. You would think that in centuries of dealing with each other we could have found a way to resolve issues without resorting to violence.

After tossing and turning with these thoughts, I slipped into a full-color dream, the kind that usually took place in the dream graveyard, but this time, I was standing in the midst of the aftermath of a battle. It could have been Shiloh or any other one of the Civil War battle sites. Smoke hung in the air, voices cried out in pain, others sobbed in grief and some called for help. Their voices echoed around the area, magnifying the intensity. Those soldiers, who dared, ran onto the grounds and attempted to pull the living from the field. Blue and Gray, the wounded and the rescuers represented both sides, while the dead lay stacked everywhere. Nearly sunset, I could feel the cold and damp settling in.

Somewhere nearby a cannon fired and I jerked when I heard the sound before my brain could register what it was. In the eyes of the men, I could see the sorrow and pain that this fighting caused as neighbors found themselves facing each other on different sides of the conflict. Brothers divided by the issues they couldn't agree on pulled rifles on each other. It was insane, I thought. All war is insane.

Then the survivors retreated from the field and it was just me standing there in the middle of hundreds of dead bodies, both Union and Confederate. A circle of light appeared in the center of the field and some souls rose and answered the beckoning radiance. Others were too broken to heed the call. These lingered, refusing to accept the salvation or comfort offered. I could pick out the faces of some of the ones I had helped, but so many remained.

I hugged my arms around my chest, dropped my head, and sobbed. A countless number of souls drifting. What could I do?

"You did enough." The warm, melodious voice floated like the touch of a breeze on a late spring day, caressing my soul with loving fingers.

I looked up to see Zac. He was the most beautiful creature I'd ever seen and if he wasn't an angel, then he must surely be a god.

"Did I, Zac? It seemed like scores of souls needed help. I could have gotten all of the ones at the first trench." My voiced cracked with the pain I felt for them.

"They were not ready to let go yet," he answered. "As long as they harbor whatever guilt holds them, then they won't respond to your call. The ones that could hear you came and you showed them the way. That was all you needed to do."

"It doesn't seem like enough."

His smile spread radiance and healing. "It may not seem like it, but even though they didn't respond to you, the others saw you and you gave them hope. It may be enough to bring them through in due time."

"They couldn't see each other, yet Hamish told me they could at first. Why did they lose the ability?"

"They didn't. They just quit looking after many years. Time has no meaning there, but it still passes and after a while, there is nothing new and nothing to say. So, they stop communicating with each other and eventually stop seeing. You were a new element in their landscape, so some of them saw you."

"But when people have a ghost sighting, doesn't that do the same thing? Disturb them?"

He shrugged. "Sometimes it does and sometimes it doesn't, but to have someone actually arrive in *their* reality, what is essentially their dimension, does affect them."

He shifted positions to stand beside me. I couldn't say walked because he was in one place one moment, then in a different place the next.

"Gillian, you have one ghost now to help and you can bring him across, but you must be prepared to forgive him as he will be forgiven on the other side. Like these ghosts at Shiloh, he has been in his private purgatory long enough. Set him free."

"Menafee," I said, understanding what he needed, then I saw Zac start to fade and my subconscious called to me. "Wait, Zac! I have a question. What are the black spirits I'm seeing."

"Black spirits?"

"Yes, a human-like figure at the cemetery in Reno attacked me. Then one at Shiloh that looked like a bat of some sort and screamed at me that the Ledbedder boy belonged to it. It started to fly at me when I jolted back to my world. What are they?"

My angel frowned, a thoughtful look in his eyes as he considered my question. I began to fear he wouldn't answer. At last, he said, "They are shades. I hoped they wouldn't find you this soon, but you did go into an older cemetery and they often stake claims on lingering souls."

"But I thought that Hell didn't exist," my weak-sounding voice objected.

"That's true, the Hell that humans perceive doesn't exist, but other layers of existence do and the shades come from one that is fed by despair and desperation. If one had earmarked Ledbedder for his world, then your actions saved the boy and angered the shade."

"That is not what I wanted to hear. Can they hurt me? I mean on a physical level?"

His green eyes warmed with a golden tone as he gazed at me, offering reassurance. "Have faith, Gillian. You are never alone."

Then the dream ended and I slept in comfort and without any other disturbances until the morning.

FOURTEEN

Modern Clarksville didn't resemble the town that the Willits brothers knew as young men. It had grown from only a few thousand in population to over one hundred thousand now. Beautiful old buildings interspersed with newer ones and the abundance of trees in the downtown area. A full-blown city with all the amenities, it now served as the Montgomery County seat. As such, the clerk's office stored the records I needed to research the Willits history.

Janna and I began by searching through the old maps of the county prior to the Civil War. With the assistance of a gracious clerk who worked there, we located the Willits farm just to the north of the city. While it would have been quite a ways from the town limits in 1862, it now formed two city blocks. Nonetheless, we drove to the address to get a look at the area where they had lived.

I climbed out of the car and gazed at the apartment building that occupied the spot where the farmhouse had been and said, "Well, I doubt there are any spirits hanging around now. But at least, we can get an idea of what the terrain looked like and the kind of view they had." I peered beyond the housing to the trees in the distance where a few rolling hills worked their way toward Kentucky.

Janna took off her sunglasses to squint toward the north and said, "It's pretty. I'll bet it was really beautiful before all this housing went in."

"I guess this jaunt is a bust, but at least it didn't take us too far from downtown. Let's go back and see if we can find the birth and death records for Menafee's family."

As I turned back to the car, a little dark-skinned boy tugged at my sweater. "Hey, ma'am," he said. "Are you looking for something?" He couldn't have been more than five or six and that Tennessee drawl in the child's voice charmed me.

I knelt down to his level and smiled. "Yeah, we were looking for something that's not here anymore."

"What was that?" He stuffed his hands in his back pockets and rocked on his heels.

Janna pulled her phone out and snapped a picture he looked so cute.

"It was the Willits family's home, but it's been torn down. This apartment building sits on it now."

His eyes grew wide. "That's my name."

Surprised, I cocked my head a little and said, "Your last name is Willits?"

He nodded with enthusiasm. "Uh huh, my name's Tatum Willits and I live there." He pointed to the apartment building.

"Well, it is a small world, isn't it? I'm pleased to meet you, Tatum Willits."

About that time, a young woman hurried out of the building, running toward us. Her dark, curly hair, which she'd pulled back into a ponytail, bounced like a paddleball as she ran. Skin the same shade of cocoa brown as the boy hinted at her relationship to Tatum. I figured she'd been watching from the window and saw him engage with us.

I straightened up as she came up and caught her son's arm to pull him back from me.

"Tatum, what are you doing? I told you not to speak to strangers." She didn't yell, but her voice was firm and no-nonsense.

"But Mama, they's looking for Willits. Maybe they wanna see you."

She shot a sharp glance at me, then at Janna. "Our name is Willits. Is there something you wanted?"

I held up a hand and took a step back. I didn't want her to get the wrong idea. "No, no. It's nothing much. We are just doing some research. There used to be a Willits Farm in this area and the family house sat here where your apartment is. Then your son mentioned his name was Willits. That's all it was."

Her shoulders dropped as she bristled down. "Oh, I'm sorry. I thought you might be from the collection agency. They've been bothering us lately. You're right that this used to be the Willits' place. My husband's family had been slaves before the Civil War, so they were kind of like Willits family in the sense that they owned them. Old man Willits freed his slaves just before the war broke out, but Michael's great-grandfather stayed with them and continued to work for them. It was all he knew."

"Really? Did any of the Willits family still own the land here before this complex was built? I'm trying to find a descendant of one of the owners in the Civil War."

She thought about it for a bit, musing as she did. "Maybe Bethany might have still owned a little bit, but most of it had been sold off over the years. Your best bet is probably the County Clerk's office. They can tell you who owned it before it was sold to the company that built this."

I thanked her, expressed my pleasure to meet her and I waved good-bye to Tatum as his mother hauled him back into the building.

"Can you believe we actually met someone who had a little information on the family?"

"As slaves," Janna said, stressing the word. "Now they're living in the housing on the property."

"True. They're the Willits family now. I wonder how Menafee will feel about this."

"Do you really think you'll find much information at the Clerk's office?" Janna asked.

"Oh sure, I've watched 'Who Do You Think You Are?'" I referred to the genealogy documentary television series where celebrities searched for their ancestors.

The County Clerk bounced on her swivel chair when I asked about looking at the records from the beginning of the Civil War.

"Oh, honey, we have so many people come in here looking for relatives that they might have lost in the war." Short, plump, and with a round face framed by long, blond hair, she looked a little like Miss Piggy. Her name badge identified her as Eloise Frasier. "But not to worry. I am sure we can find something on whoever you're looking for. Now, what is the name?"

"Menafee Thomas Willits," I said. "I believe his wife's name was Emily."

"Willits," Ms. Frasier repeated. "You mean the Willits who used to have a farm off the Higdon Road turnoff?"

I nodded.

"Oh yeah, they were well-known in this area. The family had that farm from about 1790 until 1948. But Menafee... Let me look. I believe that was the son who died in the War Between the States. Y'all have a seat over there and I'll be back in a few minutes with something." She indicated a table near a stack of books, then disappeared through a door to the archives.

"Well, at least she's heard of them," I said as we sat.

Janna raised an eyebrow. "We may have gotten lucky on this, but it still may not be that easy. You do know that those are professional researchers on those shows, don't you?"

"Oh, sure, but we don't have to dig too far into it. I just need to find out if his daughter married and had kids and her kids had kids to see if there are any direct heirs left."

I made it sound simple, but I suspected that it wouldn't be easy to follow the most recent trail. Older records were public knowledge, but stuff within the last fifty years seemed harder to find out unless they had a Facebook page. I frowned. I hadn't thought about that, but then I would need to know more than the last name and possible city before I could narrow the Willits down.

I tapped my fingers nervously on the table as we waited, drumming out a rhythm as my mind worked on a new song. Janna glared at me from across the table, but I barely registered her annoyance. When a song presented itself, I tried to run with it and this one was developing a beautiful melody. The lyrics were a little shy though, so it wasn't a major loss when Ms. Frasier returned with copies of some documents.

She set them on the table, then sat down herself. "Okay, now, I have a little bit for y'all to see. The Willits family was a house divided during the Civil War. Most of the family favored the North and the patriarch Peyton Menafee Willits freed his slaves before the war started. Now the younger brother, who was named Charles Emmett, sided with the North and the older brother, Menafee Thomas favored the South. So when the war broke out, they found themselves battling against each other."

I nodded. We already knew this part of it. "I understood that they both fought at Shiloh. What can you tell me about Menafee's wife and daughter?"

She looked up with a wounded expression that I'd interrupted her recitation. Then she flipped the page over to go to what looked like a copy of a handwritten page from a book. "Okay then, Menafee married Emily in 1859. They had a little girl, Marion, who was born in February of 1860. Now Menafee died at Shiloh in April 1862. So, I checked the next census after the war and found that Emily and Marion were living with his parents still."

"So it sounds like Menafee's parents were taking care of them after their son's death." I made a note of it on my phone so I could report that back to my lying ghost.

"Yes. It does. Now, I have a death record for Emily. It looks like she expired on June 18th in 1879. Then I have another death record for Marion Willits Johnston who died on August 21, 1877, and I have a birth record for Emily Louise Johnston who was born on the same date. So I reckon that Marion died in childbirth."

"She was only seventeen," I said, doing the math quickly. That made me inexplicably sad.

"Yes, just a baby herself. But the girl married young and

probably made a good match with the Johnston fellow. He was twenty-eight when they married and it looks like he had a little piece of property not too far from the Willits farm. The records show it right about a half a mile away." Ms. Frasier used her thumb to measure the map and I had to chuckle a little to myself. How many times had I done that as well?

"So what happened to Emily Louise? Did she marry and have children?"

Across from me, Janna shot me a bored look, then went back to reading on her phone.

The clerk turned another paper and read through her notes. "Here we go. In 1900, Emily and Edmund Johnston had a son and they called him Charles Menafee. By the 1910 census, the Johnston family showed their son, now ten, and a daughter, Elizabeth Marie, who was seven. At the next census in 1920, it was Emily, Edmund, and Elizabeth, but not Charles in their home. I couldn't find any record of a Charles in Montgomery County after that and I didn't find a death record for him. I would say that the likelihood is that he moved to a different place. By 1930, Elizabeth and Edmund were no longer in the census at the house and by 1940, even Emily was gone. Elizabeth probably married, but I can't find anything on it."

"If I wanted to visit Emily's grave, where might I find it?"

She plucked out a paper and scanned down it, then said, "She was interred in the Riverside Cemetery. It's the oldest one in town and it's right on the river."

"Thank you. So where should I go now for more information?" I asked.

"If you a computer, or you can try the library, then you can access the state marriage records and death records to see if they are recorded in Tennessee. You can also go to the state capitol in Nashville in person and ask to see the records. But to be honest, the computer is faster."

She handed me the papers and said it would be a five-dollar

copying fee. Even though I hadn't asked her to do it, I considered it worth the small amount to have the records in hand.

"Lunch," I said to Janna as soon as we left the building. We found a diner close by with a total fifties look and indulged with hamburgers and fries.

As I drew my own timeline of Menafee's family, I realized that we were stuck unless we could find whether either Charles or Elizabeth had any children.

"You know, we could sign up for a free trial at one of those ancestry search sites and see if they have any records that include either one of them," Janna said as she popped a catsup-covered fry into her mouth.

"Not a bad idea, girlfriend. We could have saved ourselves the whole trip if we'd thought about it in Reno."

She laughed. "But we wouldn't have seen Tennessee or Shiloh and we might have missed some of what Ms. Frazer told us."

"Frazier," I corrected. "It's a Scottish name, although I think it's from a French influence. You're right; I am glad I saw Shiloh, but I wish we'd had time to see more. Maybe another trip." I finished my last bite of burger, then I added, "Let's see if we can locate Emily Willits' grave."

The Riverside Cemetery sat right next to the Cumberland River in downtown Clarksville. We checked at the office and found the number and location for the woman's plot. A beautiful, green cemetery, it seemed quiet and calming as we walked the pathways. In the oldest area, not as "fresh-looking" as Janna phrased it, we located her final resting place.

Once we found the grave, I gazed at it, letting my mind wander. What would be the possibility of talking to Emily? Did she ever learn that her husband didn't die on the battlefield? That the man buried at Shiloh was her brother-in-law rather than her husband?

"I'm going to try to reach her," I told Janna.

"What? What do you expect to learn?" Her voice sounded a

little sharp, but she asked a good question and one I couldn't answer.

"I don't know. I just feel I have to do this. You can wait at the car if it bothers you."

She nodded and, while not going back to the car, distanced herself from the grave.

I cleared my mind and started singing "Church in the Wildwood", one of my favorite hymns when I was a child. At first, nothing happened, not even a whisper of connection. What did I expect? I imagined that she'd moved on long ago. But then a different image presented itself.

I saw, much as I'd seen Emmett and Menafee by the church at Shiloh, the image of a dark-haired woman dressed in black, kneeling in sorrow by an unmarked grave in a grim, dark cemetery. She sobbed at her loss, her right hand wiping at her eyes now and then to brush away the tears. Her black dress was long and full, easily a nineteenth-century design and her bodice had the form-fitted lines that looked like a jacket. I had no doubt that this was Emily Willits although I had no idea where the grave was or if it was all a symbolic message that she attempted to send to me.

As I stared at the vision grave, a raised bed of dirt bounded by bricks, I noticed the smallness of the grave. Not one for an adult but a child's grave. Had Emily borne another child while Menafee fought at Shiloh? If so, did he know that she expected a child when he left?

I spoke, not sure if she would hear me or not. "Emily Willits, I wish to speak with you if possible." I waited and repeated my request. No response.

I tried something else. "If you can't appear, perhaps you can still hear me. Your husband, Menafee, didn't die at Shiloh. He moved west where he remarried and raised a family. When he passed on, he didn't cross over. He's trapped in the graveyard. I believe it's because he feels he failed you and your daughter and deserted his obligations. I believe you should know this because I am going to do whatever I can to help him to the next plane and you might encounter him again."

I waited a few more minutes, watching the image of the weeping woman at the grave. Did the message reach her? Just as the vision began to fade, I heard a very quiet woman's voice, accented with the tones of the south, say, "I hold no grudge against Menafee, nor do I welcome him as his wife once would. He left behind a world of hardship, but my in-laws stood by me and my daughter. Tell him to come home in forgiveness but not in reconciliation. Amen."

Then the image was gone and I blinked, seeing the engraved stone in front of me again. It read:

Emily Pace Willits, born March 6, 1838, died June 18, 1876.

Gone to her Father and her husband. Peace unto her.

Her life after the Civil War must have been difficult even though she had the support of her husband's parents. To be in a place where the battle was lost would have been hard on them all. Perhaps, because the Willits family supported the North, except for Menafee, they were treated more kindly than many Confederate families.

Pulling out my phone, I snapped a photo so I would have the information. Maybe I would show it to Thomas or maybe not. If I told him the true story, it would change his perceptions about his family. I asked myself to what purpose? Would he benefit from the knowledge?

I tucked my phone back in my pocket and went back to where Janna waited. While I told her a little about the brief experience, I didn't go into detail. I realized that all of this had begun to seem a little too creepy for my friend. I couldn't blame her.

We left Clarksville around noon to head back to Memphis. Without any delays, it still took all afternoon to get back. After we checked into the hotel room, we went down to Beale St. again for some spicy barbecue chicken sandwiches and stopped in to listen to more blues for a while. More cautious after our last experience, we didn't drink much and headed back to our hotel before it got late.

As we crawled into our beds, I told Janna about my dream with Zac, but I didn't give her all the details. I only wanted her to know that he'd contacted me again.

"It's hard to ask him questions in the dream. He directs the conversation and even though I might have asked him to answer something in a mental request before I went to bed, he can choose to answer or not. So, I didn't get the answers I'd hoped to have."

"Oh," Janna said. Just that. Then she turned out the light and went to sleep.

With the morning free before we had to return the car and check-in for our flight home, we knew what we wanted to do. Situated near the airport, Graceland ranked as our number-one choice. We couldn't come to Memphis and not visit it.

I don't know exactly what I expected from Elvis Presley's home but the gaudy, packed home didn't come anywhere close to my vision. I'd seen photographs, but, to my mind, it looked grander in the pictures. My first impression marked it smaller than I expected, then I had to add in the garish decor. I'd heard that the singer had eclectic tastes, but some of it came across really wild and flashy. I guess the jungle room earned its name with good reason.

Decorated as the King had desired, it also seemed he'd crammed a lot of furniture into those rooms. However, the exhibit of his stage costumes was amazing.

Janna stared at the white and gold studded jumpsuit and whistled. "Wow. That really stands out. You know, this must have been from when he was still slim. That's a narrow hip on that costume. He looked pretty hot in his younger days."

"Yeah. I'm kind of partial to the black leather jacket and blue jeans," I answered, looking at the mannequin that wore the clothing. Behind it was a floor to ceiling photo of Elvis wearing the garment. He had been super-sexy. I could see why girls were so attracted to him.

The best part of the tour, for me, came with the grounds and the memorial garden where Elvis and both his parents were interred. It was a peaceful place, beautifully groomed, and soothed with the sound of fountains. Here, the graves bore bouquets of flowers placed by staff or his adoring fans.

How strange to have such a memorial to one person, I thought. He was a good singer and handsome, but this kind of adoration was odd. I don't know how I would feel if I were in his shoes. In my head, I seemed to hear a woman's soft voice say, *Don't even wish for it, sweetheart. It's a heartache.*

Maybe my wiser inner voice, maybe not.

We finished the tour looking at Elvis' cars and grabbed an Elvis' Fried Peanut Butter and Bananas sandwich for lunch at the café before heading to the airport. I sent a text to Ferris, who was taking care of Nygard while I was gone, to let him know I would be back in a few hours and attached a picture of me standing next to the pink Cadillac along with it.

*F*IFTEEN

*J*anna's idea to use a genealogy website to look up the state records turned out to be brilliant. With the little information I had entered, a few mouse-clicks led me to a marriage record on Elizabeth and I learned that she had divorced two years later, never remarried, and had no offspring. She expired, as Eloise Frasier would have phrased it, in 1969.

As for Charles, I didn't find any other records in Tennessee, but when I searched the surrounding states, I located him in Virginia. A death record indicated that he'd died in a train accident in 1938. As near as I could tell, he'd never married and had no immediate family other than his sister.

The sad thing about locating a family through these types of records is that they gave no sense of who they were or what they did with their lives. When you watched the celebrities on the television show hunt for their ancestors, they were able to locate newspaper articles, papers, and other pieces of documentation that provided more of a connection with their antecedents. My information consisted of cut and dried facts; birth, marriage, children, and death.

Since the program granted access to all kinds of records, I thought I'd take a look at the family names, most specifically Menafee. To my surprise, the search result tagged the name origin as Saxon and it pre-dated the invasion of Britain by the Normans in 1066. Of course, another document stated Ireland as a source. I supposed it could be both. As for Willits, it also appeared to originate in Great Britain, taken from the name Will, so it was possibly a son-of-Will name.

I finished off my timeline for Menafee's Tennessee family and thought myself almost ready to revisit him. Since I carried a full schedule for the week at Heeni's shop to make up for taking the

Monday off, I wouldn't be able to go until the weekend. Already, the Tennessee trip felt like it had occurred a long time ago.

After work on Wednesday, I hurried to the Jeep and pointed it to the promised rehearsal with Spicy Jam. This one included our two friends, Rob and Dana, who had played with us a few times before and agreed to play on this album. They were waiting for me at Ferris' rehearsal studio, formerly his garage. When I arrived my usual few minutes late, I noticed Ferris' pointed glance at his wall clock.

"Sorry," I said at once. "I ran into traffic on the way over. But I come bearing a new song." I pulled the music out of my case then began setting up my electric keyboard.

"Why don't we run through the material we're planning to record now and listen to it later?" Ferris said.

Ferris was taking charge of the band, it appeared, but he had a good point. Although I'd been excited to play the new one for them, I nodded and pulled out the set list instead.

To say it fell below the best rehearsal we'd done is an understatement. We started well with a song that we'd been doing for years, and it sounded tight and solid. Then we moved on to one that Ferris had written that had a tricky rhythm in six-eighth time with lots of short notes. I once heard it described as doing a bar of waltz combined with a bar of a fox trot. I flubbed up a little on it and Ferris hit his snare drum rim with a sharp rap.

"You've botched the rhythm on it. Pay attention to the beat, Gillian."

"Sorry. I got lost for a second. Let's try it again." I could see the annoyance in his eyes as they scrunched down to slits. Jeez, so I'd made a mistake. We all make mistakes now and then.

Then I jumped to the wrong verse on the next song we played. I'd written this one and even though I knew it like the back of my hand, I skipped to the first line of the last verse instead of the middle one and you'd have thought I'd committed a sin.

Ferris thudded his sticks onto the snare head, then climbed out from behind the drums and said, "Maybe we should take a break while the diva gets her act together." He stormed out of the garage into the house.

Digby shrugged and set his bass down. "Right. Time for a coldie," he said and went to grab a beer. Our two guest artists looked at the floor as if embarrassed, then Rob knelt and adjusted his amp pedal. My friend, Dana, cast a sheepish look my way and turned away to put her fiddle in its case before she and Rob followed the others.

Stunned, I didn't move or say anything for a few minutes. That outburst really hurt and it set me back.

Although I still felt a little tired from the trip, my sub-conscious mind continued to grapple with everything that had happened; things that neither Ferris nor Digby knew anything about, so maybe my mind floated above the music tonight. But I was trying and it *was* a rehearsal. Granted, we did contribute our time, but it wasn't as if we were spending money on the recording session. So, why did Ferris show so much annoyance with me?

Going outside, I strolled to the end of the driveway, took several deep breaths to calm myself, and attempted to gain some focus. We'd added the songs in the past few weeks, but I hadn't had time to practice them much at home. Maybe that explained why I stumbled over them a little tonight.

After a bit, Dana came out, pulled her light brown hair away from her face, securing it in a twist at her neck, and stood by me for a while before she said, "Don't worry about it, Gillian. Maybe there's something going on in Ferry's life that's set him on edge tonight. You're doing fine and we all miss something now and then."

I gnawed on my lower lip and thought that maybe she was right. "Thanks. That makes me feel a little better."

We went back into the garage and I ran through the music for the last song again on the keyboard while we waited for Ferris to come back. He returned a few minutes later, didn't say a word, and settled behind the drums then said, "Are we ready to try that one again?"

I got through that number with no more incidents, but it was a short-lived reprieve. According to Ferris, I hit a wrong note on a harmony line while I thought he had been the one who missed it. I called him on it, hitting the note on the keyboard, and singing exactly what I'd sung with him and Digby. I was right on it.

He pointed a drumstick at me. "No, you were off. You're not ready for this rehearsal," he said in a tone that carried more anger and accusation than it warranted.

"Well, crap," I muttered. It was not my fault and I snapped. "That's it, I'm done!"

Anger flowing off me like a receding tide, I unplugged my keyboard and packed it up, tossing my music back into the case while the others gawked a bit, then turned away.

"Aren't you being childish?" Ferris muttered, slamming his hand into a cymbal.

I glared at him, picked everything up, and started out the door. Behind me, I heard Digby yell, "Well, that's just great, Ferry. What the hell is your problem tonight?"

I was half-way down the drive when Digby called out to me.

"Gillian, wait up! There's no need for this."

He caught up before I reached the end. I was so angry at this point that I was on the verge of tears. The Aussie caught my case-carrying arm and turned to face me, stepping backward as I continued to walk.

"Look, babe, don't let him get to you. He's been cranky and fuming for the past few days."

"He can fume without me. I mean it, Dig. I wasn't that bad in there and he was humiliating me in front of our friends. Who knows what they think? I don't think he's ever been that rude to me before. What did I do to him?" I quit walking, the tears brimming in my eyes and ready to flood.

Digby pulled me into a tight hug. "It's more complicated than that, Gilly. Let's go somewhere and talk, okay?"

I nodded and he followed me to my Jeep where I loaded in the keyboard. "Where do you want to go?"

"How about the Perc-o-later?"

He referred to a little coffee shop in a nearby shopping center. I nodded, then reached for a tissue on the car seat. I didn't know if I wanted to talk about it, but I felt shattered. I couldn't understand why Ferris was being so nasty.

He ran back inside the garage while I loaded my things in the Beast. As I pulled away from the curb, I glimpsed him trotting toward his battered blue Volkswagen Jetta. The driver's side looked great, but a red replacement fender on the other side made it easily identifiable.

Digby pulled up right behind me when I parked at the cutesy shop that looked like it probably did forty years earlier. He led the way to a table in the back corner where no one else sat nearby. We ordered coffee, then he started talking.

"Look, I don't know what's got him riled up this time, but Ferris is getting frustrated. You weren't off key tonight. So what if you blew a lyric a couple of times? It's no biggie. But it's part of a bigger issue in Ferry's mind. We both think that you're distracted and you're not really into the music the way you were."

"What?! Of course, I'm into it. We're doing a recording session, aren't we?" My mouth hung open in disbelief.

"That's kind of part of it. We had the session and rehearsals planned and then suddenly you have to go off for the weekend with no explanation. You and Janna just suddenly need to get away. Add to it that you've set the recording date back a month. Did you use the money to go to wherever you went?"

"No," I said at once in denial, then dropped my head in shame. "Well, I did use a little, but I can replace it in a couple of weeks. It was important that I went on that trip."

"Why? What made it so important?" His earnest gaze coaxed

me to talk to him, to offer an explanation of what had more importance than our album.

I stared at a burnt spot on the table caused by someone leaving a cigarette on it instead of using an ashtray. Not that they were supposed to be smoking in there anyway, but it proved to be a good focus spot for a few moments of meditation and to avoid looking at Digby.

"See," he said after a short wait. "You don't want to talk about it. And that is part of the problem. We used to be tight, babe. The three of us could talk to each other about anything and since your accident, you've been like a clam."

"It's complicated," I said, my voice sounding meek even to my ears. I knew that he—they—needed an explanation. But how much could I tell them without sounding like an escapee from the mental ward? I felt tears in my eyes again and reached for a napkin to wipe them.

"Life is complicated," he said after a few moments. "But that's what friends are for, to help you though the complicated times. Have you told Janna?"

"She knows some of it," I answered, feeling guilty because he spoke the truth; that I had shut them out. I was even shutting Janna out on the deeper issue.

"Right now, I have a trial hanging over my head that worries me. I don't know what I can say and I don't want to talk about what happened."

"Why? You didn't do anything wrong."

My voice caught as a sob threatened to escape. "I know that. I know none of it was my fault, but it still felt so dirty!" I looked up at him with shock in my eyes. I had said it to him and I hadn't meant to tell anyone.

He slid out of the facing booth and slipped next to me, pulling me into a tight hug against his chest while his arms wrapped around me like a cocoon. The comforting gesture undid me and I burst into tears, sobbing against his chest.

He rocked me against him and said, "Hey, babe, whatever it is, we're in it together. You know you can always count on me."

It took me a few minutes to stem the flow of tears, but I got it under control and accepted the fresh napkin that he handed me to wipe my eyes and nose. A big, wet spot spread across his dark blue shirt.

"I'm sorry. I'm not usually so emotional, but there has been so much since that fall on the ice last November. I just don't know if you and Ferry need to be mired down in my problems."

He jerked his head back, looking a little like a chicken cocking its neck. "Huh? Your problem is my problem, you know. You'd do the same for us. For that matter, you have. Who did I whine at when Damien broke up with me in our junior year? Who pulled me through that depression, huh?" He poked a finger in my chest. "You did, so I am here for you."

"Okay, if you're sure you want to know." I started, speaking slowly and considering every word so it wouldn't sound too weird. "I've been having some odd dreams ever since the head injury." Then I proceeded to tell him that some of them were prophetic and they lead to my involvement with Marielle Sanders, which in turn led to becoming a kidnap victim.

"That has now given way to more bad dreams and worries and I've just been trying to cope with it all." I glossed it over and didn't tell him anything about what happened when I sang at funerals.

He hugged me again, giving me a little squeeze. "No wonder you're all stressed out. Didn't the hospital tell you to see a therapist?"

"Yeah, but I don't want to tell a stranger about it. Look how long it took me to tell someone I know really well. I've told Janna some, but not all."

I realized that the man's perception went deeper than I credited when he came back with, "You're not telling me everything now either, are you? What are you afraid of? That I'll think less of you because something happened to you that wasn't your fault?"

"I'm embarrassed," I said in a small voice, sounding like a ten-year-old.

"You have nothing to be embarrassed about. That asshat tried to rape you, didn't he? Or did he actually do it and you're afraid to tell anyone?"

"No, he didn't technically rape me, but he tried. If I'd been a kid, he would have done it; instead, he just used his fingers, then sprayed all over me like an alley cat." My voice caught as my emotions tried to overwhelm me again and I felt a hot rush of embarrassment blossom on my cheeks.

"Jesus! That bloody wanker! I'd strangle and mutilate him if I could." He kept his voice down, but the fury came through fine.

"He was going to kill me, Dig. If the sheriff's officers hadn't shown up when they did, he'd have beaten me to death. I was down to my last chance and out of options. I've never been so scared in my life."

He put his hands on my shoulders, then looked straight into my eyes. "You have got to get professional counseling, babe. This kind of thing is screwing with your mind. No wonder you're distracted and distant. Please promise me that you'll see someone. Make an appointment tomorrow."

I nodded my head, not actually saying the words. Maybe I could at least meet with the psychologist, see if I liked her, and felt comfortable talking to her. I had to admit that I did feel somewhat better for having told Digby. But that didn't solve the problem with Ferris. Could I tell him as well? Talking to him didn't come as easily as talking to Dig.

He paid for the coffee and walked me to the Jeep, an arm still snagged around my shoulder and rubbing at my top muscle. He kissed me on the forehead and said, "Look, I'll talk to Ferry and try to gloss this over some; let him know that there are some problems and you're trying to work through them. Mostly, I think he just needs reassuring that you're not leaving the band and that you've not lost the commitment to it."

"Thanks, Dig," I answered, clinging to him for a little longer. I treasured his friendship more than I could express.

I got in my car and blew a kiss his direction. As I pulled the car forward, I noticed that he'd waited until I'd turned onto the road before he started toward to his Jetta.

SIXTEEN

*E*ver since I'd returned from Tennessee, I'd wanted to talk to Madame Astrid about what happened at Shiloh and Clarksville. She'd been busy with a flurry of appointments but managed to squeeze me in for a night session. Now that I sat facing her in the parlor, a cup of tea perched in my hand, I found myself searching for the right place to begin.

She gazed at me with expectation in her attentive expression. "Something is troubling you, but you don't know how to put it. Just start at the beginning, Gillian. It will come out when it should."

So, I did, recapping the events at Shiloh from finding lost souls at the mass graves to the quest for Menafee, although I didn't tell her about the switch-a-roo that our false Emmett had manipulated. That little lie stayed between him and me.

When I got to the contact with the spirit, I said, "I hadn't made contact with Menafee, until I accidentally touched this." I pulled the button from my pocket and showed it to her. "When I touched it, the events of the war came to life for me and I could see part of the battle; the part that he was in and his confrontation with his brother. After that, his spirit came to me, a ghost on the battlefield. He had crossed over and it seemed to call him back. Is that possible?"

"Oh, yes, my dear," she answered. "It appears your gift is expanding. What happened with the button is called psychometry. It's also been called token-object reading. In your case, the button triggered visions of what happened on the battlefield. But it also links you to the spirit of the person who owned or used it."

"Wait a minute! You're saying that this object, this button from a Civil War jacket, holds memories in it and a connection to the person who wore or touched it? I I can't believe that." I rubbed my hand across my face as I sat upright, stunned by this concept. How could an object hold an imprint? It didn't make sense. I had felt the connection and the draw, but I couldn't understand how it would work.

"Can't believe or won't believe?" Madame asked. Her voice made no accusations but remained calm with a touch of amusement. "I am telling you what the explanation for what happened is, but ultimately, the connection comes from you. You have the ability to touch the object and unlock the images or emotions that are imprinted on it. It's easier to fluff it off than to accept that there is something extraordinary happening that defies scientific explanation."

Oh, Lordy. No wonder people considered psychics crackpots and frauds. While I wanted to deny what she said, how could I explain my experience unless I considered it all a very accurate hallucination? Moreover, if the illusion checks out with facts, does it make it any more real?

I cleared my throat and asked, "All right then, if I can read an object, why doesn't it happen every time I pick something up?"

"Two reasons," she answered. "First, you need to be in a receptive mode. When you sing and transport to the transitional cemetery, you've opened your mind and your spirit to the spiritual world. You're receptive to it.

"Second, not all objects are charged with impressions or scents or other sensory triggers. Usually a strong emotion or event imprints on an object. For the button, Emmett must have touched it or maybe even clung to it as he died. Or possibly the emotion at the time enveloped so much that it touched everything he wore. Sometimes, the connection may not be as strong, but a different emotion, such as love, flows through the object."

"I see," I said. And I did. It made sense, even though I found it weird. Having answered that riddle, I needed to move on to the second concern I had. "Three times now I've encountered black spirits when I've been in a transitional cemetery. The one I told you about last time and two different ones in Shiloh." I went on to describe the shade and the threat it had made. "Have you encountered anything like this?"

Madame stared at me for a few more moments as if she might be trying to see into my mind, perhaps to see the creature's image there. She blinked then said, "Only once. I was on an astral journey with Elias when I spotted one of the creatures, more of a dark gray spirit than a black, but there was a sense of evil about him. Elias guided us away from it quickly. He told me they were underworld spirits to be avoided; that they sought miserable souls and like spirits to nourish their domain."

"I'm confused. Are you saying that these shades can be here on Earth within a human body? That evil people might actually have one of these dark souls?" My stomach roiled at the mere possibility.

Madame shrugged her shoulders and her eyes looked sad. "I don't know, Gillian. I only know what little Elias told me. There are books, but they don't have answers. Only more questions. Tell me, did you ask for protection before transitioning to the cemetery?"

I looked away, not wanting to meet her gaze. "No."

"I see. It can be dangerous if you don't take precautions."

"So it seems. I forgot to take my book and I haven't memorized any of the prayers. I I haven't really studied it at all."

Disappointment showed in her scrunched up face as her eyebrows lowered and her mouth frowned.

"I know. I should have. Lesson learned. I will memorize a couple of the protection prayers and use them. Tell me, can I fight back in the spirit world? Can I learn to use my power against one of these shades?"

She picked up a deck of Tarot cards from the table and began shuffling them, hand-to-hand, as she thought. For a moment, I thought she planned to do a reading, but she set the deck down and motioned to me to cut it. That done, she flipped over the card on the right-hand side. The King of Wands came up.

Astrid picked the card up and placed it against her forehead, concentrating on it. Her eyes closed in meditation, she said, "This card indicates that you are making spiritual progress, but the feeling is that you need a mentor to guide you. You already know a man who can help but I can't see a name or face. You must discover him yourself."

She put the card on the table and opened her eyes. "I don't know if you can learn to use your energy to fight off the shades, but if you can, you need someone to train you. I am not that person and I don't know where to point you. Just please, please, my dear, say the prayers and invoke help when spirit traveling."

I swallowed down the sudden fear that these words created and said, "I will. I promise."

I thanked her and left, almost breaking into a run to my car. Wild thoughts went through my head. What if the shades could come across to me? What if they were in human bodies? How could I find whoever the man is who can help me?

Damn, why hadn't Zac told me any of this? If he was supposed to be helping me, shouldn't he tell me everything I needed to know? What happened to the guidance from my angel or guide or whatever he might be?

I pointed my Jeep toward home and tried to think this through. In order to find the mystery person Astrid mentioned, I would need to tell that person the whole situation. That meant revealing this weird gift of mine to another person, or possibly several, until I found the right one. Not a happy thought.

Later, after a large glass of wine, I pulled out a writing tablet and contemplated which of the men I knew might be the one who could be my mentor. I wrote down the names; Ferris, Digby, Mark, even Roger and I crossed them off almost as quickly. None of them gave credence to anything on the paranormal side of life. Certainly not my stalker. Both grounded in hard reality, Ferris and

Digby would think I had gone around the bend if I told them about the trips to the transitional cemetery. They already thought I was acting weird. Not Mark either. He followed a scientific path and he'd dismiss all of this as nonsense.

Who else was there? Rick at the shooting range, but I hardly knew him. Arimoto or Gregory? Of those two, I thought Ari might be more likely to be into the metaphysical, but I wasn't sure shade fighting would be on his list. Moss barely accepted that I might be psychic although his partner appeared more open to it, but not enough to participate.

I drew a blank. When I looked at the list, I couldn't see where any of them would be a mentor. I sat back, sipped at my wine, and scratched Nygard's ears while I thought about any other men in my life. My dad? No way. For one thing, he wasn't around to consider. I didn't even know if he still lived in Australia. I'd gotten a card from him when I graduated high school but hadn't heard from him since.

As I got up to refill my glass, I spotted my sweater hanging on the back of a chair and picked it up to hang in the closet. I heard something hit the floor and looked down to see what had fallen. Emmett's button. I'd forgotten about it again. I picked it up, hung the sweater, then sat down with the artifact. I needed to show it to Gavin Haines before I returned it to Thomas. With his interest in the Civil War, I felt certain he would like to see it.

Then it hit me. Gavin!

And... I dismissed him as fast. He may have been handsome, sexy, and an archeologist, but he was no Indiana Jones. Sure, he'd done a few digs, but didn't come back with priceless or paranormal artifacts. Oddly, I appeared to have that last item.

I made a note to call him the next day and I put the button into my purse.

SEVENTEEN

As I pulled into my driveway after work the next day, I noticed a familiar, and official-looking, dark-gray sedan parked at the curb in front of my landlady's house. She lived in the big brick house that occupied most of the lot, while I rented the smaller two-story place at the back. I stopped the Beast at my small front yard where the driveway turned into a garage, then got out to face Detectives Moss and Hernandez, who ambled down the drive toward me.

Moss' younger, sexier partner reminded me of a young Lou Diamond Phillips, same build, similar features, and a killer smile that he shot my way now. While Moss had dismissed my paranormal gift, Dave Hernandez kept an open mind and urged Moss to pursue the leads I gave them.

Seeing a manila folder in Hernandez' left hand, I concluded they had more than socializing in mind. Moss raised a hand in a friendly greeting and I returned it.

I opened the door and invited them in with a wave of my hand. They both took a quick visual appraisal of the small living room before sitting on the sofa. As I sank into the armchair, Nygard jumped into my lap so he could study the two intruders in his space.

"Nice cat," Moss offered as an opener. "I like cats."

"This is Nygard and he's very protective," I said, stroking his head and neck while he settled down to oversee everything. "What can I do for you, detectives?"

Dark eyes flashing uneasily to Nygard for a moment, Hernandez opened the folder in his hand as Moss said, "We ran the car and partial plate that you gave us and came up with three possible matches. We brought photos of the vehicles, not the actual ones, but the make, model and year that matched the DMV's registration records. Do any of these look like the one that caused the accident?"

I took the offered photos and looked at them closely. They were all similar and I tried to think back to the blue SUV that had sped past me, pulling an image into my mind. I held one out to them, "This one looks really close to it, but I can't swear that's it. There was a decal on the back bumper. I couldn't make out the lettering on it. I saw a red background and, I think, yellow letters. I just remembered that when I was looking at the photo."

"That's good," Hernandez said. "Any little piece of information helps. Do you remember what the shape was? Round? Square?"

I closed my eyes again, sending my mind back to that moment and focusing on the bumper. "Um, what's that shape called where the top and bottom lines are parallel but different lengths and the sides slant to form it? Do you get what I'm saying?"

"Is that a trapezoid?" Moss asked. "Is that what it's called?"

"Yeah, I think so," Hernandez agreed as he drew the shape I'd described on a blank paper in the folder. "Like this?"

"That's it," I said. "It was all red and there was a symbol like a sickle in the middle with the writing over the top."

"You don't know what it said, though?"

"No, the car was moving too fast and the print wasn't that large. It was only five letters, I think. Maybe it was a club emblem of some kind."

"We'll check it out," Moss said. "Did you get a look at the driver? Can you describe him?"

"Not really. There were two people in the car two guys, I think. The one on the passenger side and closest to me, looked like he was twenty-something and only glanced full on at me for a moment. He wore a hoodie over his head. I couldn't see the driver clearly at all, only that it looked like a man. He looked bigger, although he might be around the same age or a little older."

"Okay," Moss replied. He leaned forward a little bit and clasped his hands in front of him. "Every little bit helps. We have more pieces of the puzzle now. If we can match it all up, we might be able to find the driver who ran Willits off the road."

"That would be good," I answered. "I'm sure his son would be relieved. It won't bring his dad back, but at least he'd have justice."

As Moss nodded his head in agreement, he said, "Although, it might mean we'd need you to testify again if we can arrest the guy. But no need to worry about that now."

"Yeah, about this upcoming trial, do I really have to testify? Can't you just take a statement or something?" As much as I wanted to see that killer put away, I faced the trial proceedings with dread.

"Is there a problem with testifying?" Hernandez asked.

"I just don't want to talk about it. I don't want any of what happened to become public news. Can't I tell my story to the judge?" My voice wavered a little with my nerves and I petted Nygard a little faster.

Moss glanced over at Hernandez, then cleared his throat. "You're a key witness and you heard Coblenzer confess to killing those girls. We have the evidence and it's probably enough to convict him, but you are the surviving victim so you can tell it more personally. I know it's hard and the DA will try to protect you, but the defense attorney may try to make it seem like you were enticing the perp. You just have to tell the truth and only answer the questions you're asked. Don't volunteer any other information about how you got on the trail of a killer."

"That's right," Hernandez said. "Moss and I are the only ones who heard you talking about a spirit guiding you to him and we don't plan to say anything about it. In fact, we *did* have an anonymous tip and that's what we're going to say led us to Coblenzer."

Getting up, Moss paced over to the fireplace and leaned against the mantle. "Look, we're not going to perjure ourselves and we don't want you to either, so just keep your answers short and simple. Don't let the defense attorney draw you into blurting out more than is required to answer his questions. The three of us are the only ones who know the whole story."

"My friend Janna knows about my gift," I said. My voice came out a little squeaky.

Shooting a hard glance my way, Moss said, "Then tell Janna to stay the hell away from the trial and not talk to anybody."

I nodded, a little startled by his tone, but understanding it. "Right. I'll pass that along. Anything else today?" Giving Nygard a nudge, I encouraged him off my lap as I got to my feet.

"Nope," Moss said as he straightened up.

"Thank you for your help, Miss Foster," Hernandez said politely and started for the door, then turned back. "Try not to worry too much about the trial. It will be fine."

Before Moss got to the door, I said, "Have you got another minute, Detective?"

He paused, turning to me, and dipped his head a little. "What's on your mind?"

"This may sound a little odd, but do you have anything that belonged to Jack from Modesto? A personal item of some sort?"

"Yeah, there are a couple of things in the case file that were on his person. Not that they helped us to solve the murder. Why?"

I wrapped my arms across my chest in a protective motion as if I expected some backlash from him, although I didn't know why I felt that way. "I may have another way to try to contact him," I said.

I had Moss' full attention now.

"I recently discovered that if I touch an object that the spirit connected with, I might be able to call him to me. I've only done it once, but it might work."

Moss regarded me with an odd look, his lips pursed in thought. While he didn't believe in all this hocus-pocus stuff, he seemed to be thawing, little by little, to the possibility. "Okay, that might be worth trying. I'll look into the evidence and give you a call. If we have something that I think will work, we can try again. Thanks." His right eyelid lowered in an intentional blink and it took a moment before I realized he'd winked at me.

"Later," he said and stepped out the door.

But I had one more question for him. "Wait! When will I meet the DA?"

Moss shrugged. "He'll probably be in touch a week or so before the trial. Thanks again."

He turned away and his brisk walk carried him down the driveway. I watched from the doorway, not at all reassured. There had to be some way I could get out of doing that trial. I'd talk to the DA about it and about wanting to keep my privacy. I hadn't done anything and I should be able to remain anonymous, shouldn't I?

As I considered this, my house phone rang and I went over to read the number on it. Mark's mobile number.

I answered with enthusiasm, glad to hear from him. The calls in our relationship were few and far between.

"Good day, gorgeous," he said. "I have a rare occurrence. They've given me the whole evening off. I've gotten enough sleep to be truly alive and I have hopes that you and I could go to dinner and a movie and see what happens after that? What do you say?"

"I say fantastic! When and where?"

"I'll pick you up at six-thirty and let's go casual."

I appreciated the heads up; I would have over-dressed for the evening.

Other than just catching an hour or two for lunch and a chat, we hadn't enjoyed a real date in two months. While I buzzed with excitement to spend some time with him, I also felt nervous. I hadn't been with him sexually since before the kidnapping and my confidence about potential intimacy wavered.

While I had made an appointment to see the recommended psychologist, Dr. Elise Mannetti, it would be another week before I could get in. I still had doubts about baring my soul to someone I hadn't even met yet.

I saw a flashing light on my answering phone and checked it

out, hoping Gavin Haines had called me back. He hadn't been in his University office when I'd called earlier. Instead, the voice of a fast-talking telemarketer assaulted my ears and I deleted the message as fast as I could.

Right on time, Mark picked me up, giving me a warm, possessive kiss before we even got out the door. Even dressed casually in tight blue jeans and a pale yellow sports shirt, he looked like a lollipop I wanted to lick. I wore a pair of dark blue, mid-thigh shorts and a lightweight blue, snug-fitting sweater. He whistled when he saw how great I looked in them and the new, slimmer, fitter me reveled in the acknowledgment.

"So what have you been doing to get into such hot shape?" he asked as he drove us to the Outback Steakhouse on Virginia.

"I started running more often, instead of just when the whim struck me. I'm also taking a self-defense class. So I guess you could say that I've just gotten more active." I downplayed this aspect so he wouldn't be too curious about it.

"It's working, honey. You look terrific." He must have thought about how that sounded because he hurried to add, "Not that you didn't before, but even more so now."

Mark didn't ask many questions about what I had been doing. Like his work, my jobs kept me busy and not a lot of other things were going on, other than the defense classes, of course. I did volunteer that Janna and I had taken a weekend trip to Memphis and talked about Beale Street, the fabulous food, and of course, going to Graceland.

"It sounds really gaudy," he said after I'd described a couple of the rooms.

"Well, I think so. I wouldn't want to live in it. But I do have to say that it is unique."

From there, we went to see the newest action film with Tom Cruise. Sometimes it seemed like the same actor starred in all these types of movies. While I enjoyed the escapism, I didn't really get into this film as much I had some of the others.

By the time we got back to my place, we were laughing and ready to relax a bit. I'd put a new wine in my 'fridge before we'd left that I pulled out and poured as Nygard greeted Mark and got his attention for a few minutes. My cat, the uncanny possessor of a discerning taste, showed a fondness for the doctor. For his part, Mark had a magic touch with him that Nygard rewarded by allowing him to scratch his stomach.

I handed my date a glass of Johannesburg Riesling from a California winery that had been blessed with several online rave reviews. We tapped our glasses together before we sipped and I waited, eager to hear his reaction.

"That's pretty nice," he said. That summed it up.

Yep, it clenched that he failed as a wine connoisseur. He may be well traveled and from a well-to-do family, but his education didn't include wine *connoisseur*.

That was all right with me. At least, he wouldn't be a snob about it. I'd learned a few things from my internet reading on wine aficionado sites and, for myself, I thought it had a pleasant bouquet, a tart taste with a bit of sweetness, and I enjoyed it, but I wisely kept my opinion to myself.

I sat down on the other end of the sofa with at least a foot and a half between us. He glanced at me, then at the gap between us and back to my eyes. He patted the cushion, a clear indication he wanted me to move closer. I inched my way over to about the mid-point, still feeling this out. I tried to psych myself up.

This was Mark, not some criminal who would take what he wanted and didn't care about me. Nor would he then kill and discard me. I pushed those thoughts from my mind, replacing them with the pleasant ones from the last time Mark and I had been together.

He sensed something amiss and noticed that I tensed when he slid closer to wrap his left arm around me. "What's wrong, Gillian? You seem distracted or worried."

"Uhmm, I... I guess I'm a little nervous. It's been a while, you know."

"Yeah, but it shouldn't be too different." He leaned forward and pressed his lips against mine with a sweet kiss, not demanding, but taking his time to savor the moment and the taste of the wine lingering on my lips. Not feeling threatened in any way, my body responded with a little surge of adrenalin and endorphins. It wanted more and all I needed to do was relax and enjoy the moment. If I could just get past this little block in my mind, we should be fine. After all, I really liked Mark and he had haunted my daydreams ever since I first met him.

He broke the contact, coming back to press a light one above my lips and working across my right cheek in a feathery line of kisses. My body tingled and the old enjoyment surged. I breathed out a little sigh of pleasure. My fingers moved of their own accord to unbutton his shirt, shoving it back from his shoulders until he shrugged it off.

A warm glow filled me and every nerve sensation in my breasts seemed heightened as he continued to touch me with light teasing touches followed by sucking kisses at my nipples. They responded to beyond hard and my body cried out for his attention. His hands worked their way down to my panties.

Good lord, when had he gotten my shorts off and I failed to even notice? One hand slipped inside and he worked the silky fabric down my hips, a smooth slow movement as the fingers on his other hand began to touch my private place.

A sense of panic jolted me and my mind spun back to the dark basement. I whimpered, pulling away from the fingers touching me. "No," I moaned. "Don't do it! Don't. No, no..."

The fingers slipped away from me and I pulled my legs up, sliding out of his arms and onto the floor, my legs locked in a protective fetal position as my mind saw a different place.

"Gillian? What is it?"

I heard the voice, barely registering the words. *Not my*

kidnapper's voice; not that bastard's voice. His hands touched me, not with desire but with the professionalism of a doctor, feeling for my pulse, and he leaned forward to hear my heartbeat.

"Are you in pain? What hurts?"

I connected with the present and Mark. Then I cried as I realized what had triggered the reaction. "I'm okay," I said between sobbing gasps.

He pulled me into his arms, rocking me back and forth like a child, and rubbing his cheek against mine. "It's okay, baby," he kept repeating. "Just take slow, deep breaths. You're okay. You're safe."

The panic receded and, as I felt more in control, I pulled away from Mark's embrace, embarrassed to have flipped out on him. He hadn't hurt me, but the sensation of his touch triggered the terror and I didn't want to tell him why.

He released me and sat back on the floor, leaning his back against the sofa. "Are you okay now?"

I nodded as I reached for my shorts to cover myself.

"Do you want to tell me what happened?"

I shook my head, staring at a point on the rug between my feet. When I glanced up for a moment, I saw that Nygard watched me from his perch on top of the cushioned chair. Eyes wide and intent, the cat looked concerned and uncertain what I might do next. I couldn't blame him.

Mark rubbed a hand against his chin and sighed. He reached for his shirt and slipped it back on as I continued to gaze at nothing in silence. He'd had a rare night off and this failed to be the evening he'd been expecting. I'd disappointed him.

"I'm sorry," I said. It had sounded half-choked by the strain I felt.

The room seemed so still and quiet that I heard him draw a breath. "Baby, is this connected to what happened in February? The kidnapping?"

I nodded again, not certain I could speak.

He got to his feet, went to the kitchen, and I heard water running in the sink, followed by the sound of the refrigerator opening and the clink of ice hitting the edge of a glass. He came back, knelt by me, and handed me the water.

I sipped it and watched him.

"Look, honey, I don't know the details of what happened and you haven't confided in me, but it's obvious something is wrong. Did that bastard rape you?"

"Yes and no," I said, my voice barely a whisper.

"He tried and he hurt you?"

"Yes."

He ran his hand along my chin and looked into my eyes. "You need to get help, Gillian. This doesn't go away on its own. You need to talk to someone."

"I have an appointment with a psychol..." I faltered and grabbed a hasty breath, "...psychologist in a few days." My eyes grew watery again as I met the worried expression on his face.

"That's good. Who are you seeing?"

"Elise Mannetti. The hospital counselor said she is very good." The words came out in a tumble. "I've been afraid..."

"It's okay, baby. You're okay now and we'll deal with the aftermath."

He lifted me up and carried me upstairs to my bed, laying me on it and tucking me in like my father never did. I produced a weak smile for him.

"Stay a little while?" I asked.

He sat on the bed by me and brushed his hand through my hair, not saying much but being close. That provided all I needed. I drifted off to sleep until I heard his steps on the stairs as he left, then I lay awake listening as the door clicked shut and I heard the lock fall into place.

I tossed and turned as I tried to go to back to sleep after Mark left. I kept replaying the whole disaster in my mind. Now I feared that he'd consider me damaged goods and decide I wasn't worth the effort.

My grandmother always told me not to devalue myself, but I had never gotten past the rejection by my father. Barely fourteen-years-old, my world tilted on its axis when he came home from work one day and told Mom that he'd accepted a transfer to Australia and he planned to go without us. He'd soft-coated it saying the job was located in the Outback and that was no place for a family. I could see him kneeling in front of the chair he'd told me to sit in while he talked to me about his plan.

"I know it's a surprise, Gilly, but you're a big girl now and you'll have Mom to rely on here. This is a big opportunity for me and it's something that I've always wanted to do. I'll be working out in the field most of the time so I wouldn't be around anyway. You and your mom are much better here." He'd made it sound so reasonable, but even then, I felt that I had held him back for years while he waited for me to grow up enough to do what I had interrupted.

Then, only a few years later, when I started college Mom figured I'd grown enough that she could go follow *her* dreams to Alaska and took a job in Fairbanks. Pretty much the same story for her. She'd raised me as far as she had been obligated to do and now she could get on with the rest of her life. I'd felt rejected by both of them. They didn't want to be with me and they'd made it clear I had interfered with their plans. In retrospect, I decided it was a wonder they didn't give me away for adoption.

With all this running through my mind, I anticipated that Mark would break up with me. With a reputation and a career to think about, a woman with psychic gifts, a load of baggage, and being an attempted rape victim wouldn't help his career any. Of course, he would have to end the relationship.

Upset by the way the whole evening had gone, I cried, my tears streaking across my cheeks to dampen the pillow. Nygard made his cello-like mrrow at me as he cuddled close to my head, butting my face, and trying to comfort his clearly distraught human.

Ultimately, he got through and I sat up, cuddled my cat in my arms, and tried to get a grip on my wild emotions.

When I finally fell asleep, I slipped into a dream of the pitch-black basement where I saw myself tied up again. Unable to work my hands loose, I cried out for help, but no one came. I heard footsteps approaching and I froze in terror.

Something slapped me across the face and I opened my eyes to Nygard's blue ones filling my vision. His paw pressed on my nose, claws retracted, thank goodness. Poor cat was getting used to rescuing me from my nightmares. Ever since the kidnapping, I'd been sleeping with a nightlight. Small illumination though it provided, I took comfort from it. Never again did I want to be in pitch black and feel helpless.

I reached over to the nightstand and opened it to reveal the small handgun in it. I'd applied for a concealed carry permit a week before Janna and I went to Memphis, but I hadn't taken the weapon anywhere, not even out of the drawer. I picked it up and held it in my hand, my fingers caressing the surface. Apart from the one lesson, I hadn't done any of the regular practice I'd promised myself. For one thing, time on the range cost more money than I had to spare. Between the self-defense classes and seeing Madame Astrid, I just didn't have any uncommitted dollars.

Although it wasn't a requirement for owning a gun in Nevada or Washoe County, I'd registered my weapon. On one level, I felt like I'd betrayed all my principals in owning one, but my fear of being in a dangerous situation again drove me to want it.

I slid the gun back in the drawer. *Who was I now?*

I had trouble sleeping; I'd bought a gun, even though I abhorred violence. I studied martial arts and lived in fear of ever being in the position that man had put me in again.

This fearful version of me existed because of what Vincent Coblenzer had done to me. I would have to testify; I couldn't escape it unless by some miracle he pleaded guilty to all charges. I would not let him get away with it.

I left my bedside light on and rolled over to go back to sleep as Nygard curled up in the back of the bend of my knees.

As I dressed for work in the morning, my smartphone chirped out my current tune and I picked it up to see the caller identification. As soon as I saw Mark's name, I almost let it go to voice mail rather than talk to him. But then again, I didn't want him to either leave the breakup message on the recorder or have to call back, so I picked it up, a hard knot of dread sitting uneasily in my stomach.

"Hey, baby. How are you this morning?"

"A little tired," I answered, surprised at the cheeriness in his voice. "I had trouble sleeping."

"I should have stayed. I'm sorry. Listen, I hope you don't mind, but I did a little checking on Dr. Mannetti. She has a great reputation and from what I can tell, I think you'll like her. If you want, I can see if I can get your appointment moved up a little."

I was stunned. He called to tell me that he checked on the psychologist? Not to end our relationship? "Uh, no, that's okay. You don't have to do that. Thanks for checking on her. Mark, I'm really sorry about last night."

"Don't give it another thought. I wish I had known sooner. I could have been giving you more support. I think talking to the psych will really help you gain more perspective on it."

"You're probably right. Thanks."

As I hung up, my shoulders slumped with relief and tears of gratitude formed as I thought about Mark helping and standing by me.

EIGHTEEN

*T*wo days later, I met Egan Moss at the cemetery where Jack from Modesto had been interred. Moss said he'd found a couple of items in the dead man's possessions that might trigger something, although I detected the skepticism in his voice. In spite of that, he didn't pass up any chance at a clue.

He waited by his car, leaning against the fender and talking on his phone when I arrived almost ten minutes late. Par for the course, Ferris would say. I hopped out, strolled over, and held out my hand for whatever he'd found while he wrapped up his conversation. Digging in his right pants pocket, he pulled out a chain with a charm dangling from it and an odd-shaped piece of metal. I puzzled over that, not sure what it might be. It looked bent or melted and jagged around the edges.

"Shrapnel," Moss said. "Jack had an old wound on his right thigh. He could have been wounded in the service or been involved in some kind of explosion. But whatever the source, he had that piece of it in his pocket when we found his body."

I nodded, then studied the charm a little closer. It resembled a hammer, but the handle branched into two arms at the top. Was this significant to him? Did it represent a person or a place in his life?

"One of these might do it," I said.

I walked over to the line of graves but didn't stand directly in front of any of them. I didn't need to address the specific plot where his body rested. Clearing my mind, I said a low-voiced request for protection, hoping that Moss couldn't hear it, then held the shrapnel in my hand and began singing. The metal felt warm against my fingers and it tingled a little.

I saw a camp in a desert area, lots of soldiers in an

encampment. *Maybe Desert Storm,* I thought. But this wasn't what I wanted to see. Instead, I called out to Jack, hoping to bring his spirit to me.

A man in the vision stopped and turned toward me. He stared for a few beats, then walked closer, peering straight at me. Looking about twenty-five, he wore an Army uniform and carried himself with military precision. I thought the insignia indicated a sergeant's rank. His closely cut, short dark blond hair peeked out from under the military cap he wore. Dark blue-gray eyes met mine with a question in them.

"Are you Jack from Modesto?" I asked, almost certain I'd found him. This didn't feel like part of the vision although the background image of the camp remained.

"I called myself that in my last years," he replied in a slight southern accent. His deep voice resonated with firmness, yet held the warmth of an out-going person. I didn't doubt that he could be tough as nails when needed.

I hesitated, thinking of the best way to frame my questions. "I've come to get your help. No one claimed your body at your death. The detective working the case couldn't find a missing person's report and couldn't identify you from your fingerprints. You were military. Why weren't they on file?"

He looked around him as if he needed to confirm that we were alone, then he spoke softer as he said, "I served in covert operations for a while and my records were all sealed to protect my family and colleagues. I became a man who never existed. After Desert Storm, I began drinking a lot. I had too many memories to bury."

I nodded, moved by his simple confession. "I'm sorry. It must have been difficult for you. And for your family. Please tell me your full name, so the detective can locate them and maybe get your remains home to them."

His face stretched into a sad smile. "I'm afraid I was dead to them long before I actually died. My remains are fine where they are. I'd been named Jackson Wayne Dorfman when I was born in Austin, Texas in 1971."

"Not from Modesto at all," I said with a little laugh and his mouth quirked up into a smirk. "Do you know how you died, Jack?"

"In my sleep, drunk," he answered. "I think someone stabbed me."

"Yes. Any idea who might have done it? The detective hasn't turned up any leads."

He thought about it for a few heartbeats before he shrugged his shoulders. "Not really. This one guy hung around the same area at the bridge for a few days. Called himself "Porky", although he was as thin as a beanpole, but I didn't know much else about him. You know, he'd steal things from the others, but I don't think he would kill for anything."

"It's not much for my friend to go on, but at least we can identify you and remember your service to this country. I am glad to see you crossed over."

"If that's all, ma'am?"

"One more question, Jack, please. What's it like on the other side?"

The quirky smile returned to his face, as he seemed amused at the question. He hesitated so long that I didn't think he would answer, then he said, "Indescribable. You'll see in due time."

With a salute to me, he turned and stepped back into the light, then vanished in a blink of the eye.

As I told Moss everything that Jackson had told me, he wrote everything down, adding little reminders as he went. His mouth tweaked a little when I told him about his military service, but he didn't scoff.

When he closed his notebook, he cast a thoughtful look my way. "Thank you. I still don't understand how you do it or if it's even real. But—at least I have some answers and—," he paused to tap his notebook. "—I have a name now, so another small lead, if you're right."

"Yep. Have you found Jack Ostero's daughter?"

"Maybe. I have a lead that might be her. I'm trying to track down her location. If she's the right one, she's moved around a bit."

"How hard are you trying? You know, I promised him and he'll haunt me until you get it done." I frowned at him for emphasis.

He chuckled. "Haunt you? Are you serious?"

"Yes, I am. He's shown up in one dream and I'm expecting another visit any day now. It's not funny!" My frown shifted to an annoyed glare as a smirk started to form on his face.

He straightened up and put on his serious face. "Okay. I'll see if I can get something more solid in the next couple of days. I'll let you know."

I nodded, then started to my Jeep.

"Thanks again, Foster," he said as I passed him.

I held the Ruger in my hands the way the instructor showed me, with one hand overlapping the other and aimed for the target about forty feet away on the shooting range. Even though guns made me nervous, I was growing used to the feel of this one. In my mind, I envisioned it as more of a laser weapon from a science fiction show than a gun with bullets.

I squeezed the trigger with a steady move rather than a jerk, expecting the report when the bullet fired. The crack of the sound came through muffled by noise-cancelling headphones, but I recalled it from when Eric had first shown me how to fire the weapon. I reset my hands and repeated the position and the pull another four times, then reloaded the cartridge as the target moved toward me.

The holes in the paper ranged from the far outside right edge to almost the center of the next-to-the-middle ring. At least all five of them went into the target. I'd missed more than half the first couple of times I'd tried firing the gun.

"Better," Eric said over my shoulder. "If it had been a real target that outside one might have caught his hand. But if you were aiming for his heart, you missed by about eight inches."

Eric stood only a couple of inches taller than me, a tough-as-they-come Marine for all that he was a wiry little guy. When you think of Marines, you picture the big, muscular ones that resemble a tank approaching the enemy, but Eric served as a sniper and a darned good one at that.

He took the gun from my hand and set it on the counter. "I watched you through that round and you seem more comfortable with the weapon. Your hand didn't jerk each time you fired. Let's try something. When you start, pick the gun up, position yourself and fire at the target as quickly as you can, then set the gun down again. I'm going to time you while you do it. You want speed and accuracy, so make sure you've got the target lined up before you fire. Can you do that?"

"I can certainly attempt it," I answered.

"Okay, then, do it."

I picked up the pistol, set my hands as I pulled it into place, sighted the target, then squeezed. As I fired, the weapon's kick rocked me back a little, then I returned it to the counter.

"Go again," Eric shouted and I repeated the whole exercise.

After we'd done this another three times, reloaded and repeated for another five, my shoulder ached and I felt drained. The Ruger 9mm was a woman's gun, or so I had been told, because it was lightweight, smaller for a woman's hand and easy to fire. Although the kick when it fired was minor, after about thirty bullets, I could feel it in my arms and shoulders.

"That wasn't too bad," Eric said. "It took you about fifteen seconds to do it when you fired the first four bullets, then you got a little quicker and ended at 9 seconds. I think you can go faster, but we'll try it the next time you come out. The thing is, Gillian, if you want the gun for protection when you're out, you need to be able to get it out of your purse, release the lock, and fire the gun at your target as accurately, and quickly, as possible. The whole process shouldn't take more than 5 seconds."

"Doesn't sound like a lot of time."

"Most of it will be getting the gun out and into position. The firing is quick, but your life may be at stake, so the faster you can do it the better."

I picked up the gun and began breaking it down to clean it. "I guess the element of surprise is the biggest asset I have in the situation. That my attacker won't be expecting this kind of resistance."

He nodded. "The real question is if you can actually do it under the pressure of the situation."

"Yeah, but I am getting tougher. If it means my life, I think I can do it."

"You can't just think it. You need to know it. See you next week?"

"Yeah. I'll be here." I had signed up for a series of six lessons, determined to master using and firing my gun, but Eric had a point. Could I actually fire it if I aimed at someone? Could I kill a person?

Then, I pictured the leering face of Coblenzer and I knew I could kill him. But what would be the price to me if I did? As I reassembled the Ruger, fitting the pieces into place with more expertise than the first few times, I wondered what my mother would think if she knew her daughter now owned a gun. For that matter, what would Janna think? I hadn't even told her about it.

I tossed and turned as I tried to sleep that night, still keyed up from the shooting practice and haunted by thoughts of killing someone. It was easy to say it, but part of me worried if it would cost me part of my soul if I actually pulled the trigger on another human.

This brought me to thinking about the shades I'd seen and I

flashed back to a dream I'd had early on after I'd gotten my gift. I'd seen the dark woods and brambles, the shadows moving within it, and I recalled a frightened person running as if pursued by a demon. Even then, I'd recognized the sinister nature of those woods and had known to stay away from them. Now, they seemed to be closer, edging the cemeteries that I'd been visiting and the shades were bolder than that first one had been.

I couldn't help but feel that I was being pulled into a battle that I was ill equipped to fight; that my job entailed more than being a spirit escort and unfinished-business resolver. I needed to find the man Madame Astrid had referenced; the one who would be my mentor and help me to combat the shades.

"Zak, please help me," I murmured to my so-called angel. "I need some assistance here. If you're supposed to be my guide in this, then show me the way."

Of course, I didn't get an answer.

NINETEEN

When I forced myself to get up on Sunday, half the morning had already flown. I made coffee and considered the prospect of confronting Menafee Willits. I didn't think it would be particularly pleasant, but he was a ghost and at least, it wouldn't come to physical blows. If I thought about it long enough, I grew angry all over again with the man who had deserted his wife and daughter, as well as the rest of his family and allowed them to believe he'd died in battle. Not to mention letting his parents think that something equally as terrible must have happened to Emmett.

I tried to be rational, thinking the man had suffered seeing his brother killed by his companions, getting shot himself, and witnessing a terrible battle with friends dying before his eyes. Post traumatic stress disorder hadn't been heard of at that time, but he no doubt became a victim of the guilt, the horror, and the nightmares. However, understanding that much, for him to leave his family behind with no support hit home, especially in relation to my own father's departure, and made it hard to forgive.

By one-thirty, I had returned to the Old Hillside Cemetery, parked near the closest end to the gate on Tenth Street, and strolled down the dirt road toward it. I found it sad that most of the graves in this cemetery were neglected and had few relatives visit them. Of course, all of them would have been great grandparents or older to the current generation, so it wasn't surprising. Out of that regard, I'd brought a small bouquet of daisies to place on Menafee's grave.

I stopped at the gate and scanned the area, looking for anyone who might be in the vicinity. Not that I was concerned that someone might see me in a trance in front of a grave or anything like that. Assured of my privacy, I pushed the gate open and made my way to the grave.

Now, standing in front of the desolate-looking headstone, I placed the cheery yellow flowers on it, cleared my mind, then started to sing, going back to "Buttermilk Hill" as the tune of choice this day. A few wisps of clouds floated like veils of gauze across the otherwise clear sky and a delicate-fingered breeze blew strands of my hair free as I waited for Willits to make an appearance. Although I hadn't dressed up, I'd worn an ankle length navy blue dress with a sweater over it. The full bottom of it billowed and rippled like a flag.

As I started the second verse, I transitioned to the Tennessee-looking graveyard.

Willits stood nearby, still in the Union blue uniform. I marched toward him, the words from the song flowing in the back of my mind. Stopping directly in front of him, I said, "How did you get the Union uniform?"

"What do you mean? It's Army issue." His eyes narrowed a little at the question.

"It is. But not your army. Your uniform was gray. So tell me, Menafee, did you take it off your dead brother?"

His expression shifted from shock to anger and I began to question my assumption he couldn't physically attack me. If the shade managed to do it, then Menafee might be able to as well. But his face fell as his fury collapsed and he stared down at the clothes he wore. "The jacket belonged to my brother. Yes, I took it off his dead body. Originally, I planned to send it and his identification card back to our parents so they knew what happened to him.

"I was wounded at the same time and things happened quickly around me. When I got cut off from the rest of my unit, I took off my coat and covered Emmett with it, then put on his and made my escape with the Union soldiers coming onto the battlefield. We were near the brambles, as we called it. Later on, after the war, people called it the Hornet's Nest. I managed to slip into

some bushes and hide. Later, I found a dead Yankee soldier with pants that fit me and I took them, leaving mine behind. Dressed as a Northerner and with my brother's identification, I was soon found by a squad of Yankees and taken back for medical attention."

"So you decided to become Emmett," I said.

A pained look filled his eyes as he recalled this. "Not at first. I was going to let my family know, but as I watched the wounded being brought to the field hospital, something snapped in me. I could not bear to see any more of the horrible damage the war caused. I counted myself lucky even though I had a bad injury. At least, I had my legs. After the battle ended, they moved me to a military hospital in the North where my leg healed as much as it could, but the damage could not be repaired. I remained grateful I did not lose it."

"You had a limp. Thomas told me about it and that it had been from your war injury. Was that why you didn't want to go back home?"

He looked away, perhaps ashamed to face me. "Partially, ma'am. Even though I had healed and been ousted from the fighting, the war continued. No one had expected it to be such a bloody, deadly war and to last so long. I had been shattered by it and by the loss of my brother. I decided the only hope I had to make a decent life after this was to move to the west coast. I knew that silver had been discovered in Nevada and a lot of it went to support the North's war efforts. Hell, they even made it a state because of it, you know."

I laughed a little. "Yeah, Battle Born. It's on the Nevada flag. I was born and raised here; I learned all about it. So, you moved to Nevada hoping to get rich."

"If I couldn't do it in Nevada, I could try for gold in California. I was pretty sure they were somewhere close to each other." He flashed a quick smile at me.

Menafee had been a handsome young man and he seemed

personable enough with that southern charm. If they could bottle it and sell it, the world might be a better place, I thought, recalling how nice and polite everyone had been on our trip. But I had to think about his family.

"Your parents took care of Emily and Marion. Did you know your wife was with child when you went off to fight?" The expression of surprise on his face answered that question.

"I had another child?"

"No, your wife did. A son, who didn't live more than five months. And you never knew about him. Your wife mourned you and never remarried. She still lived at your family home when she died in 1876.

"Your daughter, Marion married and also had a daughter. She died giving birth to the child, whom she named Emily after her mother. She was seventeen at the time." I watched the pain seep into Menafee's face as I told him this. "They've gone on ahead of you, Menafee. You could have met them on the other side already instead of lingering here in this in-between cemetery. Your granddaughter married and had a son and a daughter. She also died young. The son was killed in an accident and her daughter married, divorced, and never remarried. There were no children from that line."

"I am grieved to hear that," he said as he turned and walked to a boulder to sit. He seemed weary and deeply troubled, as well he should be. He unbuttoned and removed his jacket showing a dingy white shirt underneath it. He let it drop to the ground. I hadn't thought before about how things seemed solid and real in this cemetery, but I knew that we couldn't actually touch.

"My life here was based on a lie. I had not intended it to be that, but it is what happened. I sent a message to my parents as Emmett, telling them that I had moved west to find my fortune and start a new life. I told them that Menafee had died in battle at Shiloh. In a sense, he did. The person that left there was not the same man who went into battle."

"Your brother was buried in a common grave. Did you know that?"

He nodded. "I heard later that the Confederates were interred in trenches to prevent disease. I guess no one knew who had been placed in which trench and there was no record of everyone who died that day. I hoped my brother found peace afterward and went on to God."

"He did. I spoke to him at Shiloh."

His brow wrinkled in a frown. "You spoke to him? I thought he crossed over."

"It seems that a spirit can return to talk to me now and then, so I called for him, although I actually asked for Menafee. Curiosity aroused, he answered, and through his memories, I saw what happened that day. He wants you to know that he forgives you and he says it is long past time for you to come across."

"Maybe, ma'am. Maybe soon. However, I made a promise to you and I do not always break my promises. Most of the time, I have kept them. The only vows I truly broke were the ones to Emily and Marion. I told them I would return and I did not do it."

His voice choked as he spoke and I realized he cried. Not real tears, of course, but a semblance of them in spirit form although the emotions seemed real enough.

"It's been over one hundred years, Menafee. They are not holding grudges. They have moved on. Although she didn't appear to talk to me, I think I got a message from Emily and she bears no ill will against you." I couldn't exactly say she forgave him.

"How could she not? What I did... After that, I swore I would never betray my new family and I always kept my word to them." He straightened up, then spoke with more resolve. "As I promised you, there is a treasure if it has not been disturbed. I told you I hid it in a cave and now I am going to try to show you the location."

"How?"

He locked his eyes with mine and seemed to gaze into my soul. If he was attempting to do the same sort of thing Marielle had done to show me where she had been, his technique deviated quite a bit. I wanted to blink but found I couldn't do it. I gazed deeply into his eyes and with slow progress, an image began to form in my mind. I could see the railroad tracks along the ridge of the Sierras and I recognized the bend in the river at that point. Below and following the tracks was the flume. Of course, it appeared newer in Menafee's vision, but parts of it still remained; enough that I had a good idea where to begin looking. A short distance from the Gold Ranch exit, I thought the location sat on the Nevada side of the mountain. Best of all, it wouldn't be too hard to reach.

"Did you get it?" he asked.

"I think so. It's in the lower hills before you cross into California."

"I buried another trinket with it. If you find it and the gold is still there, the trinket is yours. I think it will be worthwhile for you."

I acknowledged this with a short bob of my head, then I looked around for the silver path or the golden light to direct Menafee to it. I couldn't spot it.

"Are you ready to cross over now?" I asked.

"No, ma'am. I think I will wait a little longer. I want to know if you find the treasure and that it will be enough to help my young relative finish his school and start his life. I have failed my family enough. Come back when you find it and talk to me."

He rose to his feet, bowed his head toward me, then turned to walk away, disappearing before he'd completed five steps. As I started to turn away, I got a brief glimpse of the dark shadow lurking by the hedge. I started to take a step toward it and my foot stepped down into the Hillside Cemetery.

I stumbled a bit because my foot actually had stepped down but I was already standing so it jarred me a little. Was there a trick to doing these transitions more smoothly?

My thoughts went to the shade I'd seen and why it was hanging around. Unlike the other shades I'd encountered, this one hadn't threatened me, only observed. I pondered that before I bowed my head, then said, "Prepare yourself, Menafee Willits. I will lead you home."

As I paused to lock the gate, my eyes landed on the apartment building across the street. I decided to head over to see Thomas since I had a bit of news for him.

The young man invited me in with a sweep of his arm. His roommate, a pudgy red-haired leprechaun of a kid, was in the living room. He introduced him as Shawn McAllen, who nodded and smiled in greeting, then retreated to his bedroom. After Thomas offered a soft drink and fetched it, he sat down and asked what brought me by his place.

"I went to Tennessee," I said. "I wanted to find out more about your family and what happened to Menafee's wife and daughter. It wasn't a happy story, I'm afraid" I proceeded to tell him what little I knew about Emily and her daughter Marion.

While I had debated about telling him that the man who moved west after being injured in the Civil War wasn't Emmett, I concluded that nothing would be served by revealing the truth. Thomas and his aunt had an illusion about their ancestor and who was I to shatter that? Would it change anything other than the name on the headstone? Revealing it would do nothing except possibly make Thomas and Celeste less proud of their heritage and they didn't need to feel that. So, I kept that part of the story to myself.

I did tell Thomas about going to the Shiloh Battlefield and the mass graves and the one where Menafee was probably buried. "It's a beautiful site for all that there are around seven hundred

Confederate soldiers buried in it and it's well tended. The National Park Service ensures that no one disturbs it. The only sad thing is that no one knows who is buried in each of the trenches. I just had a feeling that your relative had been interred in the largest of them."

"That's amazing," Thomas said. "I can't believe you went to Tennessee to research this. I am very grateful to you for doing it and I wish I could pay you something."

I waved him off. I lowered my voice so that Shawn couldn't overhear what I had to say. "That brings me to something else. You know that I've talked to the spirit lingering here at Emmett's headstone at this cemetery."

I paused as a wide-eyed Thomas nodded.

"He tells me there is a treasure to be found in the foothills of the Sierras and I think I know where to start looking for it. If it's still there, it will be more than enough to put you through the rest of your education and give you a good start in your career. Are you game to go looking?"

"Of course!"

He bounced off the sofa in enthusiasm and I hissed and motioned at him to keep his voice down as I glanced toward Shawn's door.

He got the message and answered in a low voice, "When do you want to go?"

"Next weekend?"

His face fell. "Oh, I can't. I have a special workshop I signed up for both days. But I can do the one after that."

I looked at my schedule and had to say no. "That one doesn't work for me. I've got something planned. How about the end of May, over Memorial Day weekend?"

"Yeah. That sounds great. Let me know where and when to meet you." He grinned at the prospect of treasure hunting. I admitted, it did sound exciting.

With that arranged, I finished my beverage and said I'd see him soon. Going back up the long road to my Jeep, I paused to glance through the fence at the Old Hillside Cemetery, focusing on the area of Willits' plot. Under my breath, I said, "I hope you're telling the truth and the gold is still there, Menafee Willits."

Later that evening I thought about what Menafee had done and wondered if I blamed him or if I might have done the same thing in his shoes. It made me think about redemption for the kind of sins he had committed. For all intents, he had only transgressed in relation to the Civil War and the events that happened there, which led him to betray his wife and daughter. Still, the load must be a heavy burden for a man's soul to carry over the many long years he'd done it.

TWENTY

With a gig scheduled for the next Saturday evening, Ferris called a band rehearsal for Thursday night. He left a terse message on my home answering machine with the time, his place, and said, "You'd better be there or maybe I should just call someone to fill in?"

That pretty much indicated his state of mind. Even if Digby had talked to him, it sounded like he hadn't forgiven me. This suggested it could be an awkward session and I sent a text confirming that I would be there.

Since it appeared I needed to be the one to patch things up, I sent him another message asking if he could meet me at the Green Griddle, a favorite coffee shop near where I worked, at six that evening. First, he sent back "Why?" then followed with another text saying, "OK".

At one time, Ferris and I had been very close friends, but it seemed like we were moving apart in the last few months. With a flash of insight, I realized that it started about the time of the accident. More specifically, about the time I met Dr. Mercer. Jealousy? Could that be it? Or was he upset that I wasn't including him in my plans? Whatever bothered him, I had to fix it or our band, and our friendship, would soon be defunct.

Heeni had booked a full schedule for me with ten dogs to groom by four o'clock, which pleased me. It meant good money and would keep me busy, leaving little time to think about confronting Ferris.

My first "client", an apricot-colored Pomeranian wriggled with a lot of spunk. He didn't like being groomed and we battled every time I worked on him. I hummed a lullaby-rhythm tune as I clipped, which seemed to calm most animals, and his growls and barks faded away in a short time then he settled down. At least, until I shampooed him. Almost as soaked as the dog when I finished bathing him, I put the Pom in the drying cage and changed my smock.

"You losing your touch, dog whisperer?" Heeni asked with a giggle from where she worked on a sweetheart of a Russian wolfhound.

"Only with one persnickety Pom," I answered and pulled my hair back into a ponytail before I returned to take on the little beast. Honestly, bigger dogs were easier to deal with sometimes.

Then I moved on to the next dog on the list and so it went.

I adored my last client, an easygoing black standard poodle named Oswald, who never caused any trouble. He capped off my day with an easy-to-groom job and his mom always gave me a good tip. Today proved no exception. Overall, I cleared about three hundred and fifty dollars for the day, a slightly above average take.

I hadn't yet heard back from Gavin Haines, although I'd tried two more times to connect. I had a few minutes before I needed to leave to meet Ferris, so I made another attempt. The phone went right to his answering service, but the message had changed. The voice wasn't Gavin's but belonged to his student aide, who said the professor was out of the country for a few weeks leading an educational dig but if I left a message he would get back to me.

While that explained why he hadn't returned my calls, why hadn't that recording been there before now? Annoyed, I left another one asking him to call me as soon as he had time, teasing that I had an artifact he might like to see. Although I'd tucked the button in my jewelry box at home where it remained secure, I felt guilty to be hanging onto it for so long.

Taking my hair down, I brushed it out, took off my smock and stuck it in my to-be-laundered bag then smoothed my jersey top down before going to meet Ferris. Nerves unsettled me, as I still didn't have a plan for what I would say or any idea how he would take it.

I pulled into the parking lot at the Green Griddle, relieved that I managed to get there before Ferris. At least, I wouldn't have him waiting and fuming over my late arrival. I ordered a beer for him and a diet soda for me, then took a few deep breaths while I waited.

He arrived just a little after the appointed time and spotted me as soon as he came in. A dark-haired, good-looking man, Ferris fell into the boy-next-door mode, not drop dead gorgeous, but eye-catching attractive. He could get the ladies at our performances eating out of his hand, but he didn't date any of them. I had never wondered why he didn't date anyone, but it seemed a little odd now that I thought about it. As he walked over, I noticed at least three appreciative looks travel his direction from women in the coffee shop.

He slid into the booth on the side facing me, acknowledged the beer, and took a deep swig before giving me his attention. "You wanted to talk about something?"

I swallowed a sip of my drink and leaned forward a little into his space. "Yes. Thank you for meeting me. I feel really bad about how the last rehearsal ended. I know that you're upset with me, but I don't understand why."

"You don't know why?" His voice went sharp on the last word.

I held up a hand and said, "Wait. Let me talk. I know I have been late to a few gigs in the past few months..."

He held up a hand showing five fingers, then flashing two more.

"Okay, I've been late to seven gigs and I am really sorry about it. I have never been the most punctual person, but sometimes other things really do interfere in my plans. Like the car accident. I couldn't help that. Was I supposed to drive away from an overturned car in an accident that I had witnessed? So, yes, it delayed me. But honestly, Ferris, it doesn't mean that I'm not committed to the band. If you remember, I started it."

A bit of hurt showed in his eyes. "I know that. However, I've been managing it for the past four years. It feels like you're not as interested as you were. Suddenly, you have other things on your plate to be done, Mr. Wonderful to date, a trip to the Mecca of Elvis with Janna, and our music seems to be at the bottom of the list. I think even singing at a funeral would have precedence over our gigs. I bet you've even dipped into the album fund."

Wow, that amounted to quite a mouthful from my friend. I sat in shocked silence for about fifteen seconds as I tried to frame a reply. "You're right. I did borrow some, but I'm replacing it. I just needed a little money for the Tennessee trip. Janna gave me the flight there and I had some saved up, but I came up short two hundred. I just made that today and I'm replacing it. I won't take any more out, I promise." I didn't point out that I had put the majority of the money into the recording fund in the first place.

He mumbled something I couldn't hear, but it might have been an acknowledgment.

"Ferris, the recording is important to me, too. You know how long I've wanted to make an album. I'm sorry I screwed this up and I acknowledge that it is my fault. I've caused us to set the recording date back three times now and I'm well aware of that. I will not reset it again, I promise." I crossed my heart as I had when I was a little kid. "Believe me?"

He looked up, "Yeah, I do. But, what is happening with you? You're just not the same girl you were. Dig tried to tell me that you were going through some issues, but what is it that you can't tell your best friends?"

Recognizing the pain in his voice, I knew I'd found the crux of the problem; I'd quit sharing my problems with them. Since we'd met in college, we'd been close friends and we'd talked about everything with each other. Well, except totally girl things. Some things a woman just didn't discuss with male buddies.

"The slip on the ice changed me a little. It made me more aware of my mortality and I guess you could say that I've been experiencing a crisis of faith over the past few months. But the bigger change is from being kidnapped." I paused. "Want another beer? I can use a glass of wine."

He looked surprised at the sudden halt, but he said, "I'll get them," and he went to the bar rather than flagging a waitress. I could use some food also, but that could wait until after I told him what was going to be difficult to say. By doing this, I reasoned, I might be working my way up to telling total strangers in a courtroom what had happened.

When he came back, I sipped a little of the white zinfandel and began telling him the story of what had happened beginning with me innocently going into the teen club downtown to encountering Coblenzer and his attempt to rape and then kill me.

When I'd finished, I gulped half the wine while Ferris sat with his mouth hanging open. "I had no idea. I could not even guess that had happened to you. Why didn't you say something?"

"You guys are so important to me, Ferry. You and Dig... I count on you for so much. But... This has been so personal, so degrading to me that I didn't want to talk about it. I feel so violated, so damaged by what happened and the fact that I could do nothing about it." Tears began to form in my eyes as my emotions threatened to spill out.

"So, that's why you've started doing the self-defense classes? So that you might have more control if it happens again?"

I nodded. "And they've already paid off." Then I told him about the drunk on Beale Street that tried to coerce Janna. That elicited a chuckle and soon we both laughed about it. It felt good to have this connection with him again.

Then he grew serious and his eyes had little puddles in them. "Gilly, never, ever, be afraid to talk to me. I promise I will always have your back and I will never betray you. I love you, you know that."

Tears almost broke though as I nodded. "Love you, too."

While the meeting went a long way to clearing up our misunderstandings and Ferris even admitted that I hadn't been off at the rehearsals although I did blow the lyrics, it still left some guilt lingering. In spite of all I'd confessed, I hadn't told him about the biggest change in my life.

My ability to see departed souls and, now, shades may be more than even Ferris could handle.

I met with Dr. Elise Mannetti a few days later. Mark's evaluation was spot on; I did like her. A dark-haired, dark-eyed Italian woman with a figure that said, "I love food, especially pasta," she stood about five-foot-two and wore a dark gray shirtdress that worked well with her small stature. Gold hoops dangled from her ears and a matching necklace with a drop pendant draped around her neck. She greeted me with a warm smile, the kind that softens the face and eyes, as I settled into a plush chair in her office. She didn't sit behind her desk but took the matching one that angled toward me. In some ways, her technique reminded me of Madame Astrid's approach, doing what it takes to make the client comfortable, I assumed.

"Now, I want you to know that whatever we talk about in here is confidential information. I won't share it with anyone. I often make recordings of sessions for my own benefit, but if you have a problem with that, I won't do it. It helps me to be able to replay a conversation when I think about it later. But it's not necessary."

I nodded when she paused. "If I don't want something I'm about to tell you recorded, I'll tell you. Is that how it would work?"

"Yes. Exactly. So far as what we discuss, that will be up to you. I don't know what is bothering you or what problem you may be working through, but you choose the subject and we'll see where it takes us. So let's get acquainted first, shall we?"

I found it easy to talk to Elise and she didn't push me into talking about anything in particular. Testing the waters, I brought up my father's departure and how it made me feel. While she sympathized, she didn't offer any platitudes or explanations but asked me a few questions about how I thought it affected me.

"I felt abandoned," I told her. "Discarded. It was like I was nothing more than an old towel to him. Something that he'd liked once and used, but then had no further need for so he tossed it away."

"And how has this affected your relationships?"

I started to say that it hadn't, but it had and I knew it had. "I am wary of any relationships and every time a boyfriend ended one, I think it reinforced my feelings of inadequacy."

The session seemed to fly and it ended before I realized it. We hadn't gotten to talking about the kidnapping, but I left feeling that I would be able to tell her about it and she would guide me through it. I made another appointment for the following week. With the trial looming on the near horizon, I wanted to be sure I could get through it and give an accurate, but not self-damaging, testimony.

Back at the shooting range on Saturday morning, Eric stood by me, stopwatch in hand, and gave me a nod. I reached for my gun, released the safety as I positioned my hands to hold it steady, sighted my target and fired as smoothly as I could.

"Seven seconds," Eric said.

Damn... I thought I'd done it quicker than that. We hadn't been at it long, but I'd just fired my fifth cartridge and my speed failed to improve.

"You're still thinking it through too much. It has to be automatic, second nature. Pick it up, safety, sight, and fire." He went through the steps quickly without a weapon in his hands, demonstrating how fast it should be done. "Do it again."

I popped in another magazine of ammo and went through it again. The next time through proved worse as my nerves slowed me down. It seemed like the harder I tried, the poorer I did. He kept at me until we emptied the magazine. I reloaded as he gave me the times. The last one, the best of the session, clocked a little under six seconds.

"Keep practicing for another two magazines. Then do it at home with an empty gun. Pick it up from a table, from a counter, or wherever and go through the steps. If you're going to conceal-carry this, then you need to practice getting it from your pocket, your purse, or a holster to your hand and firing. The more automatic you can make this, the better chance you'll have at saving your own life if you're threatened."

I felt like the dunce in class, but I realized this just took practice to make it automatic. I picked the gun up, flipped the safety, aimed at the target, and fired. I set the gun down and repeated the steps, over and over.

TWENTY-ONE

A week before the trial's scheduled start date, I met Duarte Bourgoin, the prosecutor from the District Attorney's office, who would be handling the Holiday Killer case, to discuss my testimony. His secretary showed me to a very masculine room with lots of leather and wood accenting it. The scent of the leather hung in the air, suggesting that the sofas were new or the cleaners used a scented spray to refresh it. It's peculiar what you think about when you're nervous and waiting for someone.

About five minutes later, he arrived in a bustle of forward motion with several file folders in one hand and a smartphone in the other as he machine-gunned his side of the conversation into it. He dipped his head toward me in acknowledgment, then dumped the folders on his desk before he sat and wrapped up the phone call.

A medium-height, lean man with a tanned complexion, Bourgoin's gray eyes showed a network of wrinkles surrounding them as he studied me for a moment, then he flashed a brief smile.

"Ms. Foster, thank you for coming in. I just want to go over the schedule of the trial with you and let you know what we expect. You won't need to be there every day, as I do know about when we'll want you to testify. These things don't always run according to schedule, but we have an approximate; however, there's always a chance that something will disrupt the expected witness order, so you'll need to be somewhat flexible for the days around it. I know that can be difficult to plan with a job, but please try to make arrangements in case we need to call you earlier or delay until later."

A little overwhelmed by this opening statement, it took a few moments as I digested the gist of what he was saying. I could be called at any time during the trial. "Yes, sir," I answered with respect to the office if not to the man who so far had been brisk and non-personal in his approach to me. I suppose he had limited time, but if this man would be asking me the questions for my testimony, I didn't feel comfortable with him.

Maybe he sensed my unease as he took a breath, then smiled at me in a kinder way and said, "Now that we have that out of the way, let's talk a little about your statement, which I have here."

I knew it contained the bare bones of what had happened. I hadn't gone into any detail about what the accused actually did to me, so it recorded only a general recitation. As the attorney read it to himself, I asked, "Is it really necessary for me to make an appearance? Can't the statement stand for itself?"

He looked up, a surprised expression on his face. "Miss Foster, we're trying a man for multiple counts of murder, rape, attempted murder, and assaulting an officer. While we have the officer's testimony and the confession of the ex-con who committed these atrocities, you're the one living eyewitness to his crimes and he confessed to you what he'd done. You are a key witness."

I dropped my gaze to the floor then stammered, "I... I know that, but I've been traumatized by the whole experience and I don't want to talk about what happened, especially in an open courtroom. I don't want to hear my experience on the evening news or read it on the internet or a newspaper. While I know it will come out, the details should *not* be made public knowledge."

As he studied me for a few moments, he leaned back in his chair. "I see. I do understand your concerns. I can try to protect you from some of it while you are testifying, but the defense attorney is likely to try to get you to say something that will benefit his client, such as you came seeking him and knew what you were getting into, although certainly planned murder wasn't something anyone would expect. Why don't you tell me as much as you can of what you are willing to say on the stand?"

I pretty much repeated exactly what I'd said in my statement to Moss and Hernandez, not adding any detail. When I stopped talking, Bourgoin stared at me and arched a questioning eyebrow. "That's it? I read that. Tell me what's not in your statement. How did he find you?"

"Like I said, he saw the two officers pick me up in a place where he happened to have been with the girl he killed. He thought I knew something, so he waited until I returned to get my Jeep."

"Did you know he was the killer?"

"No. I knew that girl had been killed and I sang at her funeral, but I didn't know who did it." That was the true, but not complete, answer I planned to give.

"So, on the chance that you might be able to identify him, he kidnapped and planned to kill you?" He sounded more like the defense lawyer than the prosecutor to me.

"Yes."

"Did anything else happen that might have led him to this conclusion?"

"As it turns out, he also saw me go into a teen club downtown where the girl had also gone." Again, as little information as possible. Moss had said to answer only the question asked.

Bourgoin leaned forward in his chair as he chewed at his lip in thought. "Did you know when you went to the club that Miss Sanders had been there?"

"No, it was a coincidence."

"Why did you go there?"

I saw what he was doing. His questions worked to pick my story apart in a rehearsal for what I might expect from the prosecution. Once I understood that, I relaxed a little and continued to give him only the bare minimum answers to his questions.

I did fine until he asked, "Did Coblenzer rape you?"

"In a sense," I spoke the words slowly as I grew more apprehensive. Yes, the defense would pursue this. He would want to prove that I hadn't been raped.

"What do you mean by that?"

He rose to his feet and moved to stand in front of me at an

intimidating distance as he, or the defense attorney, might position himself in the courtroom.

"He did everything but..." I took a deep breath feeling the disgust rise in me. "... insert himself into me. He used his fingers, he pinched me, bit me, threatened me. I felt raped." I blurted this out. I hovered on the verge of tears. "And he made it clear he was going to kill me after he'd had a little more 'fun' with me."

Bourgoin's eyes showed a hint of concern, but more approval than sympathy. "That is what will convince the jury, Miss Foster. If you show emotion, they will respond. I know this is painful for you to recount, but it will be what helps to convict him of all of his crimes."

He handed me a tissue and I wiped my eyes. "And it will be on the news and the world will know."

Stepping back, he pursed his lips into a tight line and nodded. "I expect that will happen. The media can be a friend or a foe in these cases. The main thing is to not allow the defense attorney to rattle you. Don't let him force you into saying something that may suggest you're hiding something."

Those words scared me because I *was* hiding something, but I had to keep it secret. What the press would print if even the suggestion of my gift got out could far surpass what they might say about the kidnapping. I could envision my story splashed across the front cover of one of the rag magazines at the grocery store. Just the thought made me cringe.

Satisfied that he'd covered everything he needed at this point, Bourgoin dismissed me with the advisement that his office would be in touch. As I started toward the door, he said, "Miss Foster, you do know that there are photographs and reports from the hospital to support your story, don't you?"

Stunned, I turned back toward him, my mouth hanging open in horror. I managed to squawk out, "Can we suppress them?"

He shook his head. "They're in evidence. The judge and jury must see them. I can try to limit who can view them, but I might not be able to keep them confidential."

As I left the pet salon the next afternoon, I spotted Moss' car parked in the lot near the end where I'd left my Jeep. I sighed as I marched toward him. What the heck now?

Moss leaned against the side of the unmarked car as Hernandez came around.

"What are you guys doing here?" I tried to keep a civil tone, but the frown on my face might have negated it.

Moss grinned. "Just stopping to deliver a little good news. We've found the guy who cut Willits off and brought him in. He admits to it. Said he'd had a couple of drinks and his judgment wasn't the best. The sticker on the bumper was the real key to finding him. He was in some gaming group and he was late to the party, so to speak. So, thanks to your help, we've wrapped that one up. We're going over to tell Thomas Willits a little later, but we wanted to thank you for the help."

I relaxed a little. "That's great news. I'm glad you got him."

Hernandez gave me a thumb up and a nod. He was letting Moss do the talking today.

Clearing his throat, Moss shuffled a foot on the pavement into a circle. "I also wanted to check on you, see how you're doing."

"I'm fine."

"I know you saw the prosecutor on Tuesday. Any problems?"

I snorted a laugh. "Tons of them. My whole story is going to be pulled piecemeal from me and played out in the news. He said he'd try to keep it quiet, but if the defense is as thorough as Bourgoin expects, then the reporters will have a field day."

Hernandez made a cluck-like noise, his handsome face looking badass with a frown on it.

Moss sighed. "Yeah, it's going to be tough, but like I said, answer only what you're asked and we'll try to keep your involvement in this to a minimum."

"Sure, officers. Thanks for the concern. One thing, though, can you not come to where I work? People are going to think I'm dealing drugs or something with two shady characters."

Hernandez laughed at that.

"You bet," Moss said. "I have one other thing. I think I have a lead on the guy who killed Jackson Dorfman. At least I've got the description and name of a suspect and we're looking for him. Again, the little clue you managed to find gave us a start."

"Good. Now all you have to do is find him and prove it."

Moss nodded, opening his door. "See you around, Foster."

Hernandez shot a wink my direction before he went back to the passenger side.

They were out of the lot before I even got my door open, but I was kind of glad to know they'd found the reckless driver even if it didn't help Emmett Willits.

By the time I got home, I felt kind of low, a depression settling on me. Sometimes it all seemed so unfair. You do the right thing and you end up being screwed by the media. Some busybody reporter would probably want to do an interview with me and I refused to do it.

If I could be excused from being a witness, I would, but it had been clear from the beginning that I would be called to testify. No option. Now they had arrested another suspect and the possibility that I would be called in to testify against him even though I'd barely seen him increased. My reward for being helpful? It sucked.

Hugging Nygard, I put my chin on his head and he cuddled against me. Carrying him into the kitchen, I slowed, sensing something didn't feel right. At first glance, nothing appeared to be out of place, then I noticed the floor mat in front of the sink skewed to an angle as I put my cat on the floor.

Concerned, I called my landlady and asked her if she'd come into my place.

She confirmed that she had and added, "Didn't I tell you that I had the electrician coming out today to check the circuit in the annex? After that breaker tripped a couple of weeks ago, I worried there might be a problem. It's all fine and I stayed there with him the whole time."

Relief flowed through me in a wave. *More nervous than I'd realized*, I admitted as I got out food for my cat.

"Okay, Gillian, what do you want to talk about today?" Elise Mannetti asked. While she seemed willing to wait until I chose to address my real issues, allowing me to discuss other skeletons in my past, I had more immediate concerns that I needed to face.

"Please don't record what I'm about to say." I waited while she turned the device off.

"I'm a witness in a trial coming up next week. I was almost..." I stopped, steeled my nerves, closed my eyes, and forced the words out. "...raped and murdered. The man brutally killed three young girls, around twelve-years-old, and I accidentally happened to encounter him. He thought I was on to him and kidnapped me." I gasped it out, wanting so much to tell her the whole story, but afraid that it wouldn't be private if I did.

She thought for a moment, then said, "I see. Is this what has been really troubling you?"

"Part of it. It was a horrible experience and the prosecutor wants me to tell it in court. I don't want to talk about it."

"Why is that?"

I felt comfortable with her, but I found it hard to express how this affected me. In a small voice, I said, "Because it made me feel dirty, soiled. Even though I know it wasn't my fault, he left me feeling like he had put his mark on me."

She nodded her head slowly a couple of times. "What you're feeling isn't unusual, Gillian. Many rape victims feel violated. It's an attack on the most personal part of your body.

"I want to assure you that anything you say to me is privileged information. It is confidential and as you asked, I am not recording it so there will be no audio record of it. I will put it in my personal notes later so I can reference what I write. It won't have your name or details attached to it and I write in my own code. So, if you want to tell me the whole story, it will be between us. But only tell me as much as you are comfortable with talking about."

I felt like I had been drowning and she'd just thrown me a rope to pull me to safety. Or maybe it was more like everything I'd been holding inside for the past three months came spilling out along with tears and self-recrimination for my own perceived weaknesses. She handed me tissues and listened patiently as I described that horrible night in detail.

Afterward, I sat shaking and on the verge of tears, while trying not to break down again. I hated that the monster had reduced me to this state. The effect of what he created, mentally and emotionally, reached farther than his physical attack on me and a gradual understanding of just how bad began to form.

Elise's voice remained calm and soothing as she spoke to me. "You are not the only woman who's felt this way after this kind of traumatic experience. It's easy for someone to say, 'Oh, the man only had sex with you' and 'It's not something you haven't already done,' but when it's sex that is forcibly taken, it's worse than having your house broken into and your valuables stolen. It's a violation of your person. Even if this man didn't go through with the whole act, he still violated your body with his fingers and his intent. Worse, he violated you mentally. He told you what he was going to do as well as what he had already done."

"So now what do I do?" I asked between sniffles. "How do I get past this? I couldn't even have sex with my boyfriend and I wanted to." My voice became a choked whine.

From there, Elise talked to me about techniques I could use to bring my mental state around and build my confidence. Part of her suggestion was meditation. I hadn't been doing the one that Madame Astrid had told me to do nightly, but with this additional prompting, I resolved to begin doing it. Elise also wanted me to focus on my feelings and reinforce the confidence I had in myself.

Then we discussed the trial for a few minutes and how I could get through the testimony. She had some very good suggestions. For one thing, she advised that I avoid any eye contact with the defendant in the courtroom or while I testified.

"Don't even look at him," she said firmly. "You still fear him, so he still has that hold. You want to deny him any power over you and the best way to do that is to ignore his presence. Now, you may have to point him out in the courtroom, but other than that, look directly at the prosecutor, the defense attorney, or at the judge."

While it sounded easy enough, I worried if I could carry it off.

It was a cloudy afternoon with a hint of the coming summer in the air when I left work after a long, but good day that had netted me close to five hundred dollars with tips. My smartphone buzzed out the custom tune I'd assigned to a caller that was becoming familiar to me: Egan Moss. I pulled it out as I arrived at my car and said, "Hi, Moss. Is there news?"

"I believe there is, Foster. News I think you're going to like, in fact." He sounded downright cheery.

"All right, I'll bite. What's that?"

"Coblenzer pleaded guilty at the pre-trial hearing today."

"That's good, right?" I wasn't sure if I should be excited, but it had to be positive.

"Yes, it's good. It means you don't have to testify. He's pleaded guilty to all charges. The only one he fussed over was the assaulting an officer charge for hitting me. Said he thought I was a burglar." The amusement in Moss' voice was evident.

"So, I don't have to appear in court at all?" I still tried to absorb this.

"Nope."

I thanked him and ended the call, then climbed into the Beast and let out a whoop of joy. Yes! I wouldn't have to tell anyone the story in detail. My written statement had been enough and while the media might still report it, at least it didn't include any of the specific details. Most of all, it eliminated the chance that any hints of my gift might spark unwanted interest. "Thank you, God. And Zac."

I called Janna before I started the car. "I've got some great news. Can you drop by tonight? I'll pick up Chinese on the way home." I offered a bribe that I knew she couldn't resist.

"Must be something good if you're picking up Chow Stix on the way. Yeah, I can be there about seven."

"Perfect. See you then."

I arrived at home by six and shoved the Chinese containers in the oven on low to keep the food warm, then ran upstairs to change clothes. After I dressed in comfortable jeans and a Henley style gray shirt, I looked at the time. Seeing that I had at least forty-five minutes, I decided to practice with my Ruger.

From the dining room table to the fireplace at the end of the living room was about twenty-five feet, so I designated the photograph of me with Ferris and Digby as the target. I set the gun on the table, took a breath and glanced at the digital wall clock in the kitchen that had a second counter, then told myself go and went through the process.

Grab gun, release safety, aim, and pull the trigger. Between unlocking the safety and firing, I was losing a couple of seconds. If I didn't need to take the safety off, I could save the time, but it wouldn't be secure or responsible to carry a loaded weapon without the safety on. Just the idea of carrying the gun made me nervous, but I was more worried about not having it if I found myself in a situation such as the one with Coblenzer again.

At the same time, I had to ask myself if either the gun or the self-defense classes would have helped me when he nabbed me as I went to my Jeep. Unless I had been aware of him sooner, I couldn't have gotten the gun out in time. With proper training, I might have had one chance to flip him or disable him. On the other hand, if I paid closer attention to my surroundings and I found myself in that situation again with a gun in my possession, I would have my hand on it before the attack started.

I took the next ten minutes to go through picking up the gun and releasing the safety with my thumb at the same time. Set it down and do it over again. I had to feel comfortable with that quick move while picking it up. I put the gun in my purse and tried it from there. The purse location had to have easy access and be the only thing in that compartment and it had to slide out easily. I lost more seconds from the purse. Too slow.

Immersed in my thoughts and the process, I picked up the weapon again, slipping the safety off simultaneously and sighting when the front door clicked open and I swung it automatically toward the sound as my head turned and pulled the trigger on the empty chamber just as Janna stepped into the room.

She heard the click and dead silence hung between us for a few seconds before her face crumpled into a horrified, shocked look, and she shouted at me. "Good God, Gillian! Is that a freaking gun in your hand? Are you crazy? You could have shot me!"

I had already lowered the weapon and set it back on the table. "No, I couldn't. It's not loaded. You startled me."

Her mouth still hung open as she collapsed into the easy chair and anger blazed in her eyes. "What are you doing with a gun?"

"I bought it a month ago. I was just practicing to get my speed up from picking it up to firing."

"You have totally lost your mind." In a defensive gesture, she crossed her arms over her chest.

"I'm sorry. I lost track of time and you're a little early. I had planned to put it away before you got here." I slipped the gun back into its case and put it in the cabinet in the dining area for now. Obviously, she was completely freaked about this.

"Who *are* you?" Janna asked. "The Gillian I know would never even pick up a gun, let alone try to fire one. Now you're telling me you *bought* one? What has happened to you?"

"Someone tried to kill me is what!" I slammed my hand onto

the table as if that would make her understand better. "I was kidnapped and abused and he was going to kill me. I don't want that to ever happen again."

I dropped onto the chair at the table and stared at the floor in front of me, not wanting to meet Janna's eyes. When I forced myself to look up, I saw that Janna stared at the fireplace. Her shoulders slumped and she looked beaten.

I cleared my throat. "I'm sorry you walked in on that. I didn't want to tell you or anyone that I bought a gun. It's only for protection."

"What if it had been loaded when I walked in?" Her voice sounded muffled as she still looked away from me and had a hand on her face.

"I wouldn't have shot you. I was practicing for speed with an unloaded gun. But maybe you should knock before entering from now on."

She turned to face me. "I guess I should. Are you going to be carrying that thing with you?"

"It depends on where I'm going, I guess." I ambled to the sofa across from her and sat closer. "All I really know is that I don't feel safe anymore." My voice broke as I said it and I fought back the tears that threatened.

Janna's eyebrows dropped and she looked stricken. "I'm sorry, Gilly. I know what happened was terrible, but a *gun*? You know they frighten me."

"Me, too. Are you hungry? The food is keeping warm."

"Got any wine? I think I could use a glass."

"Of course." I rose to pour large glasses from the box of white zinfandel that I had in the 'fridge.

As we sipped the alcohol, letting it sooth our nerves and ease the conversation, I told her the good news about the Holiday Killer pleading guilty. At least, he wouldn't be a problem for me anymore. After two glasses, we finally got to the Chinese food. We said no more about my pistol or my worries.

However, Janna's reaction and concerns about having a sidearm bothered me as I cleaned up the kitchen, retrieved my Ruger, and went upstairs to bed. Was I overreacting? Possibly. I reloaded the offending object and put it into the drawer of my bedside table.

TWENTY-TWO

Two days later, Moss called me again with news, both bad and good.

My trial reprieve proved short-lived. As it turned out, I still had to appear at Coblenzer's trial. At the last minute, he changed his plea of the intent to murder me to not guilty. It seemed his lawyer tried to get him off on the attempt part as if it would help the evil bastard out with three charges of homicide already against him. Adding to it, Moss' lawyer also wanted my testimony that I had, in fact, broken a window and screamed for help.

On the good news side, Moss said, "I located Ostero's daughter and called her. She lives in Roseville."

"What did you tell her?" I asked.

"That he had died an indigent in Reno. I said we only recently identified him and were able to establish that he had any relatives. No mention of how we identified him. She took it well considering she hadn't seen him since she was an infant. I asked if she wanted to move his ashes to a grave near her, but she said not to disturb them. Did you want to talk to her?"

"Not really. I just wanted to keep my promise to Ostero. It meant a lot to him." I couldn't tell Amberlee anything more without revealing how I knew, so it wouldn't be possible to tell her that he'd been sorry for not being part of her life. At least that wouldn't be sitting on my conscience anymore.

As I thanked Moss, he nodded, then said, "Sorry about the trial. I'd hoped we'd dodged that bullet."

My nerves rattled me more when the bailiff called me to the stand than when I auditioned for my first musical role in high school. That had been so stressful that I'd chewed my fingernails down to the quick. The reinforced, thick-gel nails survived this time, but I remained dry-mouthed and shaking when I sat down at the front of the courtroom.

Although two attorneys sat with the prosecution, only Bourgoin, the DA I'd spoken with, handled my testimony and approached the stand to address me. He tossed a brief, reassuring smile my way before he got down to business.

"Please tell the court what the defendant did and said to lead you to believe that he was going to kill you."

Oh, great, I thought. *He wants the whole story that I've tried not to tell.* I wet my lips and spoke softly. "He kidnapped me as I was about to open the door on my Jeep. Then he took me to his basement, tied me up, and threatened me with rape. He had to leave; I think to go to work, but he promised to come back, assault me and kill me. I believed him."

"He told you he was going to kill you. Is that correct?"

"Yes." I looked at the wooden stand in front of me, avoiding any eyes that might be studying me.

"Did he do anything that specifically made you think he was going to carry out the threat?"

"Yes."

"Would you please tell the court about it?" He tapped the edge of the stand to get my eyes to look up.

"I was trying to escape. I had gotten free of the cords holding me and found a lamp base to protect myself. I hit him when he came through the door, but he managed to wrench the lamp from my hands and hit me with it hard enough to knock me across the room. I tried to hide and rolled under the bed, but he came after me and attempted to grab me to hit me with it. I believed that if he could have pulled me out that he would have beaten me to death with it." My voice cracked a little in the middle of this statement, but it didn't break.

"What stopped him from pursuing this?"

"Detective Hernandez entered the basement with his gun drawn and told him to stop. He dropped the lamp."

Bourgoin went to the evidence table and picked up the lamp, which was marked with a tag, and held it up for the courtroom to see, then showed it to me. "Is this the lamp you are talking about, Miss Foster?"

"Yes."

He turned toward the jury. "This lamp weighs approximately ten pounds and is heavy enough to bludgeon someone to death."

He set the item back on the table and told the judge he had no further questions.

It was the defense's turn then. I couldn't figure out what the defense hoped to buy from denying the charge of attempted murder when there was so much else stacked against Coblenzer.

He didn't waste any time. "When you picked up the lamp, Ms. Foster, did you intend to kill my client?"

"Objection. The witness is not on trial here." Bourgoin said at once.

"I am attempting to prove my client's claim that he was defending himself." The defense attorney made it sound like the fault rested with me. Of course, Bourgoin had warned me he would try it.

"Overruled," the judge said. "Please answer the question."

"No," I said. "I only wanted to get away and if I could disable him long enough to get out the door and to safety, that was my goal."

"So you had no thoughts of killing him?"

"Objection. Counsel is asking for speculation about the state of the witness' mind at the time."

"Sustained. Counsel, the witness is not on trial here." The judge took my side this time.

"No other questions," the defense said and the judge dismissed me for now.

Relieved that I hadn't had to go into any detail about what had happened, I burned with anger that the defense attorney tried to cast suspicion about my intent. Yes, even though I wouldn't admit to it, I probably would have killed the man under the right circumstances, but I didn't go after him expecting to do it.

Moss caught up with me outside the courtroom. "Hey, Foster," he called out.

I slowed as I heard his running footsteps behind me and turned to look back at him.

"You did fine," he said as he came up to me. "I wanted to tell you that. Don't let that line of questioning get to you. The defense just made an attempt to discredit your testimony but I am pretty sure the jury didn't buy it."

"Why is he even fighting these charges, Moss? It won't help him out in the long run, not with three solid murder charges against him."

Moss shook his head. "I don't know. With the evidence we found at his house, there's no way he can wiggle out of those charges. He may think it will help in the sentencing phase, but I doubt it."

As we talked, I became aware of a woman in business attire watching us. She loitered across the hall and down near the courtroom door. She looked familiar. When she noticed I had spotted her, she turned to look the other way and that's when it clicked. I nudged Moss, "Reporter."

He glanced over. "Oh, hell, Gayle Trumbull. Don't say anything to her."

"You can count on it," I answered. He walked with me toward the courthouse exit and, behind us, I heard the click of heels as the reporter for the local news station followed us. When I cleared the building entrance, Moss swung back inside, moving to intercept her. I set a quick pace to the parking lot as she called out, "Miss Foster, please. I'd like to chat with you. Just a few words."

I hurried around the block in a near run and could only guess that Moss delayed her enough to give me time to get away. She exemplified my exact concern with this, a reporter dogging me, trying to pick out a story. In spite of my escape now, I felt certain she, or another one, would continue to try. Ironic, if she had wanted to chat about my music, I'd be right on board with it, but I had no desire to relate the sordid details she'd sought.

A few days before Memorial Day, Spicy Jam played at a local event with several other bands for a fundraiser. Since it benefited a local charity, it attracted a large crowd as well as press and television coverage.

Feeling like a weight had been lifted from my shoulders after the trial and with the therapy sessions helping me control my anxiety more, my mood rose to a new high and I felt at the top of my game for the afternoon gig. The band had a few more rehearsals for the album under our collective belts and the recording sessions started in a couple of weeks. Everything seemed downright rosy.

Even from the stage, I spotted Roger, whom I now dubbed my stalker, and saw his big smile. Even though I had turned down his date offers, he still seemed to be a super-fan and not too creepy. I admitted that his continued attempts to connect with me made me apprehensive, but he didn't seem dangerous. If my judgment was wrong, I felt confident I could flip him on his ass.

Our first set got the crowd charged up and screaming for more. I wrapped it up with a quick promotion for our upcoming album. "Thanks, everyone. We're Spicy Jam –Digby on guitar and mandolin, Ferris on the drums and I'm Gillian. Our thanks for coming today and listening to us. If you really like us, we're putting an album out in a couple of months so you can take us home with you."

That brought a round of loud whistles and cheers.

"Thanks, mom, dad, and my siblings. This last number will be on the album," Ferris joked. Then we launched into our upbeat ending song, a folk-rock number that had everyone clapping along.

As we vacated the stage, Ferris hugged me with enthusiasm. "I think that was the best gig we've done in months. You were hot, I was hot, and Dig is always hot."

The sexy Aussie just grinned and shrugged his shoulders.

I pressed my way toward the refreshment area to grab a cold drink while the next band took the stage. We had another set to do in about two hours, so we had time to relax and enjoy the fair-like setting. Several vendors for food, drink, assorted jewelry, and summer casual clothing filled a line of booths from the amphitheater toward the entrance to the park. At the first cold drink stand, I ordered an iced lemonade and went back to the grassy hillside theater to watch our colleagues whip up a crowd-pleasing bluegrass tune. I leaned back against a tree that provided a little welcome shade and swallowed a few gulps.

"That was quite a rousing set," a woman's voice said and I turned to see the speaker, ready to say, "thank you".

She stood right next to me, sunglasses covering her eyes, and a baseball cap on her hair. Not so stylishly dressed today, she wore jeans and a tee shirt with the network logo on it. The television news reporter flashed a sly grin at me. "You're pretty talented, Ms. Foster, but I'm a curious person. Just how did a nice girl like you get mixed up with a piece of slime like the Holiday Killer?"

"I don't have any comment on that," I said keeping my voice a neutral, flat tone. "I would just as soon forget it ever happened."

"But you can't, can you?" Gayle Trumbull asked. "Why don't you want to tell your story, Gillian? Maybe it would help other women to avoid ending up in the same situation. Consider it a public service."

"No, I don't think so." I enunciated the words in a staccato. "I think you just want a story and I am not it. The story belongs to the little girls that man killed and the justice for them."

"True, that is the main story. But you're the girl who lived."

"Oh, that is really reaching," I laughed. "I was very fortunate that help arrived when it did."

"You know, I won't give up trying." She took the sunglasses off and looked me directly in the eye, so I could see the determination in hers.

I raised my own wall of stubbornness, shot a tight smirk at her, and said, "And I won't give in."

She laughed, slid the glasses back on. "For now. Like I said, I'm an inquisitive person and I just have to wonder why a talented singer, who is about to cut an album, sings at funerals and is apparently uncannily accurate in creating specialized lyrics for the deceased?"

My eyebrows went up as her words registered.

Her closed lip, smirk-of-a-smile reeked of saccharin as she turned away. It left me feeling somewhat nauseous.

TWENTY-THREE

On the beautiful Saturday morning of the Memorial Day weekend, I picked up Thomas at his apartment and we set out on a treasure hunt. I had marked a map of where I believed the pot of gold, or rather Menafee's cache, to be. We had filled our backpacks with water, food, flashlights, and anything else we thought we needed for a short hike in the forest.

We stopped at the Gold Ranch casino for breakfast and while we waited for it, Thomas and I looked over the map and formed our plan. We could only go so far toward the possible burial area with the Jeep, then we'd have to hike the rest of the way. While not high or rough terrain that we'd be going into, the dirt trail weaved through rocky and uneven ground with loose dirt that could slide. We always risked the chance of encountering snakes or aggressive animals so I'd packed a first aid kit, just in case. I felt optimistic about our chances to locate the cave although not quite as sure of whether anything would still be in it after all these years.

Back on the road, I backtracked to Verdi, then took the route across the Truckee River, which showed a decent water flow after a sizeable amount of rain and snow in the mountains over the past winter, then turned on Colichi Ranch Road. This took us west and paralleled US 80 and the railroad tracks with the riverbed between them and us. Once off the pavement, it turned to a hard grated dirt path, which the Beast took easily, bouncing us as it went, but performing as I expected an off-road vehicle to do.

We continued for several miles on an increasingly bumpy, uneven road until we got our first glimpse of the flumes to the left of the Jeep. Built along the edges of the mountain rises, they had deteriorated over the decades and looked broken and ruined in many places. The V-shaped flume transported logs for building and moved water from the lakes to the lower areas through the Sierras. In some places along the highway, parts of the system remained intact and visible. When it rained, you could see the water running off them into the Truckee.

Once we got close to the area I'd identified as the one Menafee described, I parked the Jeep and Thomas and I set out on foot, climbing up the incline to come as close to the flumes as possible. Menafee said that the cave sat below one of the structures that had been situated several miles west of the little community of Verdi.

As I looked along the ridge, I wished that Menafee had given me a vision of what he saw when he scrambled into the cave. From my view, this just looked like hundreds of feet of bushes, weeds, and a few scraggly trees all along the edge. I didn't see any hint of a pathway, so we would have to pick our way through it while trying to spot anything that looked like it might be an opening to a cave.

I heard a grunt behind me and turned to see that Thomas had tripped on something and had fallen to one knee in the dirt. He reached back to see what had caused the fall and his hand came up with a rusted piece of metal.

"What the heck?" he said as I took a couple of steps back toward him.

I reached for the four or so inches of a curved blade-like object he held up. "It looks like it might be part of a tool. Maybe a hand-pick that someone used—"

"For mining gold?" Thomas said, his voice excited at the possibility he might have stumbled, literally, onto something.

"Or some Boy Scout lost out here on a campout. There are many trails out in this area and a few camping locations. But it does look like it's been out here for a while."

As I handed it back to him, I noticed a glint of light in the area behind us, as if the sun had reflected off a mirror or a lens. Not from the area where I'd left the Jeep, I figured it didn't reflect off the windshield. Curious and maybe nothing, but I hesitated to dismiss it entirely.

If the broken pick came from either Menafee or his pursuers, then it could mean we neared the hiding place. A long shot, but better than no clue. Now that I stood here, all of this area looked the same and I couldn't single out the location Menafee had tried to show me.

After another hour of searching, getting right up to the edge of the cliff sides and shoving bushes aside, we stopped for a break and sat on a couple of boulders. I heard something rustle behind me in one of the bushes and tensed.

"Don't move, Thomas. I heard an animal."

His eyes went wide and he nodded, as he understood my concern. In a slow movement, I turned only my head to look. I didn't want to frighten a rattlesnake or a something bigger with any quick movements. I didn't see anything at first, then a chipmunk darted out of the bush and scurried to a tree. I let out my breath and laughed.

I glanced back the way we'd come to see if I got another glimpse of light, but it seemed quiet. Yet something nagged at me, some intuition, I suppose. I nibbled at some blueberries I'd brought along and tried to picture the image of the area in my mind. The flume had been almost new when Menafee traveled along here and it had connected with the one next to it at about a thirty-degree angle to go around a jut in the cliff's side.

I took a few steps back and tried to visualize the flume flowing along the area, where it would jut out enough for the slight angle change and for a few moments, I could see the flume as it probably looked when it was filled with water flowing through the V-channel coming from the mountain down to the valley. I looked at each section and how it locked together then I spotted what I believed to be the section we sought. As I blinked, the vision vanished, but I knew exactly where to look.

Grabbing up my backpack, I pointed ahead of us. "I think it's a little ways further up, maybe another hundred yards, but let's continue to look for any openings in case I'm wrong."

We started hiking uphill again. I felt the pull in the back of my calves and consoled myself by thinking it would all be downhill going back down toward the Jeep. Even though my body's strength had sharpened, I'd done precious little climbing in the past three months and I felt it now. A glance at Thomas showed his reddened face as he also felt the effort of the gradual but steady climb.

The same glimpse revealed reflected light from downhill. At mid-afternoon with the sun well overhead, the source of the glare had to be pointed upward to reflect. To my thinking, it suggested that someone behind us used either a camera or binoculars pointed toward where we stood. "Did you tell anyone we were coming out here?" I asked Thomas.

"I told my roommate. Why?"

I frowned at him, uneasy with this. "It may be nothing, but it's possible someone is following us. Did you tell Shawn why?"

"I kind of made of a joke of it, saying I was going treasure hunting in the hills. I didn't think he thought I was serious and I sure didn't tell him the whole story. I mean, that would make us sound crazy, wouldn't it?"

"You would think." However, I wondered if he might be more than just a chance housemate. "Tell me about him. Where did you meet?"

"Shawn? He's all right, a bit of a prankster, but easy enough to get along with. When I first decided to live in the University housing, I advertised for someone to share the costs of the off-campus apartment, which was all I could get at the time. He was one of the first to answer. We get along fine. He's also a second-year student so it seemed like a good match."

"You'd never met him before?"

"No. I didn't even recall seeing him on campus prior to him coming over to talk about the apartment."

"Okay. This may be nothing and not related. We'll keep an eye out on that person behind us." I hoped the possible tail didn't have anything to do with our search, but if word of a potential cache of gold got out, who knew what might happen. I pulled out my smartphone to check for a signal in case we might need to call for help, relieved to see the positive indicator. As we progressed, I continued to check behind us for any advancement.

Another fifty feet along, Thomas spotted a crevice in the hillside behind the bushes. It looked too small to be what we were looking for, but we needed to investigate anyway. With the opening about four feet wide by three feet tall, I dropped to my knees and flashed my light into it to look around enough to see it only went in a short ways, maybe four feet. Two pairs of eyes peered at me from the darkness and I clicked the light off.

I scurried back from the opening and said, "It's small and it's occupied. I think that's a pair of skunks, just judging by their pointy noses and the hiss one of them made at me. Let's move on."

We quickly put some distance between the undesired problem and us. The encounter suggested a distinct possibility the cave we sought might be inhabited. Being spring, there could also be babies and a protective parent. I tried to recall the most frequently- encountered animals that might be occupying a cave; it started with bears and ran through mountain lions. Not a comforting thought.

We came around a slight bend and just ahead of us, we spotted a jut in the cliff with a piece of the flume hanging above it. Heavy scrub bushes, common in this area, covered the ground. Desert sage and an assortment of ground-cluster weeds encouraged by the wet spring added to the natural camouflage. As daunting as this vegetation front appeared, it provided the best hope we had that, if a cave nestled behind them, it had remained undisturbed in the time since Menafee shoved some plants in front of it.

I turned to point it out to Thomas and took a long look downhill, seeking any movement behind us. I should have brought my binoculars, but I hadn't anticipated any need for them. My phone had a zoom lens on it, but I didn't think it would be enough to do any good from here. Nonetheless, I pulled it out, pointed it downhill, and zoomed it to the maximum, then slowly moved it across the area we'd come up. I didn't see anything at first, but then a splash of dark blue showed up that seemed out of place. I snapped a photo and studied it for a few seconds before I showed it to Thomas.

"Does that look like a hat to you?"

He squinted at it. "I dunno. It could be. Maybe it's one of the Wolf Pack hats."

"I don't like this. He could be trouble."

While my confidence to defend myself had been boosted by my

encounter with the drunk in Memphis, I wasn't sure if could handle someone sober. Then again, if it turned out to be Thomas' pudgy roommate, I thought I could take him.

"Let's see if we can hack our way through this brush." Setting down my backpack, I pulled out a pair of leather gloves and a small bush pruner.

"You really did come prepared," Thomas said, pulling out a pair of gloves and his flashlight.

I snipped away at some of the sagebrush limbs to make a straight line back toward the wall. Three layers of plant life blocked the curve, so it took an effort to get enough of a separation even to see anything that might be a cave. At first, I didn't think so, then I spotted a dark curve at the right edge of the bottom scrub bush.

"This might be it," I told Thomas as I clipped the branches of the bush revealing more of the opening behind it. When I'd gotten enough cut away for me to move in, I shoved more branches out of the way and slipped into the space just in front of the cave. With this much brush in front of it, I thought it unlikely that any large animal would be living in it but provided ideal accommodations for snakes or rodents to make it home. I turned my flashlight on and peered into the cave.

Not a huge opening, it provided enough space for a man to crawl in and stretch out to spend the night or shelter for a while. It looked fairly clean to me, no animal droppings or anything to indicate that any creatures lived in it. Although I did see a couple of spider webs near the entrance.

"I'm going in," I called back to Thomas. "Keep an eye out for anyone coming up the incline. If I find anything, I'll let you know."

I considered it a measure of the trust that Thomas had for me that he didn't object. I don't know if I would have trusted someone I'd only known a short time to find it ahead of me.

Inside, the cave seemed dry and unmarked. Appearances suggested no one had been inside it over the past century. While I could rise to my knees inside, the low ceiling precluded standing straight up, even for my smaller stature. Crawling, I worked my way to the back and felt around for the rock that Menafee said he'd moved in front of the smaller crevice. I flicked the flashlight ahead and noticed a change in the surface where a flat-looking boulder leaned against the rear wall. Edging my way to it, I grasped the edge and tried to wiggle the sizeable rock out of place.

Awkward and heavy, it proved more than I could move with my hands and shoulder. I shifted to the other side where a little space gave me a cramped spot to use my strongest assets, my legs, to shove against the rock. Bracing my back against the wall, I bent my knees, wedged my feet against it, then shoved as hard as I could. I grunted and the boulder shifted a little, but it seemed to be stuck against something on the other side.

"Thomas, I need your help in here," I yelled.

He ducked his head in then crawled inside. Two people in the little cave made for cramped quarters, but we managed. He studied the stone on the end opposite where I shoved and found that another rock under the dirt on that side, by accident or design, held it in place.

Grunting and pulling, he moved it away several inches and I resumed shoving the larger boulder with my hiking boots propped firmly on the edge. As it inched aside, a small opening, large enough for me to reach into with my flashlight, appeared behind it.

In the light's beam, a leather saddlebag, about the size of a gallon of milk, leaned against the rough back of the hole. Encouraged, I threw all my weight against the rock to shove it a little more, enough that I could reach the bag. As I pulled it toward me, I could feel it weighed heavy enough to be easily ten pounds and probably a few pounds more.

"Is that it?" Thomas asked. He leaned forward to see better, excitement glittering in his eyes.

My hands shook as I carefully unwound the fragile-looking wrap tie at the top, aware even through my gloves of the brittleness of the leather. A black spider climbed out of the bag and I shoved it away from me in a spasm of automatic reaction but relaxed when it scurried back into the little alcove that it called home. A little more cautiously, I spread the opening a bit more and tipped out a portion of the contents. Several small stones, including a couple of gold ones, rolled into my gloved hand.

Smiling, I caught Thomas' hand and placed them in it. "Look at that! It's your inheritance."

At the sight of those little pieces of ore, his face split into the biggest smile I'd ever seen. If this bag contained a few more pieces that size, there would be more than enough to get him through college. While Thomas took his nuggets to the cave entrance to see them in the light, I positioned the flashlight to illuminate more of the contents.

Carefully shifting items around, I saw at least a dozen more golden pebbles, but many more stones that looked like pieces of quartz. A flash of green, as well as an odd reddish-brown stone, standing out in the sea of white and tan, caught my attention. I pulled out the two objects and held them to the light, revealing an emerald ring in a silver setting and a roughly two-inch-by-one-inch, rectangular rock that could be an unpolished gem. Might this be what Menafee had offered me? Feeling just a little guilty, I pocketed the items, along a few golden nuggets, then peered back into the bag, moving the light around. Pressed against the back of the bag, I saw a yellowish piece of paper edging up from under the rocks.

Removing my right glove, I reached in to move the stones away and, with the lightest touch I could manage, eased the paper from the bag. Seeing the fold line in the fragile piece of parchment, I took pains to unfold it with care, wincing when it cracked a little across the middle. As I read the heading at the top, I realized I held the assay report from Truckee and saw the notation of the gold's weight and the source being Emmett Willits' claim. This would be as good as a will for establishing Thomas' right to the gold. I tucked it back into the bag and closed it, ready to slide outside.

At that point, I realized that Thomas had not come back. Fearing the worst, I shoved the saddlebag back behind the stone we'd shifted away from the wall. It wouldn't hold up against a search, but at least, I wouldn't be exiting the cave with it in my possession.

"Thomas," I called as I neared the entrance.

"Gillian…" His tense-sounding voice broke off, followed by an oomph-sound, as if someone had punched him. It seemed likely that trouble waited on the other side.

Damn, I should have brought my Ruger on this trip, I thought. *What good is the darn thing if you leave it at home?*

Preparing myself for whatever threat waited, I pulled my phone out and dialed 911. I cupped my hand over it and whispered help just as a male voice called out.

"You might as well come out, Gillian. We know you're there."

Even though I'd only heard him speak once, I felt sure that Shawn had followed us up and it appeared that he'd brought someone else along. I still held the line open, so I repeated help, and set the phone down near the entrance to the cave. With luck, the police could track the GPS in it and find us.

I poked my head out and crawled forward, but before I could get a clear view of the situation, a strong hand gripped my right upper arm and yanked me out like pulling a worm from the ground. A young man, built like a weight lifter with bulging muscles, wasted little effort in hoisting me into the air.

Recovering from the momentary shock, I kicked wildly, scissoring my legs, and flailing at him with my free arm as he tried to grab it. I must have resembled a toddler throwing a tantrum.

"That's enough of that," another man called out.

I twisted toward the speaker, confirming his identity as the roommate, as soon as he'd started to talk. I barely registered that he had a pistol pointed at Thomas until he stepped forward and rotated it toward me. From the way he held the weapon, I guessed that Shawn wasn't used to handling it, but my legs were already kicking out.

Shawn continued, "If you don't cooperate, I'll shoot "

And I caught his gun hand with my boot, knocking it downward where it went off and hit his foot. In a brief moment, I saw Thomas dive away from him and scramble in the dirt.

Now, the big man holding me gripped my left arm and started to pull me into a bear hug to attempt to neutralize me. Unfortunately, he held me facing him and even though I couldn't use my arms, my legs were still free and I stomped down hard on his ankles and kicked at his legs and knees. It wasn't as effective as I would have liked, but it was enough to distract him and keep him struggling with me.

I couldn't see what was happening with Shawn and Thomas, but I could hear the former cursing and whining with the pain from his wound. If he got his hands on the gun again, I wouldn't be able to do anything about it unless I could break free. I butted my head into the muscleman's chest and about that time, a ball-sized stone flew into his head, smashing just above the nose.

He screamed in anger and pain, releasing my left arm to raise it to his jaw, when another projectile slammed into his brow and he stumbled backward. Both hands shot to his face in protection and I took advantage of the moment to butt my head into his stomach as hard as I could.

Air whooshed out and he doubled over, dropping to the ground. I didn't hesitate to pound both fists into the sides of his head until he passed out.

Behind me, Shawn called out. "That's enough of that. Get up and put your hands where I can see them. And you get over here and stand by her." He used the gun as a pointer to direct Thomas.

Well, damn, Thomas hadn't gotten to the weapon and Shawn had control again.

I complied with his instructions.

He limped forward, an angry fire burning in his eyes as he growled at us. "Where's the rest of the gold?"

"That's all we found. Didn't Thomas tell you?"

I sized up Shawn, noted the nervousness with the gun. He wasn't used to handling one, but that didn't make him any less dangerous.

"He said there was a bag..." Shawn answered.

"Oh yes, there is a bag and there are some stones in it, but they aren't gold. It looks like some kind of quartz maybe, but no gold."

If I was right, those quartz stones held gold inside them that would need to be released. I gambled that Shawn and Thomas didn't know that.

I glanced down. The big bruiser I'd downed began to stir. I needed to distract Shawn now in order to control the situation.

"Why don't you take a look if you don't believe me? The bag is in there." I doubted that either Shawn or the man at my feet would be able to squeeze into the opening of that cave. Even though we were smaller and more slender, Thomas and I had barely made it.

He motioned for me to move aside and I stepped away from the muscle man to keep out of his reach while Shawn moved toward the cave opening. Seeing my moment, I swung my foot into the big man's jaw, motioned to Thomas to duck, then rolled back across him as Shawn turned to see what caused the commotion. I came up to the side of him, brought the edge of my right hand down in a sharp chop on his gun hand, knocking it down as he fired and the bullet skittered into a bush. With a quick twist, I wrenched the gun from his fingers and planted a knee into his groin.

With a sharp cry of pain, Shawn collapsed to the ground. I stepped over him and grabbed my phone while keeping the gun pointed at the whimpering redhead.

"Hello, 911, have you pinpointed my position? There are two of us and we had an attempted assault by two men who followed us on our hike. I have the situation under control at the moment, but assistance as soon as possible would be appreciated." I paused to listen as she told me to leave the line open; officers had been dispatched.

"Did you bring any rope or twine with you, Thomas?" I asked, as I ran through a mental inventory of my backpack contents and came up null.

He dug into his and held up a roll of duct tape.

I grinned. "That'll work. Get their hands taped behind their backs, and their ankles wrapped together." I knew firsthand about securing limbs to prevent movement.

Starting with the still-stunned muscle man, Thomas freely used the tape to wrap the wrists tightly together behind his back, then caught his ankles, raised the pant legs, and secured them with the tape against his bare skin. That would hurt coming off.

Shawn was now moaning from the pain in his family jewels plus the bleeding right foot. I gave silent thanks that I had been fast enough or it might be Thomas or me on the ground bleeding. A little shaky now, I still rode the high of pride that I'd managed to do it. The lessons I'd been taking and practicing repeatedly were paying off. I had managed to defend myself and disarm someone.

Once Thomas had secured Shawn, I slipped back into the cave and retrieved the leather bag, bringing it out to show Thomas. I pulled him away from our two captives, where we could talk quietly and still keep our eyes on them. The quartz rocks puzzled him.

"I thought you'd told them that as a ruse. Isn't there any more gold?"

Casting a quick glance to our two prisoners where they now sat braced against the cliff side several feet away, I said, "I think it's inside the quartz nuggets. If you look at them closely, you might get a glimpse of the veins inside. The rocks need to be split or broken up to free the gold within them."

I watched as Thomas pulled out one of the stones and held it up to the light, looking for the glint of color in it that might reveal the precious metal.

I continued. "Your triple-great grandfather must have broken up quite a few stones to get the ore out then he took a sampling to the assay office in Truckee. They verified his find and certified that he had located a certain weight of gold bearing stones that he'd brought to the office and that they were from his claim. There's a paper in the bag that states this. Be careful with it, by the way. It's very delicate and it's your claim to your inheritance."

"Was there more at his claim?" Thomas asked, still marveling over the stones that might yield a fair amount of money.

"Probably, but he died here, never returning to dig any more of it. Since then, it's probable that someone else found it and nothing's left now. Staking a claim on a portion of a stream would not be easy to hold anyway, but once he was gone, it opened it to the thousands of miners who came to the Sierras looking for a fortune."

Thomas' eyes clouded up a little as his gaze went around the area, the words I'd said registering with him. Menafee Willits, known to his grandson as Emmett Willits, had died near this area of the Sierra Nevada Mountains a little over a hundred years ago.

"Now, what brought Shawn and his friend out here today? Just a suggestion that you were hunting for treasure?" I said. "Maybe we should ask them."

Neither one seemed inclined to talk when we asked about it. "How did you even know about the gold?" I asked Shawn, certain that he instigated this attempted robbery. I only had a glimpse of my attacker at the lake, but I'd had the impression of red hair under the hoodie.

"It's as much mine as his," the roommate muttered, the only thing he'd said about it.

"How so?" I asked as Thomas shot a puzzled glance at me and shrugged.

However, Shawn refused to say anymore.

Then, a helicopter arrived overhead and a Highway Patrol officer came down on a cable toward us. "Ah, it looks like help has arrived."

I could see a second officer waiting on the chopper, but with the situation under control, the first sent the them back to Reno. As the sun began dropping behind the highest peaks, in the distance, I could just see the red and blue lights of a pair of Nevada Highway Patrol cars coming up Quilici Road to where I'd left my Jeep.

After the officer had spoken to Thomas and me, telling us he would have to take the sack of rocks into custody as evidence, I informed him that they could be very valuable and belonged, rightfully, to Thomas. He assured me that Thomas would get them back.

Of course, I didn't tell them that I had dumped half of the gold nuggets and a couple of the quartz rocks into my backpack. Out of sight of our prisoners, we'd added a few stones to the leather bag that we'd picked up from the ground to up the weight.

I figured Thomas could cash the ones I pocketed in order to have some money while he waited for the courts to release the evidence. Nor did I mention the ring and stone that I'd pocketed earlier. *Withholding evidence,* I thought, but only I knew about them.

Almost two hours passed before a pair of EMTs arrived to take care of Shawn. The emergency first aid we'd done restrained the bleeding and the helicopter from the hospital arrived to airlift him. The muscle man, a friend of Shawn's identified by the police as Kyle Statler, was taken down the incline ahead of us and escorted to a Nevada Highway Patrol car.

TWENTY-FOUR

*T*wo days later, Thomas and I met at the Nevada Highway Patrol office at the request of Lt. Parker, the officer who'd arrested our robbers. He took us to an interview room similar to the one I'd visited at the Sheriff's Office a few months earlier. I hoped this wasn't going to become a habit.

He motioned for us to sit, then took the chair across from Thomas. "I want to bring you up to date on the case as well as ask you to read through and sign the statements you gave on Saturday. We have confessions from McAllen and Statler stating that they attempted to procure the saddlebag and its contents that you had found.

"McAllen claims that the gold is rightfully his. He says that his family has known those nuggets were likely somewhere in the hills for years. His ancestor told his wife and family that he had a claim in the Sierras and would be bringing home enough to make them rich. He went off to get it and didn't come back. Later, they learned he had been killed. According to him, your ancestor, Mr. Willits, was the thief and murderer, who stole their gold."

"I can't believe that. I didn't even know about the gold until recently," Thomas objected. "But my triple-great-grandfather and all my family were honorable people. They would never do something like that."

"Besides, the certificate in the bag from the assay office says the claim belonged to Emmett Willits," I added, feeling indignant myself.

Parker smiled, "Yes, that's probably the best piece of evidence we have to prove the claim. We'll be authenticating it and checking the records, but it's going to take some time."

"Meaning that the gold will be held in evidence until it's confirmed," I said.

"'Fraid so," Parker responded. "Valid claim or not, McAllen and Statler attacked you and attempted to steal the bag that you had retrieved. At the least, there's an assault charge. Once the claim is authenticated, the attempted robbery charge will be added."

Parker handed us the printed statements, which we both took a few minutes to read before signing. Assured that I hadn't perjured myself in any way   omission of information isn't lying, is it?   I scribbled my name and pushed it back to him about the same time my companion finished up. Parker thanked us again for coming in.

Since his car was parked near mine, Thomas walked alongside me until we came up by my Jeep, then I turned to him and said, "I'm sorry this happened, but I suspected the saddlebag and its contents would be held as evidence for a while. So, I slipped out a few pieces of the gold, just in case."

His eyes went wide. "You did what?"

"Once I realized the police would be involved, I thought it prudent to keep some of the gold rather than turn it all over to them. We can try to sell them to get enough to take you through the next year of college while we're waiting for the legal process to free up the rest."

He grinned. "You're amazing."

With a pleased smile, I told him I hadn't brought them with me, but I'd call him later to discuss how best to convert the nuggets into dollars.

After I left him, I thought about the chain of incidents with the treasure, Thomas, and Shawn. If Shawn thought the Willits family knew where the gold might be hidden, it seemed likely that he'd been looking for Thomas when he offered to move in with him. I closed my eyes and tried to see the car accident again, looking over to the dark blue SUV going past. The passenger didn't look toward me; I only saw a profile of the young man and a glimpse of red hair. It could have been Shawn.

I called Egan Moss and left a message for him, telling him what had occurred and that I suspected McAllen might have been involved in creating the accident that had killed Thomas' father. It was a hunch but if anyone could get to the bottom of it, I'd bet on Moss.

With some assistance from the Internet and a recommendation from a friend of Janna's, Thomas and I found a reliable gold buyer in Reno who appraised the gold nuggets we'd found in the cave. Pleased to see the almost twenty-eight ounces of good-quality ore, he noted that a few weighed over one ounce. Something rare to find now, he told us, but during the earlier days of the gold rush, they would have been more plentiful.

"So what is all of this worth?" I asked the buyer, a man who called himself Ranger. His wire-rimmed glasses sat on the end of his nose as he looked at one of the larger stones. He held it up to the light, "Well, a nugget like this one, which is one-point-fifteen ounces but beautifully shaped, is worth more than a one ounce one with more of a boxy shape, so I could offer you two thousand for it alone."

We'd already talked to another buyer who had offered us fifteen hundred dollars for it, so we felt we'd made a good decision to try Ranger. He looked at another two of the nuggets and offered to buy those for eighteen-hundred each. However, that concluded his interest. Less than three ounces.

Nevertheless, he appraised values for several other nuggets ranging from the smaller ones that were about a quarter of an ounce to the largest one, which weighed one-point-twenty-three ounces. Then he made a suggestion that sounded odd at first.

"Put them on internet auction. You set the minimum price you're willing to take and let the buyers bid 'em up. You'll get a good price for them. Another tip; put them up one at a time so you sell them over several months."

We made the deal, Thomas picked up the pouch of gold, and we left the shop with fifty-six hundred bucks in his pocket that he could use for his education. As I drove him back to his apartment, he talked about getting good photos against a black velvet background, so it really showcased the gold, then he'd sell them, one at a time whenever he needed the money.

"What will you do with them until you get them sold?" I worried that he planned to keep them in his apartment.

"As soon as you drop me off, I'm going to the bank to get a safety deposit box to store them in. I'm not dumb."

"No, you're not," I agreed, relieved that he'd already thought about keeping the gold safe. "Let's not take any chances and get them secured now."

He nodded his agreement, so instead of dropping him off, I drove him to the bank.

An hour later, I parked the Jeep outside Thomas' apartment and got out with him. He looked a little puzzled. "Is there something else, Gillian? Do you want to come up?"

"There is something else, but it's nothing to do with you. Go on up. I'm glad it all worked out."

"Me, too," he answered. "Are you sure I can't give you at least the cost of the ticket to Tennessee for all you've done?"

"No, I'm fine. You use the money the way your Civil War great-grandfather intended." I didn't tell him that Menafee had left me the ring in payment. At least, I guessed that he intended that, but I would confirm it soon.

He thought a moment. "I want to give you something in thanks. So, keep the Civil War button. It's not worth a lot, but it may bring you luck."

I started to object, then realized that I would like to keep it. As the first object I'd experienced psychometry with, it did mean something to me. I simply said, "Thank you," and hugged Thomas.

As he went into his apartment building, I crossed the road and walked half the length of the cemetery to stand outside the fence facing the familiar grave. Time to send Menafee on his journey.

No need to go inside this time, I started singing, relaxing my body and freeing my mind. In a short time, my consciousness arrived in the now familiar graveyard where Menafee waited for me.

He smiled, a welcoming expression lighting his face. "Good afternoon, ma'am. I assume that you come bearing news today."

"I do indeed, Charles Menafee Willits. Today is a very good day for your descendant, Thomas Willits. We have recovered the gold and it looks like, at today's prices, it will give him around two hundred thousand dollars if all the nuggets yield as much gold as the samples."

While he looked impressed at the value, he also looked puzzled. "There is not a set market price for gold anymore, ma'am?"

"Well, as I understood it from the merchants we showed the gold to, the price varies not only by the purity of the gold but also by the size and shape of it. So an attractive nugget with a pleasing shape can be more valuable than one the same size and purity, but not as nicely shaped."

"If that does not beat all," he said in amazement.

"I also found a lovely emerald ring tucked in the bag. Is that the item that you said was for me?"

I started walking toward where I knew the path would be when he was ready and Menafee fell into step beside me.

"It is. It was a gift from my mother, a family heirloom. She wanted me to have it when I left to fight. In case, I needed money. I never wanted to sell it so I kept it for many years and often carried it on me for luck. When I determined I might be robbed again, I left the ring with the gold. Now, it is yours, Miss Gillian, to do with as you choose. I expect it is worth quite a bit of money now."

"Emeralds are quite valuable and the setting is gold. I am sure

it would sell for thousands of dollars if I decide to let it go. But "I hesitated, the words I had been about to say fleeing. Instead, I continued, "When Thomas graduates, I will return it to him for his children. An heirloom should be passed on." I had no idea where those words came from, but I guess I had been thinking that would be the right thing to do.

Menafee arched an eyebrow in surprise, then asked, "Did you also find an ugly brown rock in with the gold?"

"Yes."

"Once cleaned up, that might be more valuable than either the ring or the gold. That, too, is for you. You helped my family and ran my errands for me. You earned it."

"Thank you."

While I had no idea what the stone was - possibly a ruby or a garnet - maybe it would pay a few bills. "Now, it's time for you to move on. No more lingering around a graveyard. You need to go through the light and meet the Creator."

He cocked his head at me as he asked, "You do not say God. Why is that?"

"Good question. It's only been recent that I've begun to believe again. To make that clear, to believe that there is a God who cares about humanity. I believe in a Creator of the Universe and therefore, is Creator of all that is in it, but believing that God cares about His creations takes a little more faith than I've had for the last dozen or so years."

"Fair enough," Menafee said. "And yet I have feared that God for over one hundred fifty years."

"Feared Him?"

He stopped and turned to face me, his voice sounding strained as he said, "I cannot return to the promised Heaven. I have sinned and I have done evil deeds in my life. I broke a sacred promise and I fear there is no forgiveness for my sins." Tears filled his eyes as his face contorted in the anguish that ripped through him.

"Menafee, listen to me," I said with compassion and a desire to touch his arm and offer comfort. "You have more than paid for those sins in the grieving that you've done in this graveyard for so many years. It's your own personal purgatory. Do you see that? If God is truly there and, given where I am right now He must be, then the one thing I do believe is that He forgives the sins of His creations - His children - because He loves them."

"But my brother, my wife, and daughter, the false life I led, can these be forgiven?" He dropped to his knees and sobbed, the pain of what he'd perceived that he'd done crushing him under its weight.

I knelt beside him, reaching out until my hand trembled just above his shoulder, hoping that it offered comfort. "Your brother and your wife hold no grudge against you. You used your brother's name, but you used it well. You didn't disgrace him. Your life was not a lie. You were a good father and husband to your second family and you have had children who continued the line with pride. Go to your home now, Menafee. Let me sing you there."

I rose, encouraging him to his feet, as I started singing "Nearer My God to Thee". Ahead of us, the silver path began to glow to lead us to the light, his portal to the next plane.

Hat held in his hands, Menafee humbly walked the path until he reached the radiant oval and he looked up. Whatever he saw ahead gave him hope and peace as he spread his arms wide as if to hug someone, then stepped into it.

"Goodbye, Menafee," I said in a low, almost reverent, voice from where I stood again in this world, in the dirt on the street side of the fence. A feeling of fulfillment washed over me and the sense of completion from a job well done.

I turned and strolled back to the Jeep, my footsteps hastening as I went. With that long-desired recording session planned in two weeks, I refused to be late for today's rehearsal.

About This Book

*F*or many years, Shiloh has been a siren song in my mind, begging me to write a story about it. Through all those years, I only had knowledge of two things called "Shiloh", the song by Neil Diamond and the Civil War battlefield.

Back in my ancestry, there's a pair of family names that ran for a few generations from my mother's side of the tree. The names were unusual and sparked some curiosity about their origins. I suspect that even though they were first names and middle names, they likely had been surnames. In particular, my great grandfather bore the name Menafee Womack Tatum and other children had either Menafee or Womack in their names. While I still don't know a lot of the history, other than the origin is possibly Irish or Welsh or Saxon, I do know it went back to the War Between the States.

When I started brainstorming this second book of the *Funeral Singer* series, I had a rough idea for a soldier, but as it developed, it incorporated both of these elements in a tale that takes my heroine to Tennessee and Shiloh Battlefield, past and present. I almost went to Shiloh about a decade ago and didn't quite make it, but I felt the need to see it with my own eyes, not just in photographs. So, this past spring, I went there to smell, taste, and feel the historic battleground.

If you have never been to Shiloh and you have an interest in the history, then I highly recommend you pay this National Memorial a visit. I felt like I walked on hallowed ground as I passed cannons, memorials and the graves of the soldiers who died there. It is one of the most beautiful, yet oddly peaceful, places I have been in this country. I hope I paid it respect and justice as I described it in this novel. And, yes, there have been ghostly sightings at Shiloh.

While the Old Hillside Cemetery does exist in Reno and is allegedly haunted, I have taken some creative liberties with the setting and history. At one point, it had been willed to the University of Nevada, but is now privately owned.

About the Author

A sometimes musician, sporadic artist, occasional poet, and obsessed writer, Lillian Wolfe has spent most of her life writing. From fan fiction to short stories, novels, training manuals, newsletters, and other documentation, she has constantly been putting words on paper or a computer screen. She is, in fact, extremely grateful for the invention of the computer because using a manual typewriter is tedious. She loves all types of fiction, but her favorites are fantasy and mystery novels. "Funeral Singer: A Song for Marielle" was her first published novel, with "A Song for Menafee" being the second in the planned series of spirit novels following Gillian Foster and her unusual talent to see dead people.

Lillian shares her home in northern Nevada with her best friend for the past thirty-odd years, four lovingly superior cats, and one feline-dominated dog. She is a member of the High Sierra Writers Group and the Fiction Writers Group.

You can contact Lillian through her web site:

http://www.lillianwolfe.me/loft/

or at her Facebook Page:

https://www.facebook.com/LilliansLoft

Look for the third novel in the "Funeral Singer" series around summer 2017.

From the Author:

*T*hank you so much for reading my book. I have always loved writing stories, but it is much more gratifying to know that people read and enjoy what I write. So, if you've enjoyed this novel, please consider leaving an honest review at Amazon and/or Goodreads or any other website that accepts reviews.

If you would like to know what I'm working on and what's coming up next, please consider signing up for my mailing list at my web home:

http://www.lillianwolfe.me/loft/

or connect with me at my Facebook Page:

https://www.facebook.com/LilliansLoft

I do Tweet now and then, but I'm not a frequent Tweeter, just so you know. However, if you want to follow my Twitter bits: @LI_Wolfe56

Enjoy these novels from **Pynhavyn Press** available now or coming soon on Amazon.com

Funeral Singer: A Song for Marielle - Book One
by Lillian I Wolfe (Paranormal Suspense)

Singing at weddings, parties, holiday events, and street fairs with her band are all just another gig for Gillian Foster, a dog groomer and for-hire musician/singer. Following an accidental fall and head injury, she begins to have unusual dreams. When she is asked to sing at a funeral, she accepts the paying job and discovers that her music connects her to the deceased. But this new talent also leads her to more trouble than she could ever have imagined as one of her "clients" demands her assistance in locating the person who killed her.

Funeral Singer: A Song for Marielle is paranormal suspense with a touch of romance in the first book of a series of spirit mysteries.

O'Ceagan's Legacy: Book 1 (O'Ceagan Saga)
by Lillian I Wolfe (Sci-Fi Fantasy)

Trained by her grandfather to command, Grania O'Ceagan expects to one day inherit the family's space freighter, but first she must prove herself worthy to be captain. Her ambitious brother Liam is nipping at her heels and wants the ship as well. While she adores Vilnius, the dashing assistant station master, their lives are worlds apart, but they relish their time together whenever the ship docks at Earth's station.

On the return trip to their home world, they take on two unplanned passengers and run into serious, life-threatening events that could destroy everything. Grania must muster her crew and apply all she's learned to save her ship and crew from imminent destruction. Can she prove herself the leader she expects to be?

For Eleven Million Reasons
by M.L. Weatherington - Police Mystery

If you think that winning the lottery is a dream come true, then you need to read the possible dark side of publicized sudden wealth. In *For Eleven Million Reasons*, mystery author M. L. Weatherington takes you on a suspenseful ride of murder and intrigue as Lt. Arthur Franklin pursues a killer. Don't miss this thrill ride of a first novel.

Bitter Vintage
by Riona Kelly - Suspense Romance

When the heir to the Claremont Vineyards in Northern California is killed in an accident, his sister Martinique returns home for the funeral, but she finds her father reclusive and odd, her estranged half-sister in residence, and a mysterious person skulking around the property. As she learns more about her brother's death, she is convinced there is more to the story and is determined to learn the truth.

Bitter Vintage brings the suspense of treachery, greed, and ambition along with romance and betrayal as the story unfolds against the California vineyards of the Napa-Sonoma region and the migrant workers' struggle for fair wages in 1964.

Alpha's Song (Les Loups-Garous)
by Angelina Fasano- YA Urban Fantasy

In quiet little Kennington, Massachusetts, dark secrets abound and some are buried deeper than others. Mysterious club owner Daniel Hawthorne keeps them close to his heart.

Following the devastating death of her mother, Christa Ellsworth never expected to return to the town where she grew up, but five years later, she finds herself dragged back to the scene of her family's tragedy. Christa's plan to finish high school unnoticed comes to a halt following a chance encounter with the devastatingly handsome club owner she can't get out of her head and she begins to uncover the extraordinary truth about the town she grew up in and an unusual birthright that is now hers.

www.ingramcontent.com/pod-product-compliance
Lightning Source LLC
Chambersburg PA
CBHW060148180626
46813CB00007B/2678

* 9 7 8 1 9 4 2 6 2 2 0 9 3 *